Reviews

"This is a gripping first installment in what promises to be a riveting and engaging series. It is an easy, smooth read, and I found it impossible to put down. I highly recommend this series and this author!"

"I'm quite a fan already."

"Hannah is an amazing author (who) knows how to keep her readers on the edge of their seat and keeps them guessing at the right moment in the game."

"I was entranced, hooked, and wanting more when I got to the end!! I was hoping I had not gotten there yet!"

BOOKS BY HANNAH GORDON:

<u>The Shades Series</u>
The Shades of Orthea

<u>Sabella Hall Series</u>
The Vu
The Gathering

<u>Short Stories</u>
Bride and Seek

The Shades of Orthea

Hannah Gordon

To my husband, and to everyone who ever believed in me.

Playlist:

Standing the Storm - William Joseph
Across the Burren - Michele McLaughlin
The Druid's Prayer - Michele McLaughlin
Perhaps Love - James Galway
The Drift - Blackmill
Adiemus - Karl Jenkins, Adiemus Symphony Orchestra of Europe, Peter Pejtsik
Celtic Fire - Debhair the Dancer
Newgrange - Clannad
Far Away from Home - Thao Ngyen
There Will Be Fire - Boris Nonte, Vanessa Campagna
Evergreen - Two Steps from Hell, Thomas Bergerson (final battle...you'll know)

The Shades of Orthea

Hannah Gordon

CHAPTER 1

There were Norsemen about. Fiona wrinkled her nose at the acrid scent of smoke wafting through the crisp autumn air, a knot of unease tightening in her stomach. The sun hung low, casting long shadows over the golden fields, and she could almost hear the rustle of the harvest still waiting to be gathered. Of course they had chosen now to appear. There had been no Norse activity for six months, but it seemed her village's luck had run out.

The distant clang of iron echoed in the stillness, a harsh reminder of their presence. Fiona glanced toward the tree line, heart pounding, as the first chill of evening settled over the land. They were coming.

Being a forest village nestled between the sea and the main cities had its benefits. The dense woods provided cover, the nearby river an easy route to the sea, and the rich soil bore plentiful crops. But these very advantages also made them a target. The Norsemen came and went as they pleased, taking what they wanted.

Fiona had learned early on to stay out of their way when they appeared. She preferred to busy herself inside the thatched hut she shared with her family, finding solace in the repetitive tasks that filled her days. There were always socks to darn, ropes to weave, and meals to prepare.

Two mornings ago, her father had sent word that the modest dowry he had spent years trapping animals and selling their furs to prepare was finally ready, and Fiona's marriage to Jason hovered close on the horizon. The thought of her fiancée brought a smile to her lips. He was everything she could have hoped for in a husband: a gentleman with a hard work ethic and blue eyes that twinkled with mischief and kindness. She blushed as she remembered the kiss he had stolen earlier that morning behind King Rock, a massive jagged stone that stood twice as tall as the village's tallest building.

The rocky giant was a familiar landmark, dividing the village from the thickest part of the forest and offering a fantastic lookout point. It was here that Fiona often found herself, crouched near the top, scanning the woods for any sign of movement. Today was no different. As she narrowed her eyes to focus on the shadows beneath the trees, a familiar voice interrupted her thoughts.

"You hear them, too."

It was not a question, but a quiet observation. Fiona didn't need to look down to know who had spoken. Erin, her twin sister, stood at the base of King Rock, her wine-colored curls tumbling over her shoulders, and her sharp emerald eyes mirroring Fiona's own. There was a note of trepidation in her voice that Fiona knew all too well.

"Should I go get Father?"

Fiona nodded, her eyes still locked on the tree line. "Go. Quickly."

Without another word, Erin disappeared into the morning mist that clung to the forest floor. Fiona remained where she was, her heart pounding in her chest as the fog shifted, revealing the hulking shapes of the men who descended upon the village. She had seen these men before, but their presence never failed to fill her with a deep, instinctual fear.

She slid down the length of the rock, landing silently on her leather-clad feet. Her thin skirt brushed against the damp earth as she lifted it clear of the mud surrounding her. With one last glance at the woods, she turned and ran for home. As she reached the village, she saw a line of men walking down the road, their heads bowed in resignation. They moved, goods tucked under their arms and hauled in makeshift wood pallets drawn by mules.

Erin's arms reached out and grasped Fiona's before she could enter the doorway of their simple home. The girls clung to each other, listening to the creaks and groans of the pallets dragged across the muddy ground. The birds that usually filled the forest with song were silent, fear palpable in the heavy air.

"I never get used to this," Erin whispered, moving to the bench farthest from the door.

Fiona stared out the doorway, her expression hard. "None of us should."

Her father stood among the men with his horse Darcy, a beautiful black horse he'd won in a bet with his brother. Fiona knew that one day they'd take the horse, too.

Fiona moved back to join her sister, forcing a smile. "This shouldn't take long."

Her voice sounded loud in the oppressive silence that hung in the air. Green eyes wide, she looked back to the doorway. Nothing moved. The men had passed. On any other exchange, there would be the low, melodic murmur of the Hibernian men haggling with the rough voices of the Norsemen. But today, there was only silence.

"What's going on out there?" Erin started for the door, but Fiona grabbed hold of her skirt and pulled, trying to haul her back to the bench.

"I want to see what they're doing," Erin protested.

"I don't have a good feeling about this," Fiona whispered. She followed her sister to the doorway and peered out into the clearing.

The sight that met her eyes made her blood run cold. The Norsemen stood frozen, malicious grins plastered on their faces, weapons gleaming in their hands. One figure, significantly larger than the rest, stepped out from the middle. Fiona's breath caught in her throat as her eyes rested on the slender form in his arms—her mother, Aideen.

Aideen's eyes were wide with fear, her struggles futile against the beast of a man's iron grip. "Mammy!" Fiona shrieked before she could stop herself.

Her mother went rigid against her captor, her eyes wild, and her nostrils flaring like an animal caught in a trap. The harsh language grated on Fiona's ears as the man who held her began to speak. Fiona narrowed her eyes, focusing on his head, encased in a metal helmet with spikes jutting out of the top.

"He wishes to have your land," a voice translated, his tone rough and unforgiving.

Another man joined Aideen's captor, his accent thick and his words like stone scraping across Fiona's nerves. He wore the same fur garb as his comrades, his muscles bulging under his tunic. Though he stood a full head shorter than his companion, he remained as intimidating.

The men glanced at each other and the ground, shuffling their feet. Horses snorted, sensing the tension that hung thick in the air. It was almost palpable, a heavy weight that pressed down on the village like a dark cloud.

"I'm afraid I don't understand," Lochlan spoke, his voice steady but strained.

Fiona's heart raced as her father stepped forward, his jaw tight and his fists clenched at his sides. "This is our land, but you are welcome to whatever supplies you need. You always have been."

Aideen's captor began shouting, his voice rising in fury as he shook her like a rag doll. Fiona's heart leaped into her throat as she watched her mother struggle, her eyes rolling back into her head. Without warning, the man slammed her face-first into the ground.

"This is our land now," he said, a sickening smile spreading across his bulbous face. He raised his ax high, the blade gleaming in the pale light, and for one long, horrifying moment, time seemed to stand still.

Then the ax swung downwards in a brutal arc. A sickening crack flashed through the air, followed by a blanket of shocked silence. Fiona's eyes widened. A scream tore from her throat, loud and shrill, born from the depths of her soul. Lochlan dropped to his knees; his head bowed in grief as his sobs filled the air. The men standing before him roared with triumph and then charged.

The ground shook as they advanced, the thunder of their boots a harbinger of death. Fiona's only thought was of her mother. She reached out, desperate to touch her, to hold her, but hands wrapped around her waist and lifted her off the ground.

"Let me go! Mammy!"

"If I let go, you die." Jason's voice was firm, as he hauled her back into the house. He pushed her to the ground, crouching in front of her, a dagger in one hand, his other hand gripping her shoulder. He shoved his dark hair out of his eyes, his face wild with fear.

Outside, the clash of metal against flesh filled the air, and war cries instilled fear into the hearts of the people. The sound was deafening, a cacophony of violence that drowned out all rational thought.

"What did we do?" Erin moaned beside her, tears streaming down her face as she trembled. "I don't understand."

"Stay here. I have to go help." Jason bent down and enveloped Fiona in one last desperate embrace, his lips brushing against her ear. "I love you," he whispered.

Before she could respond, he was out the door, and the din of the fight drowned his footsteps. Fiona and Erin clung to each other, eyes wide and bodies trembling. Erin buried her face in her sister's shoulder and sobbed. Screams outside drove through Fiona's heart like a knife. She had never felt so helpless or hopeless.

When she glanced at the doorway and saw the Viking standing there grinning, she knew it was over. She scooted back only to meet the unforgiving clay wall, her arms squeezing her sister as the man thundered inside with a sneer. Rough laughter seared through Fiona's ears. He stood inches away, suffocating her with his hot, fleshy breath, and lifted a large hand. The blow barely registered in her mind, but her head snapped sideways, and stars cartwheeled into her vision. Fiona fell to the ground, fingers sinking into the dirt floor. She heard her sister scream, a strange gurgling sound, and reality spiraled away into a world of darkness.

Fiona's consciousness flickered in and out, the edges of her vision blurred and dark. The world around her felt distant, like a twisted nightmare she couldn't escape. The metallic taste of blood filled her mouth, and her head throbbed. Somewhere, in the haze, she was aware of Erin's screams, each one stabbing through her like a shard of ice. She tried to move, to reach out to her sister, but her body wouldn't respond. It was as if the air around her had thickened, pressing her down into the cold, unforgiving earth.

Rough hands gripped her shoulders, yanking her up from the floor like she was nothing more than a rag doll. The Viking's hot breath washed over her as he leaned in close, his words a guttural growl that Fiona couldn't understand. She struggled weakly, her body refusing to obey her, her vision blurring as tears welled in her eyes.

Erin's screams continued, more desperate now, mingled with the sickening sounds of struggle. Fiona's heart shattered with each tortured cry, but she could do nothing to help her sister. The Viking's grip tightened, and he dragged her towards the doorway, his boots crunching on the dirt floor as he pulled her out the door.

The scene outside was worse than any nightmare. The peaceful village had been transformed into a battlefield. Bodies lay strewn across the ground, mostly Hibernians with a few Vikings, the earth stained with blood. Fires raged, casting a hellish glow over the carnage, and the air was thick with the acrid scent of smoke and death. The once familiar village now felt like a foreign land, a place of horror and despair.

Fiona's eyes darted across the chaos as she struggled, searching for any sign of her father, of Jason, of anyone she knew. But all she saw was death and destruction. Her heart pounded in her chest, each beat a painful reminder of the life that was slipping away from her.

The Viking dragging her seemed to delight in her fear, his laughter loud and cruel as he hauled her towards a group of his comrades. They stood in a loose circle, their faces twisted in grotesque grins, their eyes alight with the thrill of conquest. Fiona's stomach churned with dread as they turned their attention to her, their gazes hungry and predatory.

She wanted to scream, to fight, to do anything to escape the fate that awaited her, but her body was weak, her spirit crushed. The Viking shoved her to the ground in front of them, and she crumpled into a heap, her limbs refusing to support her. The men around her laughed, their voices booming in her ears, a terrifying chorus of victory.

Fiona squeezed her eyes shut, wishing she could will herself away, back to the safety of her home before everything had gone so wrong. But there was no escape from this nightmare. The cold, hard reality of her situation pressed down on her, suffocating and inescapable.

The leader of the group, a massive man with a beard as wild as the sea, stepped forward, his eyes locked on Fiona. He reached down, his hand rough and calloused, and grabbed her chin, forcing her to look up at him. His eyes were as cold as ice, devoid of any humanity, and a shiver of pure terror raced down her spine.

"You'll fetch a good price," he muttered in a thick accent, his voice like gravel. "Or maybe we'll keep you for ourselves."

Fiona's breath hitched in her throat, her heart pounding so hard she thought it might burst. She could barely comprehend his words, her mind reeling. The world around her spun, the ground seemed to tilt beneath her, and for a moment, she thought she might pass out again.

But something inside her refused to give in. Fiona's gaze hardened, her teeth gritting together as she summoned the last reserves of her strength. She might be weak, but she would not go like this.

With a burst of energy, Fiona twisted in the Viking's grip, her nails digging into his wrist as she tried to wrench herself free. Her sudden resistance caught him off guard, and he loosened his hold just enough for her to slip out of his grasp. Fiona stumbled to her feet, her legs shaky but determined, and she turned to run.

But before she could take more than a few steps, a searing pain shot through her leg, and she cried out as she collapsed to the ground. One of the other Vikings had thrown a spear, the sharp metal tip slicing through her flesh. The pain was overwhelming, white-hot, and all-consuming, and it took everything in her not to scream again.

Fiona clutched at the wound, blood seeping through her fingers as she lay there, gasping for breath. The Vikings surrounded her again, their laughter even louder now, more menacing. They had enjoyed the chase, and it was clear she would not escape. She was theirs.

As the darkness closed in around her once more, Fiona's thoughts turned to her family, to her sister, to Jason. She prayed they had found a way out, that they had escaped this horror. But deep down, she knew the truth. Her village was lost.

Quiet blanketed everything, a silence that felt unnatural in the aftermath of the chaos. Fiona's hands trembled as she reached up, her fingers caked with dirt, nails shredded and bleeding. She brushed strands of tangled hair off her face, her movements slow and deliberate, as if any sudden action might shatter the fragile stillness around her. When she opened her eyes, the world came into focus in sharp, painful detail. Her leg throbbed, and she looked down to see a crude cloth wrapped around the wound from the spear. Blood seeped through.

Dirt clung to her palms, her hands a mess of raw skin and torn flesh. She glanced to her left, where thin, desperate scratch marks marred the clay wall—evidence of her frantic attempt to escape. But from what? The memories surged back with the force of a tidal wave, and she gasped, her chest tightening. The

Viking. The hulk of a man with his rough hands and foul breath, his presence as oppressive as a storm. She shook her head to clear it, her gaze sweeping across the devastated remains of their home.

The bench, once a sturdy piece of furniture, now lay sideways by the doorway. The deerskin flap that had served as a door was draped over an upside-down chair. Pots, bowls, metal drinking cups, and blankets were scattered everywhere. Panic seized her as she remembered Erin. Fiona whirled around, her heart racing as she searched the room with desperate eyes, but she was alone.

"Sister?" The word escaped her lips in a whisper, the sound crackling in the oppressive silence. A twig snapped outside, the sudden noise sending a jolt of fear through her. Fiona scrambled back to the far wall, her pulse pounding in her ears. She waited, every muscle tense, dreading the approach of another intruder.

A hand appeared at the doorway, grasping for support. It slid down the frame, leaving a streak of blood in its wake. Fiona's breath caught in her throat as she recognized the small hand, and she forgot her own pain. "Erin!"

Seconds later, the two girls clung to one another as if their very lives depended on it. Fiona's eyes widened in horror as she took in the sight of her sister. Black bruises curled around Erin's neck, the perfect outline of fat fingers. Fiona's stomach churned at the sight. "Are you okay? You're bleeding," she whispered, her voice thick.

Erin glanced down at her burgundy-stained frock, confusion clouding her eyes. "I... I don't know," she murmured, her voice weak and distant. She leaned against Fiona, her body frail and trembling. Fiona guided her sister to the bed, her movements gentle but urgent, her heart aching with fear. She examined Erin, smoothing her hands over her body until a sharp flinch told her she had found the source of the pain. "There."

Fiona lifted the hem of Erin's skirt and gasped at the sight of a deep gash on her thigh. The wound was jagged as if something thin and sharp had sliced through her flesh. "Oh, Erin," Fiona moaned, her heart breaking. She tore strips from a nearby blanket with her teeth and fingers, her hands shaking as she bandaged her sister's leg as best as she could. When the wound was covered, she laid Erin down on the tattered remains of their mother's quilt, the once-exquisite fabric now a tragic reminder of what they had lost.

Erin drifted into a troubled sleep, her breathing uneven and labored. Fiona tiptoed to the entrance, her nerves on edge as she peeked outside, praying she wouldn't see any more of the invaders. But the sight that greeted her was a nightmare in its own right. The village had transformed into a graveyard. Bodies lay strewn in every direction, both human and animal. Flames still flickered from a few of the homes, casting an eerie glow over the destruction. The well bucket lay in splintered pieces scattered across the grass.

The smell of burning flesh reached her on the breeze, along with the gravelly voices of the Norsemen. Fiona's stomach turned, bile rising in her throat as she pulled back from the doorway. The sound of approaching footsteps sent her heart into overdrive. They were getting closer. Fiona rushed back to her sister's side, pulling the deerskin flap over Erin's prone body in a desperate attempt to hide her. She flattened herself against the wall by the door, every nerve in her body on high alert as she waited for the inevitable discovery. The men were close now, outside the hut.

Fiona squeezed her eyes shut, bracing herself for the moment when they would find her. The seconds stretched into an eternity, the silence between each footstep deafening. But then, after what felt like hours, the footsteps began to fade. The men were moving on. Fiona slumped to the ground, her body wracked with silent sobs of relief and despair.

Erin stirred under the deerskin, bringing Fiona back to reality. She gathered herself, crawling over to her sister's side. "It's okay, sweetie," she crooned, lifting the flap to check on Erin. Her sister's face was pale and clammy, her cheekbones too pronounced, dark circles forming under her eyes. She was getting worse. Fiona's heart sank as she recalled the last time she had seen someone like this—young Cormac, mauled by a boar. The infection had spread, and within two days, he was gone. The same fate awaited Erin, but faster. Fiona felt a twisted sense of relief knowing her sister wouldn't suffer for long.

"Sister." Erin's voice was a weak whisper, barely audible. Fiona looked up and saw Erin's eyes open, her gaze focused and clear for the first time since she had found her. Fiona scooted closer, clasping her sister's hand in both of hers. "I'm here," she whispered, pressing her chapped lips to Erin's smooth hand.

Erin's smile was faint, her green eyes filled with a sad understanding. "I love you," she murmured.

"I love you too, sister," Fiona replied, her voice trembling. Tears welled in her eyes as she added, "Take care of Mammy for me." She knew it was unlikely their father had survived, but she didn't want to add to Erin's grief.

Erin nodded, her breath coming in shallow, ragged gasps. Fiona helped her turn onto her side, her heart clenching as she heard the death rattle in her sister's chest. Erin's eyes began to lose their focus, her grip on Fiona's hand loosening. Fiona kissed her sister's hand again, watching helplessly as Erin coughed, blood splattering from her lips.

Despite the danger lurking outside, Fiona did the only thing she could think of to comfort her sister in her final moments. She began to hum a soft, melodic Irish tune, the one their mother used to sing to them as children. The haunting melody filled the air, carrying Erin toward the afterlife. Fiona sang until her sister's breathing slowed and, at long last, stopped.

For a long while, Fiona sat beside her sister's body, her mind numb with grief. Leaving Erin felt wrong, but she knew she had no choice. The Norsemen would return, and they would defile her sister's body if she stayed. Fiona forced herself to her feet, standing at the doorway, her teeth worrying her bottom lip as she debated what to do.

Steeling herself, Fiona turned and peeked outside again, expecting to see a Viking waiting to capture her. But the village was quiet, the bodies she had seen earlier now gone, leaving only muddy impressions in the earth. Footprints crisscrossed the ground, a chaotic jumble that only added to her confusion. The only movement came from the Viking flag flapping in the wind by the town gates, a grim warning to any who might pass through.

The sound of gruff laughter drifted toward her from the town square, reminding her that the invaders were still nearby. Fiona knew she had to act if she wanted to escape. She grabbed her father's leather jacket, pulled it tight around her for warmth, and stuffed a few biscuits into her pockets—biscuits her mother had baked that morning. Fresh tears threatened to fall, but Fiona bit them back, squaring her shoulders. She couldn't afford to break down now.

Taking a deep breath, she limped out into the chilly air, her senses on high alert. Her leg throbbed, threatening to give way under her. She paused, listening for any signs of discovery, but none came. She ducked to her left, slipping past dark, empty buildings that had once teemed with life. Her heart pounded in her chest as she moved, each step taking her farther from her home and deeper into the unknown.

Rain began to fall.

A twig snapped behind her, and Fiona whirled around, her breath catching in her throat. Her heart hammered in her chest as she spotted a figure emerging from the shadows. "Emma?" she whispered, her voice raspy with fear.

The gray-clad figure moved closer, and Fiona recognized her cousin's familiar face. Emma flung herself into Fiona's arms, the two girls clinging to each other in desperate relief. They weren't alone. But Fiona knew they couldn't stay out in the open. "We can't stay here. They'll see us," she whispered, grabbing Emma's hand and pulling her through the mud and rain.

"Mother Earth cries for the dead," Emma murmured, her voice thick with grief as they trudged through the puddles, their soaked clothes clinging to their bodies like a second skin.

"Shh," Fiona admonished, her voice barely audible over the pounding rain. They sloshed through puddles and mud, their dark curls plastered to their faces and backs, clothes clinging to their bodies like second skins. Fiona's leg throbbed with every step, the spear wound burning with each painful movement. She gritted her teeth, willing herself to keep moving, knowing that slowing down could mean the end for both of them.

When they finally reached the gate, Fiona fumbled with the latch, her raw, bleeding fingertips trembling. She winced as pain shot up her leg. Frustration welled up inside her as she realized she couldn't get the latch open. She tried again, biting back the involuntary groan that escaped her lips as she pushed against the rusted metal.

Emma, sensing her cousin's struggle, placed a cold, wet hand on Fiona's arm. "I'll try," she whispered.

Fiona nodded and stepped aside, her injured leg nearly giving out beneath her. She leaned against the gate for support, watching as Emma worked, freeing the rusted latch with a determined tug. Emma took Fiona by the wrist and led her through the gate, the urgency in her movements keeping them both going.

Once they were through the opening, Fiona's strength finally failed her. She stumbled into the woods, her vision blurring from the pain that had begun radiating from her leg. She dared not stop until they the dense trees concealed them, but her body had reached its limit. With a final, staggering step, she collapsed against a rough tree trunk, the bark digging into her back as she sank to her knees, her injured leg screaming in protest.

The rain was less punishing under the cover of the trees, but Fiona felt no relief. Exhaustion washed over her, mingling with the numbness that had settled deep within her soul. The pain in her leg faded into the background, overtaken by a hollow emptiness that left her feeling like a shell of herself.

Emma crawled over to Fiona's side, her small body trembling from the cold and the fear that gripped them both. She lay down beside Fiona, their bodies huddled together for warmth and comfort. The occasional drop of water on their skin and the sound of leaves rustling in the breeze lulled them into a fitful slumber. Fiona's leg throbbed even in sleep. They were hidden, and that small sliver of safety was enough to let their exhausted bodies rest, if only for a little while. Their dreams filled with the cries of their dead loved ones.

CHAPTER 2

iona's eyes refused to open. Weights as heavy as iron held them prisoner. Her ears, however, caught the soft crunch of footsteps and the murmur of distant voices. Shifting her position, she realized with a start that Emma's weight was no longer beside her. Her leg throbbed. A wave of panic surged through her chest, threatening to steal her breath. Where was Emma? What had they done with her?

She forced herself upright, inhaling a lungful of muggy air, which triggered a fit of coughing and gasping. Her eyes flew open, and she rubbed at them, trying to bring the blurry world into focus.

When her vision finally cleared, Fiona's breath hitched. The sight before her was not what she expected. Gone were the towering, menacing figures of Viking warriors she had feared. Instead, she saw simple peasants, their clothing a patchwork of drab, earthy tones that blended with the forest around them. Their tunics and skirts were made of rough, homespun fabric, dyed in muted greens, browns, and greys.

The campsite itself was a haphazard collection of rugged tents, their canvas worn and patched in places, staked into the uneven ground. Wooden poles, some crooked and others straight, jutted up from the earth, supporting the tents or serving as makeshift drying racks for strips of meat or bundles of herbs. The ground beneath was trampled and muddy, with pathways worn smooth by countless footsteps.

Despite the rudimentary setup, there was an air of quiet industry. Some crouched near a fire, stirring pots of something that smelled savory, while others busied themselves with sharpening tools or repairing gear. As Fiona stirred, a few heads turned her way, their expressions curious but not alarmed. It was as though her sudden appearance was nothing more than a minor distraction, an everyday occurrence in this strange place. Then, they returned to their tasks, the rhythm of their work uninterrupted.

Hugging her knees to her chest, Fiona's eyes darted around, searching desperately for someone familiar. Where was Emma? Was she safe? Her gaze fell to her leg, where blood oozed through the bandage, staining the cloth a dark crimson. Ugly bruises, black and blue, mottled her arms.

The tree branches above her rustled, and a boy dropped down in front of her, landing with a soft thud. He smiled brightly. "You're awake!" He looked no older than nine or ten, with sandy hair and dark brown eyes, dressed in an off-white tunic that stopped at his elbows, and deerskin pants, and he stood barefoot on the earth. "I was starting to think you'd never wake up. Looks like Julian was right, but then again, he usually is."

"Where am I?" Fiona's voice cracked, and she realized how parched she was, her lips dry and chapped.

"In the Wickard Forest." He eyed her curiously. "Where else would you be?"

"Wick...what?" Fiona's muscles tensed as unease spread through her body.

"Wickard Forest," the boy said patiently, but concern flickered in his eyes. "Are you okay?"

"No," she stammered. Trembling, panic surged as she scrambled to her feet, her hands searching for the reassuring roughness of the tree bark behind her. "I don't know anything about a Wickard Forest!" Her voice dropped to a whisper, fearful of the people nearby.

The boy said nothing as he studied her impassively, his thin arms crossed over his chest. One eyebrow raised, he waited for her to calm herself. Get a grip, she thought, closing her eyes against her swimming vision. She slid back down to sit at the base of the tree, resting her head against the solid trunk, seeking comfort in its familiar texture. This was all a dream, and any moment now, she would wake up to find Emma beside her, the rain pouring down on them, and the village still in ruins.

When she opened her eyes again, the boy was still there, watching her with mild concern. "Fine," she sighed. "So, I'm in a place called Wickard Forest. Who are you?"

The boy broke into a crooked grin. "Dax." He plopped down next to her with boyish enthusiasm. "It's only fair I know your name, too. You know, before I get all personal with you." His accent was strange, and difficult to place.

"Oh, sorry. I'm Fiona."

He nodded, processing the information. "Where are you from?"

"Well, I'm starting to wonder that, myself," she smiled wanly. "But I'm from Hibernia. Aren't you?"

Hibernia." The boy tasted the word on his tongue like new food, then shook his head. "Never heard of it, miss."

Fiona's heart sank as she shook her head in disbelief. "We're in Hibernia!" she insisted, her voice rising with frustration.

"No, we're not," Dax said, his eyes narrowing as he studied her as though she were a madwoman. And maybe she was.

"Where are we?" she yelled. Her outburst froze the encampment. The people around them paused, turning their eyes toward her. Dax leaped back, retreating to the safety of the women standing near a cart laden with beans and corn. Silence blanketed the camp as they all stared at Fiona, waiting to see what the strange girl would do next. She clenched her fists, daring them to say something, to challenge her.

"Go back to the tent, Dax," a deep voice commanded, breaking the tense stillness. The tone was familiar, though it carried the same odd inflection as Dax's. The boy obeyed without question, slipping into the gathering of people whom continued to watch Fiona warily.

Footsteps approached from the left, and Fiona turned her head, hope flaring in her chest at the sight of close-cropped, curly dark hair, piercing blue eyes, and that familiar stocky build. He stared at her with a mix of incredulity and…something else. Not speaking. She would know him anywhere. "Jason?" she whispered, hardly daring to believe it.

At the mention of the name, the man paused, exchanging glances with those around him. Frustration welled in Fiona's chest, tears blurring her vision. "What is your problem?" she screamed, slamming her fist into the ground. The people around her shuffled back, putting more distance between themselves and the wild girl.

But Jason stepped forward and knelt in front of her, his movements cautious, like one might approach an injured deer. He reached out and gently took her hand, his touch warm and reassuring. "Does your head hurt?" he asked.

Fiona nodded, salty tears spilling over her cheeks and dripping onto her smock. Relief and disbelief warred within her as she raised her free hand to his face, tracing his familiar features with dirt-smudged fingers. He had survived.

"Do you know your name, love?"

Reality shattered around her. "What?" Fiona's voice laced with incredulity. "You know my name!"

"I'm afraid I don't." His voice was soft, and gentle, as though she were something fragile that might break under the weight of his words.

"Jason, it's me! Fiona!" Her voice broke, a sob choking in her throat.

"Fiona," he repeated as if the name were foreign to him. "My name isn't Jason."

Ivar was not an ordinary man. His mother often recounted

how he had entered the world too soon, a frail, premature infant she almost left to perish. She had placed him on a cold, rock outside the village, intent on letting nature take its course. But then, he cried—a sharp, desperate wail that cut through the air like a blade. The strength of his lungs pierced her resolve, compelling her to scoop him up and return home. Ivar's father saw this as a dreadful omen, a sign that the child was cursed. He abandoned them both, often passing them on the street without so much as a glance. The villagers pitied Ivar's mother, tossing her a few coins or giving her laundry to wash for a living.

When Ivar turned fifteen, he finally confronted the man who had discarded them. His father, sneering, laughed at the boy's demands for repentance. But Ivar, his rage simmering, reached up and, with a swift motion, slit his father's throat. The gurgling sound of his life draining away was music to Ivar's ears, a symphony of vengeance.

From that day forward, no one dared to cross Ivar or his mother. Not that they could have, even if they tried. On his eighteenth birthday, Ivar locked the entire village in the small church during their morning service and set it ablaze, watching with cold satisfaction as the flames consumed everything.

Afterward, Ivar took his mother to a new settlement where marauders were beginning to establish themselves. There, she set up a bakery, making a decent living while Ivar put his formidable size and unbridled rage to use in the Marauder army. He learned quickly, excelling in the art of pillage and destruction, his talents earning him the respect and fear of his peers. His mother beamed with pride as he rose through the ranks, eventually leading his own war band of men.

A decade later, Ivar had forged a name for himself as the most feared berserker in the known kingdoms. With three hundred men at his command and a dozen loyal commanders ready to drop everything at his call, Ivar channeled his fury into the one thing the Marauders desired most: conquest. Now, as he stood in the empty town they had overrun, dissatisfaction gnawed at him. The village was devoid of life, its people either dead or enslaved, yet his patience wore thin.

"I'm here, my lord." Aldo bowed as he spoke. There was an

unspoken affection between them—a bond that rendered them inseparable. Though he would never admit it, Aldo was the closest thing he had to a friend. Ivar fixed his gaze on the weathered map spread across the crusty wooden table of the town's meeting hall.

"We waited too long," Ivar said. "The village was not as supplied as I hoped."

"It's enough." Aldo stepped to his friend's side. "The men are satisfied."

"Satisfaction is laziness," Ivar growled, slamming his fist onto the table with enough force to make the lamp perched on the corner teeter. A nearby soldier, quick on his feet, caught the lamp before it fell, then retreated to the shadows, blending into the wall as if hoping to disappear. Being noticed by Ivar rarely ended well.

Unruffled, Aldo shrugged. "We've refilled our bags and the supply wagon. We shouldn't stay long. I don't like the feel of it."

"Of course." Ivar's eyes remained on the map, tracing their path with a finger. "We are not far. Maybe four days."

"What will I tell the men?"

"We leave at first light." Ivar stood to his full imposing height and crossed massive arms over an equally formidable chest. His armor gleamed silver in the lamplight, a stark contrast to the dim, rustic surroundings. The metal was polished to a mirror finish, with intricate engravings running along the edges of the plates, catching the light with every slight movement. A heavy, black leather belt cinched his waist, holding a sheathed sword with a hilt as intricate as the armor.

"Load the survivors into the wagon and lock it down. Take it back to the main city. I want one guard at each corner of it."

The men began moving to the door to make his commands happen. There was always a sense of urgency when Ivar gave a command. Aldo led them out, leaving Ivar alone with the flickering flame of the lamp. With no one to observe him, Ivar reached into a small satchel at his belt and pulled out a vial filled with a gritty, sand-like substance. Removing the lid with his teeth, he poured a small amount into his palm, then set the vial on the table.

Ivar turned to the candle, its flame dancing in the still air, and sprinkled the sand in a circle over it. The fire flared, burning white-hot, twisting with violent energy. The candle began to melt, wax dripping over the metal holder and onto the table. Two small, blood-red dots appeared within the flame, rotating at first before settling in one spot.

Ivar was no meek man, but the sight both frightened and pleased him. He saw the eyes of the soul trapped in the vial--the sorceress Alena. Though disembodied, her presence filled the room like a heavy blanket. He cleared his throat, trying to maintain his composure. The sound startled her, and the red eyes spun wildly before focusing on him.

"We are close," Ivar murmured, his voice low and reverent.

The eyes narrowed, their crimson gaze piercing through him, probing his mind with tendrils of unseen energy. It was as if they were unraveling his thoughts, sifting through his memories. The sensation was invasive, yet it stirred something within him—a twisted pleasure that curled his lips into a subtle, dark smile. He allowed his thoughts to wander, guiding them to the blood-soaked town, the screams of the fallen, and the nearness of their ultimate goal. Each memory, each vivid image, fed her insatiable hunger for knowledge. Only when she had consumed enough did the flame recede, pulling back from its ferocious brightness to a small, steady flicker within the confines of the lamp.

Ivar shifted in his chair, the movement causing the flame to flicker. "We are alone," he whispered, his tone softer now. "No one knows yet."

The flame began to warp and stretch, a thin, translucent face emerging from the fire. Alena's visage, though ghostly, retained the beauty she had possessed in life—high cheekbones, full lips, and long, flowing hair. The sight was unnerving, yet Ivar forced himself to remain calm, knowing how her temper could flare. It was this temper, after all, that had made them such a formidable pair.

"Your men wonder about your motives," Alena said, her voice hollow and echoing. "They question you."

"They will do as I command," Ivar replied with unwavering confidence. He knew better than to falter in front of her. Many seasoned warriors had met their end at her hands, and he had no intention of joining them.

Alena was guiding Ivar to Oldgrange, a thousand-year-old mausoleum of stone. The ancient tomb stretched a mile in each direction, its dome-shaped structure protecting the graves of shades and kings. The only entrance was a meticulously carved doorway, the gateway to unimaginable power. If Ivar could reach it in time, he intended to access the tomb's hidden secrets and the immense power they contained.

For now, he watched as Alena's face merged back into the flame, leaving only the eerie red dots behind. They, too, soon faded, retreating back into the vial. She never lingered long; it drained her strength too much. But she would return, as she always did. Ivar had secured a vessel for her, a young woman captured for the sole purpose of giving Alena a physical form once more. Oldgrange would be the key to restoring her, to restoring them both.

CHAPTER 3

Fiona stared at the man crouched before her, a mixture of disbelief and frustration churning within her. "You're Jason," she scoffed. "I've known you for years.

"There must be some mistake," he replied, his eyes narrowing as if trying to solve a puzzle. His expression was blank, clueless even, but she knew him. Didn't she? Doubt gnawed at her as confusion blossomed in her chest.

The resemblance was uncanny. He had the same solid build as Jason, the same tousled brown curls that she had run her fingers through a thousand times, and those piercing blue eyes that had always held her captive. His nose even had the same slight curve at the tip, pointing down toward his top lip in a way she could have drawn from memory. Yet here he sat, denying everything.

"If you're not Jason, then who are you?" Fiona's voice wavered as she crossed her arms over her chest, trying to shield herself from the unsettling uncertainty.

He met her gaze, his eyes gleaming with a mischievous twinkle as a smirk tugged at the corners of his lips. "If you must know, my name is Julian."

That smile—so familiar, yet entirely foreign—caught her off guard. It was the same smile that had once made her heart skip a beat, but there was something in it now that made her stomach twist with unease. He took her hand, his grip warm and firm, and pulled her to her feet. "You are in—"

"Wickard Forest, yes, I know." She cut him off, the words tumbling out of her mouth before she could stop them.

Julian snorted, a sound that was eerily like Jason's amused chuckle. She tried to convince herself that this man was a stranger, but her heart rebelled, refusing to let go of the image of Jason seared into her soul. Every fiber of her being wanted to smother him with kisses, to pull him close and pretend this nightmare wasn't real. How could he look like Jason, as if her fiancé had an identical twin she had never known about?

Fiona's leg continued to throb.

"So, you've never heard of Hibernia?" Fiona hesitated as if the very word would shatter the fragile reality she was clinging to.

"I'm afraid not."

"Then, what do you call your country?" she pressed.

"Orthea is our homeland," he said.

"Never heard of it," she muttered, more to herself than to him.

Julian laughed, a sound that made her heart ache. "That seems to be a common problem today."

"I don't understand." Fiona's voice was a whisper as she gazed around her in wonder, taking in the familiar yet strange surroundings. The trees, the grass, the people moving quietly about—it was all just as she remembered, but there was an undercurrent of something... different.

"Before I woke up, I was in my town, it was raining, and I had..." Her voice trailed off as memories came rushing back, each one more horrifying than the last. She saw her sister Erin, feverish and moaning on a cot. Jason's eyes wild with desperation as he told her to stay put. And then, the sight that haunted her the most—her mother's head, severed and lifeless, her mouth twisted open in a silent scream.

"Fiona! Fiona, can you hear me?" Julian's voice broke through the haze of her memories. Her muscles ached from trembling, her mind reeling from the onslaught of horrors. She felt the quiet descend like a thick fog, and it was only then that she became aware of the fact that she'd been screaming. The sound of her own ragged breathing filled her ears, and she felt arms around her, strong and steady. Julian held her tightly, grounding her as her breaths began to even out, the fog in her mind slowly dissipating.

Fiona collapsed against him like a child, her body racked with sobs. She was vaguely aware of the other people in the camp, some casting curious glances her way, others pretending not to notice. Dax rushed to her side, his hand grasping hers as if he could anchor her to reality.

"You need more rest, love," Julian murmured after what felt like an eternity. His voice was gentle, but there was a distance in it that made Fiona's heart clench. As he stood, the coldness of his absence seeped into her bones, leaving her shivering. She clutched at the collar of her frock, trying to ward off the chill that seemed to permeate her very soul.

She felt herself lifted into the air. Her eyes fluttered open, and she found herself nose-to-nose with Julian, his expression unreadable. The impulse to connect with him, to hold on to the man she once knew, overwhelmed her. She grabbed his face and pressed her lips to his, greedily soaking in the warmth of his kiss. But as quickly as the connection was made, it broke. Julian pulled back, staring at her with a mixture of disbelief and something else— something she couldn't quite place.

"Sorry," she whispered, the word barely audible over the sound of her own heartbeat. He said nothing, began walking again, his pace steady but his hold on her firm. Fiona buried her face in his shirt, hiding her burning cheeks. She felt the jarring rhythm of his footsteps, each one sending a jolt through her already frayed nerves. When he finally stopped, she felt him lower her onto a cot inside a small brown tent. She stared up at him, her teary eyes searching his face, hoping— praying— that he would recognize her, that he would tell her this was all a terrible dream.

But his face remained impassive, neutral as he covered her with a soft, downy quilt. "I'll be back. Get some sleep," he said, his voice distant, as if he were already miles away. Fiona shrank beneath the blanket, her body curling into itself as if she could disappear into its warmth. She listened to the sound of his footsteps, each one a dull thud in her ears, like the pounding of a hammer on iron. The noise stopped a few feet away, and she peeked over the top of the blanket to see the flap of the tent door swing down and Julian and another man standing outside.

This man was wiry with a perpetual smirk that seemed etched into his weathered face. His sharp, angular features were framed by scraggly black hair that fell in uneven lengths, giving him a disheveled appearance. Despite his unassuming height and lean build, there was a quickness in his movements and a glint in his dark eyes that hinted at a mind always working a step ahead. His voice, raspy and low, carried an edge of sarcasm as if every word he spoke was a private joke meant only for him.

"This can't be a good sign," he said. "What's her condition?"

"She seems physically okay," Julian replied, "but her mind... I think she's gone mad. She keeps thinking I'm someone else."

"You are, in another world," the man chuckled. "She's a looker. Maybe you should go along with it."

Fiona's heart raced. No! I am not to be made a fool! She yanked the blanket over her head as if the thin fabric could shield her from the cruel reality outside. She longed to wake up in her own bed, with her sister Erin beside her, the rain tapping on the ground.

"You know me better than that," Julian's voice was sharp, tinged with annoyance.

"Well, I'll be off to fetch the doctor for you," the smaller man said, his voice fading as he walked away.

"Thanks, Demas."

Silence fell over the camp, broken only by the distant shouts of people going about their day and the gentle murmur of a nearby stream. The sound of splashing water, children wading through a creek, laughing as they threw water into the air, filled Fiona's mind. It was a peaceful image, one that slowly pulled her into the embrace of sleep.

Fiona awoke to the cold, clammy sensation of hands on her bare abdomen. Pain shot through her body like a jagged bolt of lightning, forcing a scream from her lips. Instinctively, she launched herself from the bed, stumbling across the tent. Leave. She could get out. The tent walls buckled under her weight, and she collapsed in a crouch, her breath coming in ragged gasps.

Chaos erupted around her as several figures rushed to her side, their voices overlapping in an attempt to calm her. She trembled with exhaustion, the last remnants of her strength evaporating.

Through the haze of panic, she spotted Julian. He stood near the tent's entrance, his hands buried in his pockets, his expression unreadable. Though he wasn't Jason, the resemblance was close enough to offer a shred of comfort. Desperate, Fiona reached out to him, her hand trembling. The room fell silent, all eyes turning to Julian. For a long moment, he hesitated, his jaw clenched, and the tension in his neck visible.

Finally, he moved, crossing the space between them and taking her hands in his. "I can't stand very well," she whispered, her voice barely audible. Julian nodded, understanding without words, and lifted her back onto the bed.

Fiona curled in on herself, trying to make her body as small as possible, her eyes darting among the strangers in the tent. She hated the way they stared at her, the pity in their eyes searing into her like a brand. The silence grew unbearable until Julian cleared his throat, breaking the tension.

"This is our doctor, Stelios, and his nursemaids, Lia and Natalie," Julian introduced, gesturing to the three people who hovered nearby. The doctor, an elderly man with a lined face and a shock of white hair stared at her with a mix of concern and curiosity. Lia and Natalie were young women with stern expressions and tight buns standing next to him. They both folded their arms and studied her.

"And," Julian added with a faint smirk, "the fat guy over there is Demas. He owns this tent."

"Fat?" Demas snorted, crossing his arms over his round belly. "I prefer 'well-rounded.' Someday you'll look like me— only taller."

Fiona's cheeks burned with embarrassment. "I didn't mean to cause trouble," she stammered, her voice small.

"Trouble?" The doctor chuckled, revealing a mouthful of brown teeth. "No more than any of these young whippersnappers around here. But I'd like to finish my exam and get on to supper."

Reluctantly, Fiona lay back on the bed, forcing herself to remain still as the doctor's cold hands resumed their examination. She flinched at his touch, the chill seeping into her bones. "Easy," Stelios muttered, his fingers pressing gently on her abdomen and sides. "Can you tell me what happened before you woke up here?"

Fiona hesitated, her mind flashing back to the rain-soaked night, the weight of Emma next to her. "I was lying on the ground in the rain, holding my cousin Emma," she murmured, her voice hollow.

"Why would you be lying in the rain?" Stelios asked, bewildered.

"It seemed as good a place as any to wait for death."

Out of the corner of her eye, she saw Julian shift, moving back to the edge of the tent. His arms were crossed, his face a mask of neutrality. She longed for him to come closer, to hold her like Jason used to, to offer the comfort she desperately needed.

"What happened?" Stelios pressed.

Fiona tensed, unsure how much she should reveal to a stranger. The doctor's concern seemed genuine, but she had learned not to trust appearances. She remained silent, her hands clenching into fists over her stomach. After moments of tense silence, Stelios sighed, realizing she wouldn't answer.

"Do you know where you are?" he asked, his voice softer now.

"Hibernia," Fiona responded, seizing on the easier question.

The nursemaids exchanged puzzled glances, while Julian fixed his eyes on the ground. Stelios continued his examination, his fingers pressing into her skin with practiced care until he reached a spot on her hip. Pain exploded through her, and she cried out. Julian stepped forward, but Demas placed a hand on his chest, stopping him with a slight shake of his head.

"What was that?" Julian asked, his voice laced with concern.

Stelios gently turned Fiona onto her side, his examination meticulous and slow. Each touch sent fresh waves of pain up her spine, and she bit her lip to stifle her cries. The doctor's brow furrowed as he stepped back, rubbing a palm across his wrinkled face. "Hm."

"What does that mean?" Julian's concern was palpable, and despite her discomfort, Fiona felt a flicker of hope. Maybe he did care.

"There's some pretty deep bruising, and of course her leg," Stelios replied, stroking his chin. "She needs to rest for today, and we'll know more in the morning."

Demas grinned, his eyes twinkling. "Well, she'll have to go to your place, Julian. My wife will be home soon, and she might not take kindly to finding another woman in her bed."

"My place?" Julian hesitated.

"I'll find somewhere else," Fiona interjected, forcing herself to sit up. A sharp pain shot through her wounded leg, but she clenched her jaw, refusing to show weakness. As she swung her legs off the bed, a searing agony coursed through her, causing her muscles to betray her. She crumpled to the ground, her hurt leg folding beneath her as she caught herself with trembling palms. The pain from the spear wound pulsed with each heartbeat.

Before she could struggle to her feet, strong arms lifted her into the air. Fiona found herself cradled against Julian's chest once again. He stepped out of the tent into the cooling evening air, his steps steady and sure. Despite her earlier resolve, Fiona gave in to the exhaustion weighing down her body. She rested her head on his shoulder, letting the sway of his walk lull her into a sense of fragile security.

Closing her eyes, she tried to conjure the comforting image of home— Jason, Emma, Erin, and her parents gathered around a crackling campfire, sharing stories and laughter. She could almost smell the scent of roasted rabbit and feel the warmth of the flames on her face. The memory was so vivid that she opened her eyes, half-expecting to find herself back at home.

But all she saw was the deceivingly familiar landscape of a world that was no longer her own.

CHAPTER 4

Another bed?

The walls, fabric stretched taut between slender poles, creating a cozy, circular space. The interior was simple, with a low cot covered by a thin, red quilt. A few personal items were neatly tucked away in a corner, including a rolled-up map, a leather-bound journal, and a small pouch that looked like it contained herbs. A single, hanging lantern cast a gentle glow, illuminating the tent in soft, flickering light.

The snapping of flames echoed in the quiet, and one side of the tent glowed with the light of the campfire beyond its walls.

Fiona could hear the steady chirping of crickets, telling her that night had fallen. How late, she couldn't say. She pushed aside the quilt and sat up, stretched her arms, then extended her legs, bracing for the sharp pain she had felt when the doctor examined her. But nothing came.

Surprised, she rested a hand on her side and noticed the odd bulkiness beneath her shirt. Her ribs were bound with several layers of cloth, wrapped snugly around her midsection. Someone had taken the time to stabilize her while she slept, no doubt to help the bruises heal more quickly. She had seen it done in her village before.

The murmur of voices drifted through the tent's entrance. Fiona recognized Julian's deep voice, but the lighter, melodic tone responding to him was unfamiliar. She could make out only fragments of their conversation: "bruising," Hibernia," "baffled." They were discussing her.

She rubbed a hand over her face and sat up, trying to clear her head. The voices halted. Surely, they hadn't heard her? But when two figures appeared in the tent's doorway, she realized they had. Julian stood with his hands on his hips, looking uneasy. Next to him was a slender brunette, an older, elegant woman despite the dirt streaking her clothes and smudging her face.

"You're awake." She had a soft, feather-light voice, carrying an accent like the others Fiona had met earlier. "How do you feel?"

Fiona hesitated, then stretched again, testing her body for any lingering pain. "I feel fine," she admitted, astonished. "How is that possible?"

"I gave you a potion," the woman explained, moving closer and resting a cold hand on Fiona's forehead.

Fiona stiffened at the touch, instantly suspicious. "A potion? Are you a witch?"

Julian snorted from the doorway, but the woman only smiled. "We don't use that term, dear."

"She's a shade," Julian interjected, his tone respectful. "A sorcerer. She's the best."

"I wouldn't go that far," the woman—Melaney—replied with a gentle laugh.

Fiona shook her head, the idea of magic striking fear cold in her chest. "I don't know anything about magic, and I don't want it used on me."

"If not for the potion, you'd likely be dead," Melaney said matter-of-factly.

"It was just bruising," Fiona protested, her voice rising in alarm. Magic had always been something to fear in her village, something unnatural and dangerous. "Stay away from me!"

Melaney's expression tightened, her lips pressing into a thin line. Without another word, she turned and swept out of the tent, leaving Julian and Fiona alone. Julian sighed, shaking his head. "Best not to speak out of turn," he advised quietly before following Melaney out.

Left alone, Fiona let out a frustrated breath and lay back down, staring at the ceiling as her thoughts churned. She was in Hibernia— or so she thought. But it wasn't Hibernia anymore. Her mind wandered back to the takeover of her town, to the horrors she had seen, but nothing seemed to explain what had happened to her. She was in a new place, a new reality, it seemed.

When Julian returned sometime later, he carried a plate of food and a metal jug filled with cold water. Fiona was too hungry to care about anything else. She devoured the biscuits and venison, washing them down with the water until Julian took the jug from her. "Easy. You'll make yourself sick."

She reddened, heat prickling the back of her neck, and nodded. "Of course. Sorry."

Julian sat on the edge of the bed, his gaze fixed on his boots. Fiona sensed his unease, and she couldn't blame him. If a stranger had appeared in her world, confused and out of place, wouldn't she feel the same?

"Look," she began, trying to find the right words. "I'm confused. I apologize for any trouble I've caused."

He gave her a small smile, taking her hand in his. Fiona hesitated, uncertain whether to pull away or allow the comfort of his touch. "Melaney explained it all to me. You've done no harm." But the smile faltered slightly, betraying lingering doubts.

"Explained it all to you? What does that mean?"

"She said you come from another land. One like this, but separated by a veil."

Fiona frowned, trying to make sense of his words. "I'm not sure I understand."

"It's why you say you're in Hibernia, and we say we're in Orthea. They're identical lands, parallel to each other."

"How does she know this?"

"She's a shade. A powerful one. She knows all about the levels of existence."

Fiona considered this in silence. Oddly, it made sense. "So, my cousin Emma… she's—?"

"We don't know," Julian interrupted gently. "She could be anywhere or nowhere. Not everything is guaranteed to be exactly as it was in your world."

"If there's a chance she's here, I have to find her," Fiona insisted, her voice filled with determination.

"And if she isn't? Will you spend the rest of your life searching for someone who might not exist in this world?"

Fiona stared at him, her desperation clashing with his calm logic. She wanted to argue, to insist that she had to try, but the words wouldn't come. Frustration welled up inside her, choking off any reply.

Julian broke the silence first. "You should get some rest. I'll check on you in the morning."

Julian released Fiona's hand, and she shuddered. The separation was almost physically painful. She closed her eyes, trying to hold back the tears that threatened to spill over. Sensing her distress, Julian reached out and took her hand once more.

"I promise it will get better," he said softly. "We'll help you any way we can." He placed her hand gently on her abdomen and left her to the quiet and her troubled thoughts.

Fiona found her new group to be more welcoming than she expected. When she stepped out of the tent the next morning, broad smiles and shy waves greeted her. The camp bustled with activity, a mix of large families, and a few stragglers like Julian and Dax. Most of the people seemed to be peddlers, their wagons lined with goods and supplies, while children played nearby, their laughter echoing through the camp.

Lia and Natalie, the nursemaids who had tended to her, approached with warm smiles. They took away her tattered and stained frock and presented her with a new one, made of soft, clean fabric. They led her to a nearby stream for a bath, an experience that was mildly embarrassing for Fiona, but the two women clucked their tongues and assured her that it was nothing for them.

Lia, who was twenty-two like Fiona, had curly orange hair pulled back into a severe bun, though her features were soft and round and her face full of more freckles than Fiona had. Her laughter was infectious, with deep dimples on each cheek, and it wasn't long before Fiona found herself smiling along with her.

Natalie was a mere wisp of a woman but older at thirty years old. She was half Fiona's size, with mouse-brown hair that reached below her elbows. Despite her plainness, her chocolate-colored eyes sparkled with amusement as she recounted stories of her childhood on an apple farm.

The two were endlessly chatty, which suited Fiona just fine; it allowed her to listen, losing herself in their stories as they scrubbed her clean in the cool stream water. She closed her eyes, letting the sensation wash away the horrors of the Hibernia attack.

At some point, Fiona drifted off to sleep, lulled by the rhythmic motion of the women's hands and the soothing cadence of their voices. She awoke with a start, sitting up and rubbing her eyes. Water streamed off her shoulders, merging back into the stream like a homesick child returning to its source.

"I'm so sorry," Fiona mumbled, feeling guilty for having dozed off.

Lia and Natalie grinned at her. "Never you mind," Lia said. "We're finished now. You need to rest."

They helped Fiona out of the stream, drying her with soft linen before helping her in the new dress. Fiona noted that her leg wound was closed and less painful now, something she wondered if Melaney's brew had something to do with. In its wake, a scar stretched from her ankle bone to her calf. Lia combed Fiona's long hair with a white bone comb, then braided it neatly down her back, securing it with a thin leather string. "Before you sleep, you need to eat," Natalie said, guiding her back toward the camp.

As they climbed the hill to the encampment, the supper line was already forming, with women at the front. The men stepped back to let the three women pass, bowing their heads as they did. Fiona felt a bit out of place and leaned closer to her companions. "I'm not used to this kind of treatment," she whispered.

"It's the way of our people," Lia whispered back. "Women are the birth givers, and as such have the first choice among. . . well, anything."

Fiona couldn't help but smile at the notion. "I could get used to that." Her comment drew a chorus of giggles from Lia and Natalie, and Fiona found herself laughing along with them. "I could get used to being around the two of you as well," she added, her voice warm. More laughter.

At the front of the line, an elderly woman with a wrinkled face ladled stew into a wooden bowl and handed Fiona a hard biscuit. She flashed a toothless grin and waved her on. Grateful, Fiona hurried to an open patch of grass, where she waited for her friends to join her before digging in. The stew was hearty and filling, and Fiona savored each bite, feeling the warmth spread through her body.

When they finished eating, they handed their empty bowls to the dish man by the food wagon. Fiona glanced around the camp and spotted Julian sitting on the other side of the supper area. His legs were crossed, and he balanced his bowl on his knee as he ate. Dax stood beside him, his fingers curled around his bowl and biscuit as he ladled stew into his mouth. Despite the amount of food he consumed, the boy remained thin, his shirt hanging loosely off his frame.

Julian's eyes lifted and locked onto Fiona's gaze. Her face flushed, and she dropped her eyes to her hands, knotted in front of her. She couldn't read his expression; his face was set, unreadable, and she didn't know what to make of it.

"You should talk to him at the bonfire tonight," Lia suggested, startling Fiona.

"Dax?" Fiona feigned innocence, stealing a furtive glance at Julian. He had resumed eating, as if Fiona's presence didn't matter at all. She couldn't decide what was worse—being invisible or being too noticeable.

Natalie rolled her eyes. "Julian, of course."

Fiona would now stay in the nursemaids' tent, and Julian had been avoiding her. She figured her arrival had left him with a bad taste in his mouth, and she couldn't blame him. But as she turned to follow her friends back to camp, she couldn't shake the feeling that he had glanced at her again. She hurried forward without double-checking... in case she was wrong.

CHAPTER 5

The marauders assembled after nightfall in the dining hall of a conquered town, the stench of burning wood and flesh still heavy in the air. Outside, the fires blazed, consuming homes and bodies, leaving nothing but smoldering ash in their wake. It was their way—ensuring that nothing remained for the scavengers, or worse, for the survivors. Though, in truth, the men took pride in making sure there were no survivors. Each man received his share of the spoils, a reward for his part in the massacre. It was how Ivar kept their loyalty, secured through fear, respect, and greed.

Ivar lounged on the edge of a rough-hewn bench, his keen eyes sweeping over the chaos of the feast before him. His men, wild and untamed, ripped into the charred meat with a ferocity that matched the bloodlust they'd shown earlier. Mugs of ale slammed back with reckless abandon, the liquid spilling over bearded chins and down bare chests. Supper was always a raucous affair, a cacophony of guttural laughter, chatter, and grunts, like wolves gnawing on the bones of a fresh kill. Ivar shoved his empty plate aside and rose to his feet, sliding one hand into the hidden pocket of his belt to check on the vial nestled within. It was a treasure he'd kill every last one of them to protect.

"Listen up!" A voice boomed through the hall, cutting through the din. Silence fell like a shroud as every eye turned to Aldo, his sinewy arms crossed over his broad chest, his presence a force of its own. "Pack your things. We leave at first light."

He glanced at Ivar, who gave a single nod, his approval as subtle as it was commanding. "Get going! The night is growing older, and so are we!" Peals of laughter filled the air.

Ivar waited for Aldo to approach him. "Is she secure?"

Aldo nodded. "Pavlo and Niklaos are on watch. She won't be going anywhere."

"She better not," Ivar muttered, distrust gnawing at him as it always did. He trusted no one, not really. Aldo came closest, the only one who hadn't yet betrayed him. Even his own mother hadn't been spared his doubt.

"I'll check on them throughout the night."

Ivar nodded. Without another word, he turned and stepped out into the chilly night air. The stars glittered overhead, the moon a swollen orb casting its pale light over the landscape.

The rugged hills of Orthea stretched out before him, their jagged edges softened by the night's embrace. Wisps of fog curled along the ground, clinging to the heather and gorse that dotted the terrain. The wind whispered through the ancient oaks and twisted yews, carrying with it the scent of earth and distant sea. They were traveling alongside the Wickard forest, but had not entered it. Yet.

A scream shattered the stillness, a sound that sent a ripple of anger through Ivar. The woman. He cursed under his breath and took off at a run, his powerful frame moving with a speed that belied his size. He reached the tent in a few strides and burst inside, his eyes immediately locking onto the scene before him.

The prisoner, a slight young woman with dark hair matted to her tear-streaked face, sat huddled against the cot frame. Her wrists were bound, her mouth gagged, but her eyes—those dark, wide eyes—were filled with a terror that even Ivar found unsettling. Pavlo stood over her, his wiry frame casting a shadow that seemed to swallow her whole. "Shut up!" he snarled, backhanding her with enough force to snap her head to the side. Blood welled from a cut on her lip, staining the gag a dark red.

"What is the meaning of this?" Ivar's voice was a thunderous growl, his fists clenching at his sides. Aldo appeared behind him, his presence a silent threat.

Pavlo spun around, fear flashing in his eyes. "She tried to escape, sir," he stammered, his voice shaky. The woman shook her head frantically, her eyes pleading, her body trembling.

"Where is Niklaos?" Ivar's voice was cold, his gaze piercing.

"Nature called," Pavlo mumbled, his attempt to stand tall failing as he shrank under Ivar's scrutiny.

"You laid your hands on her without my permission," Ivar said, his voice low and lethal, a warning that Pavlo was too slow to heed.

"N-no, I—" Pavlo began, but his words cut off as a younger, blond-haired man entered, his eyes wide as he took in the scene.

"What's going on?"

Ivar's gaze never wavered from Pavlo. "She is not to be harmed. She is for a special purpose. You're done here, Pavlo."

Without waiting for a response, Ivar turned and stalked out of the tent, the cold night air hitting him like a slap. Behind him, Aldo yanked a begging, pleading Pavlo out of the tent and dragged him to the front of the camp, where the other soldiers were already gathering, drawn by the commotion.

"You will follow orders without question!" Ivar's voice rang out, sharp and commanding, as he addressed the men. "You will not defy me in secret!"

Aldo shoved Pavlo to his knees, forcing him to face the gathered soldiers. With a swift, practiced motion, Aldo drew a long knife and pressed it against Pavlo's throat. The blade flashed in the moonlight before slicing through flesh. Pavlo's eyes widened in shock as blood poured from the wound, his body convulsing before slumping to the ground.

"Are we clear?" Ivar's voice was a blade itself, cutting through the cold night air.

In unison, the men dropped to one knee, their fists over their hearts. The message was clear.

The night was silent once more, save for the crackling of distant fires and the whisper of the wind. Ivar stood tall, his gaze sweeping over his men, the weight of his authority palpable in the air. Fear, respect, and loyalty.

"Why are we packing?" Fiona's voice was tight, her hands clenching the soft, worn leather of the bag as she stuffed garments inside. The tent was filled with the muted sounds of Lia and Natalie's efficient movements, each motion practiced and precise. They wrapped their medicines and potions in strips of cloth with the kind of care that spoke of long experience, tucking them away as if this routine was second nature.

"We never stay in one place for too long," Lia replied, her voice gentle but distant, as though her mind was already on the road ahead. She exchanged a look with Natalie, one that Fiona noticed but couldn't quite decipher. Lia's hands were deft as they secured the glass jars, her touch steady and unyielding. "It's just our way."

"Everyone?" Fiona asked, her tone carefully neutral, though she felt the question settle in her chest.

"Yes, even Julian," Lia said with a soft laugh, the sound incongruous with the tension that had been building in Fiona's mind. "We go together. We're all one big family."

Family. The word twisted in Fiona's gut. She inhaled deeply, the scent of damp earth and wood smoke filling her lungs, grounding her in the moment. But despite her best efforts, her thoughts kept straying to Julian. She caught herself glancing at him whenever she could, though he never seemed to notice. It was as if she were invisible to him now, another face in the crowd. But sometimes, just sometimes, she felt his gaze on her— a fleeting sensation that made her heart skip a beat. Yet whenever she turned to look, he was always occupied elsewhere, his attention never lingering long enough to confirm what she so desperately wanted to believe.

"I don't think he cares much," Fiona murmured as she returned to her packing, the words tasting bitter on her tongue.

"Perhaps," Lia said softly, her eyes never leaving her work, "but perhaps he does."

Fiona's heart twisted with doubt, the sharp edge of hope too dangerous to hold on to. "I'm not holding out much hope."

Natalie, ever blunt, chimed in with a frown. "Why are you so stuck on him anyway?"

"It's... complicated," Fiona admitted, her cheeks flushing. She hadn't spoken of her feelings since her first day in the camp, and even then, only in passing—a brief mention, nothing more.

"We've got time," Natalie pressed, her tone leaving no room for retreat.

Fiona hesitated, her fingers stilling over the leather strap she had been tightening. She took a steadying breath, her chest tightening with the weight of what she was about to say. "Melaney told me... she said I switched worlds."

"Ah, she knows a lot, that one. It's handy having a shade 'round here," Natalie remarked, casting a quick wink at Lia.

Fiona began, her voice low and measured. "The land I came from was called Hibernia. I lived there with my parents, Aideen and Lochlan, and my sister, Erin." Her voice wavered, the names tasting of loss and distant memories. Lia and Natalie stilled, their expressions softening with understanding as they waited for her to continue.

"My father was a hard worker, as were all in our town. We were all like family, close-knit, but then... we were attacked." She swallowed hard, forcing herself to push past the pain that clenched her throat. "They were Norsemen. They came without warning, slaughtering and plundering. They killed my sister and parents... and Jason."

Her voice broke, the name slipping out like a secret she had kept locked away for too long. Silence filled the tent, the weight of her story hanging in the air like a dark cloud. When she finally spoke again, her voice trembled. "Jason and I were betrothed when we were twelve. It wasn't something I wanted at first, but over time, we became friends, then more than friends. We loved each other. My father worked tirelessly to gather the dowry his mother demanded. He had managed to complete it when the Vikings came. Jason disappeared in the fight, and I never saw him again."

Lia and Natalie exchanged a glance, their eyes filled with unspoken sympathy. "He looks like Julian?" Lia asked gently.

Fiona nodded, relief washing over her that they understood, even a little. "Exactly like him. I thought... I thought he was Jason. I must have scared Julian with my mistake."

"No one could blame you for that," Natalie said, her tone kind. "Not many have traveled the way you did."

"Not many at all," came a new voice from the tent's entrance, smooth and calm.

The three women turned, and Fiona's heart clenched at the sight of Melaney standing at the flap. The shade's dark eyes were inscrutable as if they held secrets Fiona would never fully grasp. A subtle tension crept into the air.

"May I come in?" Melaney's voice was polite, but there was an edge to it that put Fiona further on guard.

"Of course," Lia said, gesturing with a smile.

Fiona forced herself to remain outwardly calm, though inside, her thoughts churned like a stormy sea. Melaney was a shade, a magic wielder, and everything in Fiona screamed to be wary. Her father's voice echoed in her mind, a stern warning from a world that felt both distant and achingly close. "Magic is dangerous, Fiona. You can never trust those who use it."

As Melaney stepped into the tent, Fiona shifted slightly, instinctively putting more distance between them. She knew that Melaney had saved her life, that the shade had been the reason she was still breathing, but that didn't erase the unease that coiled in her gut. Magic wielders bent the world to their will, and Fiona despised the thought of someone having that kind of power over her.

Lia and Natalie seemed unfazed, their conversation flowing easily as they welcomed Melaney. Fiona couldn't understand it. Didn't they see the potential danger standing right in front of them? Her eyes tracked Melaney's graceful movements, noting how the shade seemed to glide rather than walk. It made Fiona feel like a mouse caught in the gaze of a predator, powerless and small.

When Melaney's gaze finally settled on her, Fiona's breath caught in her throat. The shade's eyes seemed to pierce right through her as if she could see all of Fiona's doubts and fears laid bare. It took every ounce of Fiona's willpower not to flinch under that intense scrutiny. She had always prided herself on her ability to hide her emotions, but around Melaney, she felt stripped bare, vulnerable in a way that made her skin crawl.

"So," Melaney said, her voice like silk over steel, "what are we discussing?"

"Fiona was telling us about her world," Lia said.

"Ah, the other world," Melaney said, nodding. "It's always fascinating to hear about the places people come from."

Fiona stiffened at the mention of her world, feeling a protective surge over the memories of her family and the life she had lost. She didn't want Melaney's magic anywhere near those memories. The thought of someone like Melaney, with her strange powers, meddling in Fiona's past sent a shiver down her spine.

She forced herself to speak, keeping her tone as neutral as she could manage. "It was a simple place. No magic, just people living their lives."

Melaney's lips curled into a smile, but she didn't press the matter, her attention shifting as Natalie broke in with a playful tone.

"Where have you been, young lady?" Natalie crossed her arms in mock sternness.

"Meditating," Melaney replied with a slight smile.

Fiona averted her eyes, focusing on the task at hand as the others chatted. But her thoughts kept circling back to Julian—or Jason, whoever he was. She longed for the warmth of his arms around her, for the sound of his voice saying her name as if it meant something. But she knew it was a fantasy, a cruel illusion that she needed to let go of.

She became aware of the others watching her and looked up, startled. "What?"

"We asked if you were planning to stay in our tent or move to Melaney's," Lia said with an amused eye roll.

"Oh. Why would I move?"

"If you're going to learn, it's best to stay with me," Melaney said, her voice carrying an edge of authority that set Fiona's nerves on edge.

"Learn? Learn what?" Fiona bristled.

"The only ones who can cross worlds are current or future shades," Melaney explained, her words grating on Fiona's already frayed nerves.

"I'm not one of you!" Fiona snapped, her anger flaring like a spark in a dry field.

"I wish you had a choice," Melaney said, irritation flickering in her eyes. "In reality, I didn't ask for this either, but the sooner you accept it, the easier it will be for both of us."

"Reality is where I come from!" Fiona's voice cracked, a raw edge of desperation slicing through the words. "That's where I belong! It's where I want to go back to!"

"To what?" Melaney's voice turned to ice. "A burned town? A place that no longer exists?"

The words stung like a slap to the face. Fiona stared at her a moment, before whispering, "If I must."

"There's nothing left for you there," Melaney's voice was a cold, bitter truth. "Even if you could go back, it's gone. You'd do well to get used to that." Without another word, Melaney turned and strode out of the tent.

As the tent flap closed behind her, Fiona's strength crumbled. She fell to the ground, the weight of Melaney's words crashing down on her like a tidal wave. Tears streamed down her face, hot and unrelenting, as the truth of it all clawed at her heart. Melaney was right, as much as Fiona hated to admit it. There was nothing left in her old world, nothing to go back to. The loss felt like a jagged wound, and the thought of staying in this strange place felt unbearable.

Fiona whispered, "I'm staying with you two."

Lia and Natalie exchanged a glance, their eyes soft with understanding. "Stay with us or not," Natalie said, kneeling beside her, "you're still destined to be her apprentice. There's no changing that, Fiona."

"For what it's worth," Lia added, "being a shade is a coveted gift here."

But Fiona couldn't find the strength to respond, her heart too heavy, her spirit too shattered. The words fell around her like a shroud, the weight of her new reality pressing down, suffocating in its intensity. And as Lia and Natalie quietly left her to her grief, Fiona felt the crushing tide of despair pull her under, drowning in a world she didn't know, in a life she didn't want.

As they left camp, the group moved in silence beside the supply wagon. The dawn's chill lingered in the air, wrapping around them like a shroud. Fiona pulled her new brown hooded garb tighter around her, her arms crossed protectively over her chest. She bowed her head as if she could hide the turmoil inside. Lia and Natalie flanked her, mirroring her posture, each lost in their own thoughts. Since their confrontation the day before, Melaney kept her distance. Fiona didn't mind.

The dense forest closed in around them as they trudged through the underbrush, the canopy above filtering the weak sunlight into fragmented patterns on the ground. When they reached a small valley, the group halted for a midday rest. The old couple from the food wagon handed out chunks of smoked ham and water skins to everyone.

"Best keep your strength up for all this walking," the old woman said with a wink as she handed Fiona her portion. "Would hate to see you riding on some young man's shoulders." She shuffled off, leaving Fiona bristling as Lia and Natalie giggled behind their hands. Fiona shot them a withering glare, her irritation flaring. They fell silent, but the mischief in their eyes remained.

"Ladies." The voice was casual, but it sent a jolt through Fiona's heart. She turned in time to see Julian passing by, a small smile tugging at his lips as he went.

"Oh, for goodness' sake," Lia muttered. "When will he fall for you already? I'm so tired of all the pining."

"Hush," Natalie scolded. "These things take time. Besides, who knows if they're meant to be?"

"I'm sitting right here," Fiona reminded them.

"So you are," Lia said with a sly smile, turning her attention back to her food.

Around them, the camp stirred to life as everyone prepared to resume the journey. Children dashed about, gathering whatever the adults needed. Fiona spotted Dax among them, lanky and limber as he ran up to Julian and handed him a freshly filled skin of water. Julian ruffled the boy's hair with a broad grin, his expression so warm and genuine that Fiona felt a pang of envy. She should be the one there, basking in that easy camaraderie.

"He's not Jason," Natalie murmured in her ear before slipping away to join the others. The camp moved forward again at a slow and steady pace that left Fiona feeling both anchored and suffocated. She lingered where she stood, the temptation to turn and disappear into the forest gnawing at her insides.

She backed away, inching toward the edge of the path, her heart hammering in her chest. She could slip away, vanish into the trees, and find her way back to where she belonged. To Jason. She reached behind her, seeking the rough bark of a tree to steady herself, but instead, her fingers brushed against fabric. Startled, she spun around and found herself face-to-face with Melaney.

"Going somewhere?" The shade's eyebrow arched in question.

Fiona blushed, feeling the heat rise to her cheeks. "I'm sorry. I thought—"

"Thought what?" Melaney cut her off, her voice sharp as a blade. "That leaving would be better for us? For you? Are you so delusional that you refuse to see the danger that lies in wait for anyone who strays?"

"Says the person who thinks I know magic," Fiona shot back, her temper flaring.

"You don't know magic," Melaney retorted, her voice cold. "You have the blood of a shade in you, but that doesn't make you anything unless you learn to harness and wield it."

"Where I come from, sorcery and magic were not only forbidden but punishable by death."

"You aren't in Hibernia anymore, or do I need to remind you? Where will you go?" Melaney's words cut through her.

Fiona's heart sank, the fight draining out of her. She dropped her gaze to the ground, taking a deep, steadying breath. "Fine," she muttered, the word bitter on her tongue.

Melaney's expression softened, just a fraction. "That's better. Walk with me." She took Fiona's hand, leading her back to the rest of the travelers.

They continued in relative silence, the murmur of conversation around them a muted backdrop. The old couple from the food wagon was particularly noisy, embroiled in a heated argument over cooked better. The debate escalated until a male voice—strange and unfamiliar—boomed above the clamor, "You'll both kill us with your veal, so shut up and never make the stuff again!" Laughter erupted, the argument dissolving into the warm hum of camaraderie.

"Nice couple," Fiona managed, grasping for something to say to the woman beside her.

"They'll poison us one day with their food," Melaney said, but there was a hint of amusement in her voice.

A cry cut through the noise, silencing the crowd. It was a man's voice, frantic and full of fear. Melaney's eyes narrowed, her posture stiffening. "Something's wrong," she said, already moving toward the front of the caravan. Fiona followed, her heart racing.

A man on horseback appeared, his steed galloping at full speed as he waved one arm wildly. "Get off the road! Marauders!"

"Off the road!" The crowd responded in a frantic chorus, panic spreading like wildfire.

Melaney whirled around, her voice urgent as she shouted, "Get off the bloody road!"

Fiona stayed close to Melaney as the caravan turned and plunged out of the clearing and into the forest. They stumbled through the loose dirt and wet leaves, the urgency of their retreat palpable in every hurried step. Two men lingered behind, brushing over the wagon's tracks to conceal their path.

The wagon halted, and the cooks frantically threw sticks and leaves over its sides, camouflaging it. Women herded the children deeper into the underbrush, hunkering down behind the wide trunks of ancient trees, their breaths shallow and tense.

The scout, a lean, sharp-eyed man, took charge, his voice a low hiss as he warned, "They'll be here any minute."

Melaney positioned herself between the wagon and the road, her dark hair blending seamlessly with the forest's shadows. Fiona crouched beside her, her heart thudding in her chest, her hand clutching her skirt so tightly her knuckles turned white.

The creak of leather and the heavy thud of boots reached their ears. The marauders made no effort to conceal their approach. Fiona's pulse quickened, her fear mounting with each step they took. How many were there? She dared a glance around the tree, her breath catching in her throat.

"Stay down," Melaney whispered, pulling her head back to hide it from view. "Hopefully, they'll go right on by."

The line of men moved with a brutal efficiency that sent a shiver down her spine. Fiona's blood ran cold as she spotted two figures—a hulking giant of a man alongside a shorter, squat one. Recognition slammed into her like a physical blow. These were the men who had killed her mother.

Vikings.

CHAPTER 6

Melaney felt Fiona tense beside her and rested a thin, comforting hand on the girl's shoulder. "Shh," she whispered tensely.

Fiona dropped her face into her hands, fighting the urge to cry out, to leap from her hiding place and confront the men who had stolen everything from her. These were her parents' killers—walking free as if the blood on their hands was nothing more than a forgotten memory. It wasn't right. Every muscle in her body screamed to grab the nearest sword, to plunge it into their chests until the armor shattered and their blood ran like rivers.

But Melaney's hand pressed against her, anchoring her to the spot. It was as if the shade could sense the dark, violent images flashing through Fiona's mind. No, there would be no rash moves, no screams of fury or terror. They could only watch, listen, and pray that the marauders would pass by without detecting their presence.

The dirt in the air threatened to choke them, and those hiding in the brush pulled out handkerchiefs, pressing them against their mouths and noses to suppress the desperate urge to cough. One sound, one slip, and they were all as good as dead. The marauders were heavy-footed and brutish, their presence so oppressive that even the birds in the trees had fallen silent.

Several agonizing minutes crawled by, each second stretching out like an eternity as the marauders trudged through the underbrush. The air was thick with tension, so suffocating that it felt like the forest itself was holding its breath. Every crack of a twig beneath their boots, every rustle of leaves, sent a jolt of fear through Fiona's body. She could hear the low murmur of their voices, harsh and guttural, like the growl of some predatory beast. The men spoke in a language she couldn't understand, but the tone was unmistakable—one of violence, of conquest, of men who took what they wanted without a second thought.

Fiona's heart pounded in her chest, each beat a painful reminder of how close they were to being discovered. She pressed herself further into the rough bark of the tree, the texture digging into her back as if trying to hold her there, to keep her safe. The fear was so intense it made her stomach churn, her muscles tense and ready to spring at the slightest provocation. Her eyes darted to Melaney, who remained calm, her gaze fixed on the path ahead. It was as if the shade had seen this all before, had lived through worse, and knew that the only way to survive was to stay still, to be silent, to let the storm pass.

Time seemed to warp, the seconds dragging on. Fiona could feel the sweat trickling down her back, the dampness of her palms as they clenched into fists at her sides. The marauders were close enough now that she could make out the glint of their weapons through the trees, the flash of steel that caught the dappled sunlight. Her breath hitched in her throat as one of the men paused, his head turning as if he had heard something—a twig snapping, a breath caught too sharply. The entire camp seemed to freeze at that moment, every person holding onto the fragile hope that they would remain unseen.

The man lingered, his eyes narrowing as he scanned the area, his hand resting on the hilt of his sword. Fiona's heart felt like it might burst from the strain, her body coiled like a spring ready to snap. But then, after what felt like an eternity, the man turned away, satisfied that there was nothing of interest. He barked an order to his comrades, and they continued on, their heavy boots leaving deep impressions in the soft earth.

It wasn't until the last of them had finally passed, until the sounds of their footsteps had faded into the distance, that Fiona allowed herself to breathe again. The relief was almost overwhelming, her legs trembling as the adrenaline began to wear off. Around her, the other members of the camp began to stir as well, moving cautiously, as if afraid that the marauders might return.

The scout who had warned them earlier mounted his horse and rode off to ensure the marauders were truly gone, that they were safe to move again. Until he returned with the all-clear, no one dared make a move toward the road. In the meantime, Fiona busied herself by wiping down the horses and clearing debris from the wagon, her hands trembling.

"Are you okay?"

Fiona jumped, startled by the sudden voice beside her. Julian stood there, concern etched into his features. "Oh," she breathed. "I didn't hear you."

"You seem upset. I wanted to make sure you were okay."

Fiona tried to muster a smile, but it came out more as a grimace. "Not really," she admitted. "They looked like the men who killed my family."

"They are not the same," Melaney's voice cut in from nearby. Fiona had forgotten how keen the woman's hearing was—like a bat in the darkest of caves.

"Yes, I know," Fiona replied, rolling her eyes, though her heart wasn't in it. "Just like Julian isn't Jason." The frustration was bubbling up inside her, threatening to spill over. She wanted to scream, to punch a tree, to do anything to release the pent-up rage and grief that clawed at her insides.

"There will be many things in this world that remind you of your old one," Melaney said, her tone patient, though her lips pursed into a thin line.

"Too bad there isn't a little more of what I liked," Fiona muttered under her breath.

Julian stepped closer, gently taking her hand. "I'm sorry for everything you've been through," he said, his voice sincere in a way that made her heart flutter despite herself. "For what it's worth."

She watched him walk away, back to where Dax waited for him, her heart still thudding in her chest. "Are they brothers?" she asked Melaney, unable to keep the curiosity from her voice. Jason never had siblings.

"Yes, but not in the traditional sense," Melaney replied, gathering her belongings and slinging her pack over her shoulders. Fiona did the same, falling into step beside her as the caravan moved back onto the dirt road. The trees swayed in the breeze, the sound soothing, a reminder that life went on, even after moments of terror.

"And?" Fiona pressed.

They began walking with the caravan, pulling back onto the dirt road. The trees swayed with the breeze, the sound comforting in its normalcy.

"Julian found Dax lying beside his mother's body, trying to wake her," Melaney said, her voice thick.

Fiona felt a lump form in her throat as she listened, imagining the scene. The image of a young Dax, desperate and grief-stricken, clinging to the last vestiges of hope, was almost too much to bear. The horror of it was palpable, a cruel reminder of the world they lived in—a world where innocence shattered in an instant, and where children grew up far too soon.

"Julian buried her," Melaney continued. "He dug the grave himself, with nothing but his bare hands and a small, rusted spade he found nearby. The ground was hard, frozen from the night's chill, but he didn't stop, didn't rest until she was laid to rest. He wrapped her in what little cloth they had and he laid her in the earth with all the gentleness he could muster. Dax... Dax didn't leave her side the entire time, not until the last clod of dirt fell on the grave."

Fiona's eyes stung with unshed tears, the story cutting deep into her heart. She could see it all so clearly—the small, lonely grave in the middle of the forest, the cold wind biting at their skin, and Julian's hands, raw and bloody, as he tried to offer some semblance of peace to a woman he hadn't known but for whom he now carried a deep sense of responsibility.

"And then," Melaney went on, her voice trembling, "Julian took Dax in. He didn't hesitate, didn't question whether it was the right thing to do. He just knew. Knew that this boy, who had lost everything in the blink of an eye, needed someone to hold onto, someone to guide him through the darkness. They've been inseparable ever since, those two—like a father and son, though Julian would never claim such a title. He's too humble for that. But he's been everything to Dax, and Dax… well, Dax saved him, too, in a way."

The silence that followed was heavy. Fiona's chest tightened with sorrow and admiration for Julian, for the man who had stepped in when no one else could, who had given Dax a second chance at life.

Melaney's eyes glistened. "It's a rare bond they share, one forged in the fires of loss and grief. They're lucky to have found each other, in a world where so many are left to fend for themselves."

The caravan traveled until sundown, the eerie calm clinging to the group like a shroud. The rhythmic crunch of boots against dirt and the occasional clink of metal were the only sounds that marked the passage of time, each one a reminder of how far they still had to go. When the decision was finally made to stop and set up camp for the night, Fiona's relief was palpable. Every step had become a trial, her feet throbbing from the relentless terrain—rocks and twigs that had felt like tiny daggers with each painful jolt.

As they halted, Fiona moved gingerly, her legs stiff and aching as she joined Melaney in hammering stakes into the unforgiving ground. The stakes required more force than Fiona could muster, but she gritted her teeth, ignoring the pain that shot through her hands with each blow. Together, they wrapped thick ropes around the stakes, pulling the canvas of the tent upright. A long wooden rod was thrust into the center, hoisting the tent into its final form. It was rudimentary, but sturdy— a temporary haven in the wilderness, and for that, Fiona was grateful.

Once they secured the tent, Fiona unrolled the thin bedroll Melaney had given her and collapsed onto it in an exhausted heap. The rough fabric scratched against her skin, but she didn't care; the ground beneath her could have been a feathered mattress for all she knew. Her eyes closed almost immediately, her mind drifting back to thoughts of her mother, father, and sister. The memories were a bittersweet balm, soothing the aches in her heart even as they deepened the longing she felt for them. As the exhaustion took hold, she surrendered to the pull of sleep.

"You must be hungry."

The voice startled Fiona awake, yanking her from the depths of sleep. She blinked up at Melaney, who stood by her side with arms crossed, her face a neutral mask. "Better hurry," Melaney added.

Fiona scrambled to her feet, rubbing at her sleepy eyes as she tried to shake off the lingering fog of sleep. "How long was I asleep?" she asked.

"A couple of hours," Melaney replied, her gaze sliding to the darkening sky. "It's dusk now."

"I'm so sorry!" Fiona's voice rose in panic. She had slept while everyone else was hard at work setting up the camp.

Melaney said nothing in response, but instead turned on her heel and exited the tent. The silence was as much an invitation to follow as any words would have been, and so Fiona did. Outside, the fires crackled in several places, their warm glow casting long shadows that danced across the ground. People chattered, their voices a soothing murmur that filled the cool evening air.

"You're up!" Natalie's cheerful voice rang out, cutting through the hum of conversation. She appeared at Fiona's side, her hand slipping into Fiona's. "I hope you feel better. Come on, let's get some food in that empty belly of yours."

Fiona's stomach growled in response, a sharp reminder of

how long it had been since she'd eaten. The old woman at the food wagon offered her a plate, steaming with a modest portion of food. "Last of the pork, miss. You're just in time," she said, her weathered face softening with a kind smile. Fiona accepted the plate with a grateful nod and followed Natalie to a spot near the fire where Lia sat waiting, knees drawn to her chest, her dress arranged around her ankles. Her hair, piled atop her head in a haphazard bun, framed her face with loose strands.

"You shouldn't have let me sleep," Fiona admonished her friends as she sat down, her voice filled with guilt. "I fear the camp hates me now for not pulling my weight."

Lia threw her head back and laughed, the sound light and carefree. Her pale throat glowed in the flickering light of the nearby flame. "Pulling your weight? You'll be pulling more than yours soon enough," she teased, her eyes twinkling with amusement.

Fiona puzzled at the remark, but before she could question it, Melaney chimed in. "Right so."

"These women giving you trouble?" a deeper voice interjected, causing Fiona to tense. She didn't need to look to know it was Julian.

Dax, ever the energetic bundle of chaos, plopped down beside Fiona with a wide grin. Julian followed more cautiously, settling himself next to Melaney. The little boy tore into the remains of a chop, his small teeth tearing into the meat with unrestrained enthusiasm. "I'm the trouble 'round here," Dax declared, his grin widening.

"No one will contest that," Julian chuckled, his deep voice rumbling like distant thunder.

What could have been an awkward gathering quickly turned into one of the most pleasant evenings Fiona had experienced in a long time, thanks to Dax's infectious energy. The boy chattered away, his stories and jokes drawing laughter and amused scoffs from the adults. Fiona marveled at his ability to captivate an audience, his bright eyes and animated gestures keeping everyone entertained. Even Melaney, who was so often reserved, smiled ear to ear as she listened to the boy's antics. Maybe she is human, Fiona thought.

As the night wore on and the moon reached its peak in the sky, people began to retire one by one. Fires were doused, the flames hissing as they were smothered, and the camp fell into a peaceful quiet. Fiona sat watching the glowing embers of the fire, mesmerized by the way the strips of wood turned to ash, the last of the flames licking at the air in a final bid to stay alive. It was almost fitting, she thought—a symbol of something fleeting, something beautiful that would soon be gone.

A hand appeared in her line of sight, long, muscled, and calloused. She looked up to see Julian standing over her, his face shadowed in the dim light. "May I see you to your tent?" he asked, his voice a low murmur that sent a shiver down her spine.

Fiona hesitated, her heart pounding in her chest. She was afraid to accept, afraid that her own desires, buried deep but not forgotten, would surge to the surface and overwhelm her. But the warmth of his hand, the sincerity in his eyes—it was too much to resist. She reached out a pale, trembling hand and grasped his. He smiled at her, and she could see the effort it took, the vulnerability in the gesture.

"I don't want to trouble you," she whispered, releasing his hand and turning away. She took two steps before she felt his hand again, pulling her back, gently spinning her to face him. His lips brushed against her ear, his hot breath sending a shock of desire down her spine.

"I'm sorry," he murmured. He pulled back just enough for her to see the sincerity in his eyes, the concern etched into his handsome face. "About how I've been, I mean. Let me make it up to you." He searched her eyes for some sign of forgiveness. "Please. At least let me escort you to your tent tonight. Then, in the morning, maybe we can be friends."

Fiona sucked in a deep breath and held it for a moment, her mind racing. Her fingers, still wrapped in his, tingled with a mix of uncertainty and something deeper, something she wasn't ready to name. "Julian," she began, her voice shaky.

"Yes?" His face— too handsome, too close— filled with an expectant tension as he waited for her answer.

"My tent is right here." Fiona nudged the open flap with the toe of her boot, a small smile playing at her lips as she watched the realization dawn on his face.

Julian was momentarily speechless, his eyes widening in surprise. He straightened, clearing his throat. "Oh. Right," he muttered.

Fiona couldn't help but smile—a real, genuine smile, the first in what felt like weeks. "Thank you, kind sir," she said, dropping into a playful curtsy to mark her words. "Will I be escorted from my tent in the morning?"

Julian chuckled, the sound warm and relieved. "Of course! Have a good night's sleep, m'lady," he replied, bowing in return. He lifted her hand to his lips, brushing a soft kiss across her knuckles before vanishing into the night.

Fiona watched him go, her heart lighter than it had been in days. As she ducked into her tent and settled onto her bedroll, she found herself looking forward to the morning.

CHAPTER 7

Pavlo's death had been exquisitely orchestrated, its effect rippling through the ranks with a chilling finality. Not a word had been spoken for an entire day, the silence as suffocating as a shroud pulled over a corpse. Niklaos had tethered himself to the prisoner as though his very life hung in the balance—which, in truth, it did. Ivar had relished the silence. He had left Pavlo's broken body to rot in the dirt, leading his men northeast with a cold, unyielding purpose.

Now, Ivar sat astride his warhorse at the crest of a hill, the sun casting long shadows over the marauder army assembled below. Aldo stalked between the rows of soldiers, each one standing at rigid attention. Their polished armor gleamed in the sunlight, sweat running in rivulets down their arms and legs.

"The next village lies two miles ahead!" Aldo barked, his voice carrying over the ranks like a war drum. "We'll take it as we have the others— swift and lethal! No prisoners! Take what you can carry! Fill the supply wagons! I want it quick, I want it deadly! Are you ready?"

The response was a feral roar, a cacophony of voices that reverberated through the air and shook the ground beneath their feet. Ivar's smile widened as he watched the fervor in his men, their bloodlust palpable. He nudged his horse aside, making room for Aldo to mount the steed waiting beside him.

"They're ready," Ivar murmured, his voice laced with satisfaction. "Well done, Aldo."

"Always an honor," Aldo replied, gathering the reins of his horse.

"Marauders!" growled the captain, a wiry but tenacious old soldier whose presence alone could command a legion. "Arms at the ready!"

Lances pounded the earth in unison, the sound echoing like thunder. "Forward march!"

The thunderous rhythm of boots against the earth was a symphony to Ivar's ears, a prelude to the carnage that awaited. His hand drifted to the vial concealed beneath his cloak. Her power thrummed faintly against his hip, growing stronger, craving blood spilled. Soon, she would be ready—soon, she would be reborn.

As the army advanced, the distant figures of villagers could be seen fleeing towards the cluster of huts. It was a pitiful attempt at escape, a futile effort to warn the others of what was coming. Ivar's scouts had already confirmed that there were no warriors among them. It would be a slaughter, nothing more.

The marauders drew closer, their excitement rippling through the ranks like a wave. They lived for this—the kill, the bloodshed, the sheer thrill of overpowering their enemies. Ivar could feel their anticipation, could taste the fear in the air.

When they were close enough to see the frantic faces of the men below, Ivar raised his hand, signaling a halt. The army obeyed, every man freezing in place, weapons at the ready. Only Ivar and Aldo continued forward, dismounting their horses and dropping the reins to the ground. Their steeds stood obediently, awaiting their next command.

With a swagger that spoke of absolute confidence, Ivar and Aldo strode into the heart of the village, their presence alone enough to clear the streets. Doors slammed shut, and shutters drawn, but it wouldn't save them. They had nowhere to run.

"Where is your leader?" Aldo's voice rang out, a demand that brooked no disobedience.

A frail, hunched man emerged from one of the huts, his eyes wide with terror. He shuffled forward, trembling as he fell to his knees before them. "Please, take what you want, but spare us," he begged, his voice a nasal whine that grated on Ivar's nerves. "We are peaceful folk, we mean you no harm."

"We will take what we want," Aldo replied, his tone dripping with contempt. "We don't need you to offer that."

The man's eyes darted nervously, desperate to appease. "What is it you desire? I will make it so."

Aldo stepped closer, towering over the cowering figure, his expression one of cruel amusement. "We want blood."

Before the man could react, Aldo's hand shot out, plunging a dagger deep into his gut. The man gasped, his eyes bulging as he looked down at the blade embedded in his flesh. Aldo twisted the hilt with a sickening crunch. Blood gushed from the man's mouth, and he collapsed, twitching, to the ground.

The metallic tang of blood filled the air, and Ivar inhaled deeply, savoring the scent. This was what the marauders had been waiting for. With the village leader dying at their feet, the men surged forward, a tide of violence that swept through the streets, cutting down anyone in their path. They spared no one—men, women, children—every life in a relentless, bloody advance.

Ivar led the charge, his sword a blur of steel as he cut them down with ruthless efficiency. The vial's power thrummed faintly against his hip, a constant, subtle pulse that synced with his own heartbeat.

With every life he took, Ivar could feel the energy within the vial intensify. It started as a gentle warmth, barely noticeable against his skin, but with each drop of blood spilled, that warmth grew into a searing heat. The sorceress's power was awakening, no longer content to remain dormant, and Ivar could feel her presence more clearly now, as if she were whispering to him, urging him to continue, to kill, to destroy.

He could almost hear her voice—a faint, seductive murmur that echoed in his mind. It was as if she were guiding his hand, directing his blade to the most vulnerable points, ensuring that every strike was lethal, every death efficient. She was a part of him now, their fates entwined by the bloodshed he wrought in her name.

As the final villager crumpled to the ground, life draining from their eyes, Ivar stood amidst the carnage, wiping the blood from his blade with a deliberate, almost ritualistic motion. The air was thick with the stench of death and smoke, the village reduced to smoldering ruins. Bodies lay scattered like broken dolls, their lifeless forms contorted in grotesque displays of their final terror. Blood pooled in the dirt, mingling with ash, as the remnants of what had once been a peaceful settlement now lay in utter devastation.

Ivar's gaze swept over the destruction with a sense of grim satisfaction. His men had done their work well. The marauders moved among the dead, looting what remained, their faces gleaming with sweat and blood lust. They were like wolves after a feast, sated but still eager for more.

At his side, the vial pulsed with searing heat, the sorceress's power burning against his flesh like a brand. The pain was sharp and intense, but Ivar welcomed it. It was not merely a sensation; it was a promise, a harbinger of what was to come.

The pain intensified, spreading from his hip and radiating through his body like wildfire. It was agony, but it was also ecstasy—a reminder of the power that awaited him. Each throb of heat was a whisper of her impending rebirth, a sign that the time was drawing near. The sorceress was more than a phantom bound to the vial; she was a living force, straining against the confines of her prison, eager to be unleashed.

With one last glance at the ruined village, Ivar mounted his horse, the vial's heat still burning against his side, a constant reminder of the power he was about to wield. The journey was far from over, but he knew, with every fiber of his being, that the end was in sight. And when it came, the world would bow before him—or be destroyed like this village.

The smell was not a pleasant one. It lingered in the air, tugging at Fiona's memory, elusive yet hauntingly familiar. The caravan halted at the bottom of the hill, the travelers uneasy and unwilling to press forward until word came back from the scout. Finally, they spotted him cantering through the tall grass on his horse. The wind picked up, rustling the branches of the trees that bordered the clearing, and with it, the scent returned— stronger this time, more pungent. Fiona's stomach twisted, bile rising into her throat.

Spinning around, she stumbled toward the edge of the caravan, her legs turning to rubber and refusing to support her. Desperation overtook her as she slapped a hand over her mouth, trying to contain the inevitable. She barely made it to the ground before her body betrayed her, and she began to retch. The bile scorched her throat, and her eyes watered as she heaved and coughed, her body wracked with the force of it.

When it was over, Fiona collapsed onto the ground, exhausted, the cool earth against her forehead offering a small measure of relief. She coughed again, dry and painful, and closed her eyes, willing herself to find some semblance of calm. The spinning in her head began to slow, and she felt herself lifted, cradled against a familiar chest. Without thinking, she reached up, fingers clutching a fistful of his shirt, drawing herself closer to the comforting warmth.

"Are you okay?" Julian's voice was soft, concerned, but Fiona struggled to find the words to explain the dread gnawing at her insides. Instead, a sob escaped her, shuddering and raw. The world around her seemed to fade as she clung to Julian, the sound of a horse's snort barely registering in her mind. The scout's panicked words, however, cut through the haze like a knife: "Dead bodies, all burning."

Julian's grip on Fiona tightened as he listened, his face grim. Fiona took a ragged breath, trying to pull herself together. She knew she needed to be strong, but the tears flowed down her cheeks. "The marauders leave no survivors," she choked out, her voice trembling.

"You survived an attack on your world," Melaney said, her arms crossed, her expression stern.

"I did, with my cousin Emma."

"Maybe there are some here that still live," Melaney suggested, though her tone was doubtful.

The elderly cook shook his head, his weathered face creased with concern. "I don't like it," he muttered, his voice rough. "Bad stuffs happened there. We should circle around it and be on our way."

Melaney pursed her lips, considering his words, but before she could respond, Stelios, the good doctor, stepped forward. "I cannot, in good conscience, skirt around such a scene," he declared. "If there are any living beings in that village, I must do what I can. I will go alone if I must."

"You won't be alone," Melaney said. "I'll go with you."

"I will, too." Natalie piped up.

Searching wreckage and human remains was no small feat, and none too desirable, yet one by one, people began to step forward, volunteering to help. Summoning what strength she had left, Fiona began to rise, and Julian stood, pulling her to her feet. He didn't release her hand, his grip a steady anchor in the storm of her emotions.

"I'll go, too," Fiona said, her voice steadier now.

Julian nodded. "Me, too."

In the end, only the cook and the children stayed behind with the wagon. The rest of them began the slow, somber trek up the hill, each lost in the dread of what they might find on the other side. As they neared the top, the stench of burning flesh and wood grew stronger, more suffocating. Fiona was certain that if it weren't for Julian's hand gripping hers, she might have turned and fled back down the hill.

The wind grew hot, carrying billows of dark smoke that obscured the sky. Crows cawed from the nearby trees, their cries harsh and foreboding. The group cautiously entered the village, their eyes darting from one ruined structure to another. The town was eerily quiet, with belongings strewn across the ground, as if a rampaging beast had torn through. Window flaps hung in tatters, and doors lay shattered on the ground, broken and splintered.

"They kicked in the doors," Fiona whispered, realizing only then that she was squeezing Julian's hand much tighter than she intended.

As they reached the center of the village, the crackling of flames grew deafening. Fiona's gaze fell upon a sight she had hoped to never see again—a mass grave of burning bodies, the villagers piled atop one another in a horrific mound of death. The smell was overpowering, the heat from the flames searing her skin even from a distance.

Fiona's breath caught in her raw throat, and she wished desperately to be anywhere else. She shut her eyes, forcing herself to take slow, deliberate breaths. In the darkness behind her eyelids, she envisioned a vast green field, every blade of grass sharp and clear as if viewed through the eyes of an eagle. The wind whistled past, a dizzying sensation that made the world spin. She squeezed her eyes shut tighter, fearing that the motion might send her spiraling into oblivion.

When she finally dared to open one eye, she found the world drifting beneath her. The sun shone down, warm and comforting. There was no wind, no noise, only silence. Peace. The sensation of it flooded through her, swirling in her belly, expanding into her chest, and stretching down her arms and legs until it enveloped her entirely. She closed her eyes again, basking in a blissful calm she had not felt in what seemed like an eternity. It was as though all the tension, all the fear, had melted away, leaving her weightless and free. She closed her eyes, happy for a moment.

But when she opened her eyes once more, the burning bodies were still there before her, the crackling flames still roaring. The devastation was real, and yet... she felt nothing. She braced herself for the familiar wave of nausea to return, but to her surprise, it did not. The peace remained, a protective barrier that shielded her from the horror surrounding her. The overwhelming sense of calm held firm, steady, like an unbreakable shield around her heart.

Fiona blinked, confused. She glanced up at Julian, whose hand was still wrapped around hers, his grip warm and grounding. But when she met his gaze, she saw something in his eyes that made her stomach lurch— a mixture of concern, shock, and something else.

"Are you okay?" Julian asked quietly. His face was pale, his eyes wide as he searched hers for answers. He looked stunned, as if he couldn't quite believe what he was seeing. What had he seen?

Fiona's heart began to race, her thoughts spinning in a dizzying whirl. What had just happened? How had she managed to pull herself out of the darkness so completely? A part of her wanted to embrace it, to let it wash away the fear and uncertainty that had plagued her for so long. But another part of her— deeper, more instinctual— was terrified. This wasn't right. This wasn't how things were supposed to be.

"I... I don't know," she finally whispered, her voice trembling. She tore her gaze away from Julian's, her eyes darting around as if searching for some clue, some explanation. But the village was still burning, the bodies still smoldering in the flames, and there was no sign of anything out of the ordinary— except for the fact that she was standing there, completely unfazed.

Melaney appeared before them, her eyes narrowing as they locked onto Fiona. The piercing intensity of her gaze sent a shiver down Fiona's spine. It was as if the sorceress could see straight through her, into the very core of her being, peeling back layers to reveal the truth that Fiona herself didn't yet understand.

Before Fiona could answer, Melaney stepped in front of them, her gaze piercing, studying, as if seeing straight into Fiona's soul. "We will talk later," she said, her tone leaving no room for argument. Then, without another word, she turned and walked away.

The cleanup that followed was half-hearted at best. The bodies were already consumed by the flames, so the travelers focused on gathering whatever supplies they could salvage. As the sun began to dip below the horizon, they trudged back to the waiting caravan, weighed down by the somber reality of what they had seen. There was no question of staying overnight in the village—the stench of death was too strong, and no one had the stomach for it.

When they returned, they found that the cook and the children had already set up camp at the bottom of the hill. A modest meal of chicken and beets awaited them, but the mood was subdued, and everyone ate in relative silence. One by one, they retired to their tents for the night, seeking the solace of sleep to escape the memories of the day.

As Fiona lay in her tent, listening to the quiet rustle of the wind outside, she couldn't shake the feeling that something had changed within her. The peace she had found amid the horror lingered, a strange, unexpected gift. She didn't know what it meant, but she held on to it, clutching it like a lifeline as she drifted into a fitful sleep, haunted by the flickering images of flames and the scent of burning flesh.

# CHAPTER 8

The next morning, the travelers wasted no time scarfing down berries and bread, their movements brisk and mechanical as they packed everything up. A heavy silence hung over the caravan as it left the town behind. The once roaring flames had died down, leaving behind a somber landscape of ash.

Fiona couldn't resist turning back, her eyes searching for the last remnants of the village. From the distance, all that was visible was a plume of black smoke and the tops of a watchtower. Her chest tightened as she gazed at the futile structure, a stark reminder of the destruction. She closed her eyes and took a deep, cleansing breath. Then, she turned away and continued on with the caravan, her footsteps heavy.

Melaney appeared beside her, breaking the silence that had settled like a shroud. "You tranced," she said. "How's your vision today?"

Fiona blinked, confusion knitting her brow as she looked around her. "A little blurry. I did what?"

"You tranced. Back in the town yesterday," Melaney repeated patiently as she held up a cup. "Tea?"

"I'm afraid I don't follow," Fiona replied, accepting the cup, her mind scrambling to make sense of the word.

"Your eyes became blank, pure white as porcelain," Melaney explained, her gaze steady. "Only you saw something—a vision."

"I flew. Like an eagle," Fiona whispered, sipping the tea as they walked. The memory rushed back to her in a wave of surreal clarity that left her breathless.

It wasn't just a fleeting thought or a mere vision; it was as if she had been ripped from her body and flung into the sky, where the world stretched out beneath her in a tapestry of green and gold. She could feel the wind in her hair, the sharp sting of the cold air against her skin, and the exhilarating rush of freedom that came with every powerful beat of her wings. Her wings. The realization made her gasp, her heart thundering in her chest. She hadn't imagined it—she had felt it, lived it.

The air had been alive around her, vibrant and humming with an energy that she had never known. Every blade of grass below had been sharp and distinct, every shadow a whisper of secrets she could almost understand. It was a different world, a different reality, one that pulsed with life in a way that the ground beneath her feet never had.

As the memory surged through her, she felt a strange, almost painful pull in her chest, as if a part of her longed to be up there, soaring through the clouds. Her pulse quickened with the thought, and she found herself reaching out, as though she could grasp that feeling again, pull it back to her. But it was gone, as elusive as smoke in the wind, leaving only the echo of that impossible flight in her bones.

Fiona's eyes darted to Melaney, searching for answers in the older woman's calm, knowing gaze. But Melaney simply smiled, a soft, secretive smile. "It was a trance," she repeated, "Your mind harnessed your inner energy. You saw through your familiar. It's not something most shades experience."

Familiar?" Fiona repeated, still grappling with the unfamiliar terminology.

"Yes," Melaney continued, her expression softening. "We each have something—a creature—our minds connect with, a bond more powerful than any love forged in the world. It helps us, loves us, protects us, and befriends us." She cocked her head to the side. "And curious that you can do this now."

Fiona let the information sink in, her mind turning over Melaney's words as the caravan moved on. The smoke behind them faded from view, replaced by the fresh scent of dewy grass and rustling trees. Chatter among the travelers rose up, the tension easing.

After a long pause, Fiona broke the silence between them as they walked. "What is yours?"

"Pardon?" Melaney asked, her focus drifting back to Fiona.

"Your familiar. What is it?" Fiona clarified, her curiosity piqued despite her weariness.

Melaney smiled, a knowing glint in her eyes. "You'll see soon enough."

Fiona frowned. "You won't tell me?"

"There is no need, my dear," Melaney replied, shaking her head. "All in time."

Though curiosity burned within her, Fiona set her jaw and remained silent. She knew it was futile to try and pry more information from Melaney than she was willing to give. So, she let it go, though the questions continued to swirl in her mind.

They made camp early that night, everyone exhausted. The cook was more irritable than usual, grumbling as he served the evening meal. "The ol' woman is asleep," he muttered to Melaney and Fiona as they took their food from him. "Under the weather, she is."

"You would do well to have Stelios look her over," Melaney suggested.

"Aye, I will be doin' that." The cook bobbed his head and turned to the next in line.

Fiona and Melaney joined Lia and Natalie, who were already seated on the ground giggling over some joke. "What's so funny?" Fiona asked as she dropped into a heap next to Natalie.

"Oh, just boys. Nothing you should be worrying about, oh powerful sorcerer," Lia teased, bowing low with a mischievous grin.

"Ladies," Melaney raised an eyebrow, causing the two girls to quickly sober. Fiona couldn't help but grin at their sudden change in demeanor.

But as she picked at her food, a feeling of restlessness began to grow in the pit of her stomach. She tore a morsel of goat flesh from the bone on her plate and popped it into her mouth, the rich, salty flavor bursting on her tongue. They never ate goat in Hibernia, and she wasn't entirely sure why. Yet even the unfamiliar taste couldn't quell the unease bubbling within her.

Finishing her meal, Fiona pushed her plate to the side and looked up, only to find Melaney's dark, intense gaze fixed on her. Had she been staring at her this entire time? Fiona's muscles tensed as the restless feeling surged, turning into an almost unbearable need to move. Her arms and legs twitched with pent-up energy, making it impossible to sit still.

She couldn't take it any longer. "Excuse me," Fiona muttered as she shot to her feet, nearly knocking over her plate. Without waiting for a response, she hurried to the edge of the encampment and plunged into the thick brush.

She ran, her feet pounding against the earth, her breath coming in quick, shallow gasps. She didn't know where she was headed. It felt as if an invisible force was pulling her along, guiding her through the dense forest. Branches whipped at her face, scratching her arms and tearing at her clothes, but she paid them no mind. Nothing mattered except the urgency to reach...somewhere.

Her foot caught on a large branch, sending her sprawling to the ground. The impact knocked the wind out of her, leaving her gasping for breath. Agonizing seconds stretched on before she managed to suck in a long, ragged breath. Air burned into her lungs, and she stayed prone a moment longer.

Looking around, Fiona pulled herself up and sat on the log she had tripped over. The sun filtered through the leafy branches above, casting dappled light across her face. It was warm, soothing, and as she sat there, the restlessness that had driven her to flee began to ebb away, replaced by a strange sense of calm.

The warmth from the setting sun seemed to intensify, swirling around her in a golden cone of light. She felt it seeping into her skin, filling her with a gentle, radiant energy. Invisible fingers wrapped around her waist, lifting her effortlessly into the air.

Melaney stepped into view, her expression serene as she watched Fiona rise above the ground. There was a smile on her lips, and a twinkle in her eye, as if she had been expecting this. She waited, her presence both comforting and unnerving.

Fiona's attention snapped to her hands as a strange warmth began to pulse beneath her skin. Her breath caught in her throat, and her heart pounded against her ribcage. A soft, golden light glowed from within her, spreading like liquid fire beneath her skin. Rays of light burst from her fingertips, shooting into the air like beams of sunlight. They flickered and danced in a breeze, weaving intricate patterns in the space around her, as though the wind itself was alive—sentient and aware of her every thought, every movement.

Fiona moved her hands, hesitantly at first, then with growing wonder, marveling at the way the wind responded to her will. It followed her every will, swirling and twisting in a graceful dance, as if it were an extension of her very soul. She could feel its power coursing through her, a vibrant energy that filled her with a sense of awe.

Her body began to lower back to the ground, the light around her dimming as she was gently set down on the log.

"Melaney!" Fiona gasped, her voice ringing out in a hollow, melodious tone that reverberated through the air like the chime of a bell. She barely recognized the sound as her own, and the shock of it sent a shiver down her spine. "What's going on?"

The older woman approached her, her hands outstretched in a gesture of invitation. Fiona grasped them, and was pulled to her feet as if she weighed nothing.

"This, Fiona," Melaney said softly, her voice a soothing balm to the chaos swirling inside Fiona's mind, "is the beginning of your awakening. Your power has lain dormant for so long, waiting for the right moment to surface. And now, it has chosen to reveal itself."

Fiona's breath came in ragged gasps, reality washing over her like a tidal wave. The light still shimmered around her hands, a reminder that this was no dream. She could feel it in her bones, in her very soul— this was real.

"But... how?" she whispered, her voice trembling as she tried to understand. "I've never—this shouldn't be possible."

"Power often manifests when it is needed most," Melaney replied. "You've faced something that would have broken others. But instead, they have forged you into something stronger."

"What do I do now?" Fiona asked, her voice a whisper, her heart pounding with a mixture of fear and exhilaration.

Melaney's lips curved into a gentle, knowing smile. "Now, my dear, you learn to harness it. To control it. This is only the beginning."

The sun set, and the moon rose.

Melaney released Fiona's hands and took a step back, her eyes gleaming with quiet wisdom. "Look. Listen. Learn."

Fiona did as she was told, her gaze sweeping across the world now bathed in the silver glow of the moon. It was as if she were seeing it for the first time. The moon, large and luminous, cast its ethereal light over the landscape, making the trees shimmer with a soft, otherworldly glow. The leaves, vibrant green in the sun, now appeared as silken shades of silver and blue, their edges kissed by the moonlight. A nightingale sang from a nearby branch, its song more than a melody—it was a haunting, beautiful refrain that echoed in her soul. The wind whispered through the trees, each breath a gentle caress, carrying with it the scent of night-blooming flowers, rich and intoxicating. Everything around her pulsed with a quiet, intense magic, as if the world itself had transformed under the moon's gaze, revealing a hidden beauty that had always been there, waiting for her to see.

She turned to Melaney, her eyes wide with astonishment. The older woman smiled, a knowing look in her eyes.

"Refreshing, isn't it? The senses of a shade," Melaney said, her voice as gentle as the wind.

"A shade," Fiona echoed, her voice tinged with both awe and apprehension. The word felt foreign, yet it resonated deep within her, as if it held a truth she had always known. "You mean a sorcerer?"

"A shade," Melaney repeated. "It is what we are. We exist in the space between life and death, guardians of the balance, protectors of the very core of existence."

Fiona felt a rush of wonder and disbelief. "This is incredible," she whispered, closing her eyes to fully embrace the sensation of the wind caressing her skin.

It was no longer just air; it was a living entity, alive with a pulse and purpose, wrapping around her like a lover's embrace. The cool breeze traced the contours of her skin, tender and possessive, as if it knew every inch of her, every secret hidden deep within. Each gust seemed to breathe with a life of its own, swirling around her, filling the space between them with a tangible presence that left her breathless. The sensation was intoxicating, a heady mix of power and vulnerability that sent shivers down her spine. She moaned, a sound of pure, unadulterated pleasure, as the wind enveloped her, filling her with a sense of connection she had never known. It was as though she had become one with the night, with the moonlight and shadows, with the very earth beneath her feet. She could feel the heartbeat of the world in every breath, a rhythm that matched her own, and she lost herself in the sheer bliss of it, surrendering completely to the moment, to the sensation, to the overwhelming force that had claimed her.

Melaney took a step back, her voice cutting through the euphoria. "Come, sister."

Fiona's eyes snapped open, her body resisting the call. "Do I have to?" she asked, her voice tinged with reluctance. The wind's caress had immobilized her, its delicate fingers making her feel as if she were part of the very earth itself.

"We must return before the others come looking. It is our duty to ensure their safe passage," Melaney replied.

"Duty?" Fiona repeated, the word snapping her back to reality. She shook her head, trying to clear the fog of enchantment that had settled over her. As she did, the wind's touch faded, leaving her feeling exposed, almost naked without its presence. "We have a duty?"

"Always," Melaney said, her voice carrying the weight of a thousand unspoken responsibilities. She took Fiona's hand, leading her out of the clearing and back toward the caravan.

As they emerged onto the road, Fiona was surprised to see Julian standing ahead of the others, his arms crossed and a look of concern etched across his face.

"You okay?" he asked, his voice filled with a mixture of worry and something else—something she couldn't quite place.

She nodded. "You ask me that a lot."

Julian's expression softened, and without a word, he gestured for her to go with him. As the caravan began its slow march down the path, he walked beside her, his presence a comforting anchor in the shifting tides of her new reality. Behind them, Melaney pulled the hood of her shawl over her head, her eyes sharp and watchful as they moved onward in the fresh night.

The caravan made good progress even in the wee hours of the night, the miles falling away behind them. When they stopped, they set up camp a ways off the path. No one spoke of it, but there was an unspoken agreement that they needed to stay off the road for the night. The memory of marauders was too fresh, too real, for anyone to risk lingering on the open path.

Fires stayed low, voices hushed, and the cook bustled about with an urgency that suggested he believed his very life depended on getting it out to a hungry crowd.

"This is good," Fiona said as she chewed on the venison steak, the rich, smoky flavor grounding her after the evening's strange events.

The cook snorted, wiping his hands on his apron. "Hope you're ready, missy. We're nearly out of meat."

"We'll find something," Julian assured him with a wink.

"Damn right you will," the cook grumbled, gesturing as he moved on to serve the others.

"He's so gruff," Fiona observed, watching the cook with a mix of amusement and curiosity.

Julian shrugged, his expression softening as he watched the older man. "He's had his tribulations. More than most."

Before Fiona could ask more, Melaney appeared, settling herself between Fiona and Dax. "Good evening, you two," she said with a slight smile. "Three, sorry," she added, kissing the top of Dax's sandy-colored head.

"Thanks," Dax muttered, though his tone was distant. He was drawing patterns in the dirt with a twig, his usual energy replaced by a quiet, brooding mood.

"I'd better help get the tents ready." Julian stood.

Fiona glanced up at him, half expecting him to walk away, but to her surprise, he hesitated. The moment stretched, and then, in a move that caught her completely off guard, Julian leaned down and pressed a quick, almost absent-minded kiss to her cheek. The touch was brief, a fleeting brush of his lips against her skin, but it sent a flush of warmth rushing through her, leaving her stunned.

Fiona blinked, her heart skipping a beat. Her skin tingled where his lips had touched, the warmth spreading through her like wildfire. She opened her mouth to say something, anything, but the words stuck in her throat.

"I'll come find you before we sleep," he promised, his voice soft, but Fiona could only nod, still too startled to respond. As he turned and walked away, Fiona's hand instinctively rose to touch the spot where his lips had been, her fingertips brushing the warm skin as if trying to hold onto the sensation.

Melaney's eyebrows arched.

Fiona turned crimson. Dax peeked up at her and smiled and she averted her gaze to avoid his.

Melaney shook her head and finished dinner in silence.

CHAPTER 9

True to his word, Julian appeared sometime later. Fiona's breath caught in her throat when she saw him standing by the tree line, his silhouette almost melding with the shadows. She was thankful the darkness concealed the scarlet warmth that crept up her cheeks, tracing circles across her skin as she waded through the tall grass toward him. As she drew closer, the cool night air was replaced by the warmth of his presence, the heat of his body radiating toward her like a beacon in the night.

"Come," Julian said, his voice a low, comforting murmur that sent shivers down her spine. Without hesitation, he reached out and took her hand, his grip firm yet gentle, and led her into the woods.

They moved with a steady rhythm, Julian's free hand parting the dense foliage to create a path. He kept her close behind him, never once releasing her hand, as if afraid she might disappear into the night if he let go.

"Do you know where you're going?" Fiona's voice wavered, her usual confidence eroded by the uncertainty that gnawed at her. The deeper they ventured, the more the shadows seemed to press in, the unknown stretching before them like an endless abyss.

"Is that a requirement for an outing?" Julian's voice remained low, teasing even in the darkness.

"I hardly think I need to answer that," Fiona retorted, her voice rising slightly in response to the unease that fluttered in her chest. She was met with a sharp look from Julian.

"Keep it down. You never know what lurks out here."

Fiona sighed, rolling her eyes even as her heart pounded in her chest. She had just opened her mouth to reply when she collided with Julian's back, her nose smashing against his shoulder with a painful thud.

"Ow!" she exclaimed, rubbing her stinging nose.

"Let's stop here."

Fiona rubbed her stinging nose and took a step back and released her hand from his. "Thanks for the warning," she said dryly.

Then she realized where they were.

A clearing like the previous one she and Melaney had left earlier, this one draped in the deep, velvety shadows of the night. The nearly full moon hung high above them, casting a pale, silvery light that filtered through the treetops, creating a mosaic of glowing patches on the forest floor. Fiona raised her hand, her breath catching as she watched the soft, white light dance across her fingers, the wind swirling and caressing her skin like a living entity. The sensation sent shivers racing up her arms, her entire body humming with the energy that crackled in the air.

"I don't believe it!" Julian's voice was barely more than a breath, his wide eyes reflecting the awe that Fiona felt deep in her bones.

"What?" she asked, her voice just as hushed, the words almost drowned out by the thundering of her heart.

"You're really what Melaney said you are," Julian murmured, his tone laced with a mixture of disbelief and reverence.

"You didn't believe it?" Fiona felt a pang of something— relief, maybe— that was quickly overshadowed by a lingering doubt. "I didn't either. Still not sure I do."

Julian's gaze softened, his lips curving into a small, almost reluctant smile. "It's pretty clear now, love."

As he spoke, the swirling air in Fiona's hand began to condense, gathering into a tight, round shape in her palm. It pulsed with energy, twitching as if staying still was an unbearable strain, as if it longed to be set free.

"What is this?" Fiona whispered, her voice trembling with both fear and wonder.

"Your affinity, of course," Julian grinned. "We all have them."

"We?"

"Oh, sorry," Julian said, though he didn't sound sorry at all. "Here, let me show you."

He raised one arm, snapping his fingers with a practiced ease, producing a small, flickering flame that danced above his skin, illuminating his face in a warm, golden light.

"Amazing," Fiona admitted, stepping closer, her curiosity piqued despite her growing frustration. She examined the flame from every angle, her eyes narrowing as she tried to make sense of the impossible.

"So all this time, you've been one of them and just conveniently left it out of the conversation?"

Julian's smile vanished, replaced by a look of guilt. "I wasn't sure you were genuine."

"How could I not be if I didn't even know what a shade was until now?" Fiona snapped, her anger flaring like the wind that picked up around them, rustling the leaves in agitation.

"You'd be surprised," Julian muttered, his voice carrying a weight that made Fiona pause, her anger flickering like the flame on his finger.

"What's that supposed to mean?"

"Nothing. Let's head back." Julian's grip tightened on her hand.

"Why did you bring me out so far?"

Julian paused, his gaze softening. "Certain spots centralize the strength of our affinities. This is one of them. We're drawn to them."

Fiona considered his words, realizing that must have been why she felt such a connection to the clearing earlier that day. "Makes sense."

"Of course it makes sense. I said it," Julian replied with a smirk, his teeth gleaming in the pale moonlight.

"Very funny." Fiona huffed, yanking her hand free as she turned to trudge back toward the caravan. She pulled her tunic closer to her body, crossing her arms against the sudden chill that seemed to fill the woods, the cold pressing in like water in a lake. She wondered if the cold was her doing or the work of nature.

"Is it something I said?" Julian asked, appearing beside her with ease, his longer legs matching her stride. He had shoved his hands into his pockets, a gesture that struck Fiona as awkward, almost as if he didn't know what to do with them. Part of her suspected he'd rather be holding her hand, a thought that made her brows furrow in confusion.

"Fiona?"

She glanced at him. "Sorry, yes. I don't like that you hid this from me."

"You had Melaney. It didn't seem important."

"It was very important." Fiona's voice reached a higher register and the wind gusted. Julian fell silent, his gaze dropping to the ground as they walked. When they finally reached Fiona's tent, she stopped, turning to face him.

"Good night, Julian," she said, her tone final as she pushed the tent flap aside and stepped inside.

When she turned back around, he was already gone. Natalie's soft snores filled the tent, the sound a soothing backdrop to the thoughts swirling in Fiona's mind. She threw herself onto her cot, burying her face in the down-filled pillow as the events of the night replayed in her mind. Sleep claimed her quickly.

Aldo walked beside Ivar, his hand ever resting on the hilt of his thick sword, like a coiled serpent ready to strike. He was a faithful guard dog, eager to please, loyal to the bone. In exchange, he tore out the throats of anyone who dared to cross his master, leaving only blood and terror in his wake.

The village had done wonders for the men. Now they marched with their chins held higher, pride swelling in their hearts, and loyalty stronger than iron. Ivar didn't give a damn about their pride. It was their loyalty that mattered, an unwavering devotion that was priceless. And he would do anything to secure it, even if it meant slaughtering a few of them to make a point.

The vial at his belt still radiated a faint warmth, though not enough to burn. Alena had fed ravenously on the energies of the dead and dying in the village massacre, and he could almost see her in his mind, licking the blood from her lips as she devoured their souls. The image sent a dark thrill through him, desire curling like a serpent in his stomach, a craving he had only known once before. It took all his self-control to swallow it down.

Alena would be ready soon. Her energy now throbbed within the vial, barely contained, eager to be unleashed. They were nearing reaching Oldgrange, perfectly timed for the solstice.

Ivar's thoughts drifted to the young woman bound in the wagon, her fate as certain as the sun's rise. He hadn't bothered to order her gagged; there was no need. No one under his command—or even those who whispered his name in fear— would be foolish enough to challenge him, especially for her. She was an afterthought now.

The woman had been a fiery spirit once, her defiance flickering in those sharp blue eyes like the last embers of a dying fire. But now, those same eyes were dull, their once-vibrant color glazed over like ice that had settled over a winter river. She had slipped into a deep silence, the kind that only comes when hope is thoroughly extinguished. Her shoulders slumped, her body limp against the rough wood of the wagon, as if she had melted into the very boards beneath her.

It was almost pitiful, that complete and utter surrender. There was no fight left in her, no spark of resistance. It was as if she had already accepted the inevitable, her spirit broken so completely that even if he cut her bonds, she wouldn't lift a finger to escape. She was a shell, a hollow thing, drained of the will to survive.

Ivar found a twisted satisfaction in it, watching the last vestiges of her rebellion fade into nothingness. It was proof of his power, his dominance so absolute that he could crush the spirit of even the most defiant. Yet, there was a flicker of something else—something dark and buried deep within him. It wasn't pity, no. Pity was for the weak, and Ivar had no room for such things. It was more like...curiosity. A sick, twisted curiosity about how far she could be pushed, how much more she could be broken before there was truly nothing left of her.

Ivar's thoughts were interrupted. "Sir, may I request a halt?"

Ivar snapped his gaze to the right. A scout, young and wiry, sat astride a sweat-flecked horse, its sides heaving from exertion. The boy's eyes were bright, eager. Ivar sucked in a breath, annoyance flickering in his eyes.

"It better be important," he growled.

"It is, sir."

Aldo raised a fist, and the entire procession ground to a halt. Horses snorted and pawed at the earth, men whispered among themselves, puzzled by the unexpected break in their march.

Ivar reined in his horse, turning to face the scout. "What is it?"

The boy, no older than eighteen, grinned, revealing the gap where two front teeth were missing. He was scrappy, with knuckles white from gripping the reins too tightly. His chest heaved with barely contained excitement. Ivar lifted an eyebrow.

"Sir," the boy said, "there are travelers on the road."

Ivar's impatience flared. "We'll catch them. That's all?"

"No, sir. They're behind us, about three days."

"Soldiers?" Aldo asked, a thick hand resting on the hilt of his sword.

"No, they look like merchants."

"I wonder what they carry." Aldo's eyes glittered.

"There's only one way to find out." Ivar's lips curled into a cold smile. He turned to his men, voice booming. "Men! Change of plans! We march back west to relieve these travelers of their bounty—and their lives."

As if in response, the vial at his side flared with heat, searing through his belt until it burned his skin. Ivar snatched it up, holding it before him. The vial glowed with a dangerous red light, pulsing with Alena's eagerness.

"Too much," he muttered, a sharp admonishment. Aldo glanced sideways, as if he'd heard, but said nothing.

The vial's glow dimmed to a dull red, obedient for now. Ivar knew the upcoming bloodshed would feed her well, making her more than capable of resuming her earthly form. The thought sent a shiver of anticipation through him, a dark hunger gnawing at his insides. Oh, the things he would do.

The men, once halted in the dust and heat of the afternoon, now moved as one, a living tide of armor and steel. With practiced precision, they turned to face the direction from which they had marched.

The men were already turning, the wagon creaking as it circled to take its place at the rear. Ivar and Aldo urged their horses to the front of the new formation, leading the way. The sound of leather and metal-clad feet striking the earth, the rhythmic pounding of hooves, stirred up dust that swirled like a storm behind them, before settling back to the ground.

The air grew thick with the scent of dirt, sweat, and something more—an unspoken anticipation that blanketed the men as they readied themselves for the kill.

CHAPTER 10

Breakfast was short and sweet. The cook, in high spirits, had prepared hotcakes that filled the air with the scent of warm syrup and butter. Cider, served in thick pewter mugs, was passed around, its sharp, sweet taste a welcome respite.

Fiona indulged in a second helping of hotcakes, savoring the blend of sweetness and the slight tang of the cider. By the time the caravan resumed its journey, the sun had begun its slow ascent, casting the first golden rays through the dense trees lining the path.

Julian fell into step beside Fiona, his hands stuffed into his pockets, as if he hadn't a care in the world. She pretended not to notice, her gaze locked straight ahead, fingers laced together in front of her waist, trying to maintain her composure.

But when Fiona didn't respond, Julian's demeanor shifted. He began to whistle a tune, a breathy, aimless melody that wormed its way into her mind, each note more aggravating than the last. The sound seemed to echo in her skull, the rhythm clawing at her nerves. Fiona clenched her teeth, the heat rising from her chest to her jaw, her temper simmering below the surface. Her ears burned, her patience fraying with every passing second, the relentless whistle digging deeper. Finally, she couldn't take it anymore and shrieked, "Will you stop that?"

Julian stumbled to the side, arms raised in mock surrender. "Whoa!"

Fury clouded Fiona's vision, tears of anger threatening to spill over. Before she could think, she reached up, put her hands on his chest, and shoved as hard as she could. To her surprise, Julian didn't just stagger back; he was flung through the air, crashing into a tree several feet away. He slid down the trunk, his eyes wide with astonishment. For a moment, he sat there, dazed, shaking his head as if to clear it.

"What—Oh, Julian," Fiona's voice trembled as she saw the cold fury settle over his features. He pushed himself up, advancing toward her, his hands igniting with flames that danced across his skin.

"So that's how it is?" he snarled. "I did nothing to you."

Fiona's fists clenched at her sides, a battle waging within her. Common sense urged her to back down, to bow her head and continue along the path. But something stronger, something fiercer, kept her rooted in place. By now, the entire caravan had halted, eyes fixed on the confrontation. Even Melaney crossed her arms and observed.

"Nothing?" Fiona stepped closer. "Nothing must include avoiding me when I first arrived, acting like I had the plague because I mistook you for someone else. Lying to me about being a shade. Am I wrong? Shall I continue?"

"I didn't lie," he interjected, "I just didn't tell you."

"Why not?" she asked hotly. "I guess I had to earn that privilege, eh?"

The tickling sensation in Fiona's palms intensified, and when she glanced down, she saw white swirls of wind coiling around her fingers. Wind, her affinity, had come to her just as fire had to Julian. The realization brought a smile to her lips, a small but dangerous curl that made Julian pause.

Raising her hands, Fiona felt a click in her mind, and the wind exploded from her palms, hurtling toward Julian with terrifying speed. But he was quick, too. His flames flared brighter, forming a barrier against the oncoming wind. The two forces collided, fire and wind battling for dominance between them. Sweat beaded on Fiona's forehead as she pushed harder, fueled by pure, seething anger.

A calm voice cut through the tension. "Fiona, that's enough."

The rage pooled out of her as quickly as it had come. "I—I'm sorry, Melaney." Her words were a mere whisper. Her heart fluttered in her chest, clinging to an irregular beat. Darkness edged her vision, and she felt her legs give way beneath her.

She barely registered the strong arms that caught her as she fell. Julian's face swam into view, closer than she liked. His usual cocky grin was back, a glint of amusement in his blue eyes. "This is why Melaney keeps me around," he quipped. "I'm good at catching damsels."

"I'm not a damsel," Fiona muttered, trying to push him away, but her arms felt like lead.

"Oh, by definition, you are," he teased. "You don't have a husband, right?"

"I nearly did."

"That hardly counts." Julian lifted her to a sitting position, still supporting her with one arm. "Anyway, you should spend more time working on that wind of yours rather than worrying about a beau."

Despite herself, Fiona cracked a smile. "Whatever."

Melaney tisked from nearby and Julian stood. "We have to get moving again, if you are past this whole nonsense."

Fiona scowled at Julian but let him help her to her feet. She couldn't deny the strength in his arms as he supported her, making it look effortless. Even after she was steady, he kept his hand around hers, and though her pride wanted to pull away, she was too depleted to argue. The truth was, she might fall again if he let go.

Later that night, Fiona sat on the edge of the camp, her knees tucked to her chest as she gazed into the flames, lost in thought. The campfire crackled, casting flickering shadows on the trees as the night deepened. The night was quiet, save for the occasional murmur of the others settling down for the evening. Yet, her mind wouldn't still.

She thought of her parents, her sister. Would she have ended up in this world still if they hadn't been attacked? Was this inevitable? Had she died there? There were so many possibilities she didn't know the answer to.

A twig snapped behind her. She glanced up to see Julian standing just out of the fire's light. She hadn't noticed him watching her, but now that their eyes met, she couldn't look away. He hesitated, as if debating whether to approach her or leave her to her thoughts. For a brief second, she thought he might turn around and walk off like he usually did.

But he didn't.

"Couldn't sleep?" His voice was softer than usual as he moved closer.

Fiona shook her head, her gaze returning to the flames. "Too much on my mind."

He sat down beside her, watching the fire, too. She wasn't sure why he'd decided to join her, but she surprised herself when she realized she didn't mind.

"I never imagined I'd be here," she said after a while. She waved vaguely at the camp, the firelight flickering across her face. "Relying on people I barely know, with whatever this is." She twirled a finger around and the wind wrapped around her finger for a moment. "I don't know what I'm doing. I'm not even supposed to be here."

Julian shifted beside her, his expression thoughtful as he stared into the flames. "I think..." He paused, choosing his words carefully. "You're doing the best you can. And you absolutely belong here."

Fiona turned her head to look at him, surprised. The Julian she knew—the one who kept his distance, who only ever offered lighthearted remarks—never spoke to her like this. She didn't know what to make of it, of him.

"You actually think that?" she asked, her voice quieter now, almost afraid of his answer.

He met her gaze, and the smirk she'd come to expect softened. Affection flickered in his eyes—an emotion she hadn't seen from him before. "I wouldn't say it if I didn't."

A small, almost disbelieving laugh left her. Julian had always kept a wall between them, making jokes, keeping things light. But now… now he was here, looking at her like he actually saw her. And for the first time in a long while, Fiona felt seen.

"I know I've been…distant," he admitted, his eyes flicking away, as if embarrassed. "You were a stranger not so long ago, and you came off so strong in the beginning. And then, I started seeing who you are, what you're made of."

Fiona blinked, caught off guard by his honesty. She didn't know what to say at first. "Sometimes I feel like I'm pretending to be strong when all I want is to… to rest."

For a moment, she regretted the confession, but Julian didn't laugh or dismiss her. Instead, he surprised her again. His hand, warm and rough, settled gently on her shoulder.

"You don't always have to be strong," he said. "You've got people around you now. Shades support each other." The warmth of his touch lingered even after he pulled his hand away.

"Thank you," she whispered, her voice soft, her gaze lingering on his face.

Julian stood, offering her a hand. "We should get some rest."

Fiona took his hand, allowing herself to be pulled to her feet. For more than a brief moment, she wondered what it might feel like to close the space between them, then dismissed the thought and returned to her tent.

"They're burning up your mind," Melaney said, casting a sideways glance at Fiona as they walked through the forest the next day.

The group moved along a narrow path, their footsteps muffled by the thick layer of fallen leaves. The air was crisp, filled with the scent of pine and the occasional rustle of wildlife. Melaney walked with a graceful, purposeful stride, while Julian and Dax trailed beside her. Julian's close proximity was new, and though Melaney's brow arched in surprise and she hid a smirk, she had kept her thoughts to herself.

Now, Fiona turned to Melaney, puzzled. "What are you talking about?"

Melaney's gaze remained fixed ahead, her eyes scanning the dense foliage. "Your questions. They're churning inside you like a storm, and it's distracting you. If you have something on your mind, ask it. We can't afford to waste time tangled in uncertainties."

Fiona frowned, her thoughts racing. "Is it that obvious?"

Melaney's expression softened, a hint of understanding in her eyes. "It's not about being obvious. It's about being honest with yourself. If something is troubling you or if you need clarity, speak up. Holding back only hinders your progress."

Julian and Dax exchanged glances, clearly intrigued by the exchange but remaining silent.

Fiona took a deep breath, weighing her options. "Alright," she said finally, her voice steady. "I've been struggling with my place here, with how I fit into all this. I don't understand everything about the Shades."

Melaney nodded, her gaze still fixed on the path ahead. "That's a good start. We're here to guide you, but you must also be willing to confront your doubts and seek the answers you need. Sometimes, the answers aren't given freely; you have to seek them out."

Fiona glanced at Julian, who was listening intently. She felt a flicker of uncertainty but pushed it aside, focusing on Melaney's words. "That sounds like you're not answering the question."

She thought she heard Julian snort.

"I can help if you're more specific." Melaney's tone remained patient.

Fiona took a deep breath. "What happened to me in the other world? Am I still there? Did a body get left behind? Am I actually dead and in some sort of Purgatory?"

Melaney raised an eyebrow. "Ah, existential questions. There are various philosophies about that, Fiona, but the truth is, we don't have concrete answers. The best I can offer is that, no, there's probably no physical body left in another world. You are you. Mirrors don't often bridge worlds, but when they do, it's a rare occurrence."

"Is there any significance to it?" Fiona pressed.

Melaney looked around her for a moment. The others seemed to be leaning in, acting as if they weren't listening but eavesdropping anyway. "Such events typically coincide with major upheavals—nearly catastrophic occurrences."

Fiona's stomach churned, and she came to a sudden halt. "Are you saying I've doomed you all?"

Melaney turned. "I don't know what it means."

Fiona felt the wind pick up as her heart beat faster. "I don't want to hurt anyone."

Her mentor stepped closer to her. "You won't," she said. "If anything, this means this world needs you here to help us." She straightened. "Now stop being dramatic. We need to stay focused."

Fiona sensed Melaney's attempt to ground her, to pull her out of her distress. She placed one foot in front of the other, resuming her pace, but the anxiety gnawed at her as they continued.

CHAPTER 11

It had all begun with the thirst for blood; that thick and red essence flowing on the ground. The desire for the heart-pounding rip of flesh, the crack of bone—it was a hunger that had been gnawing at him since dawn. He could already taste the defeat of the travelers just around the bend in the path, the crooked finger of the trail winding through the trees as if beckoning him closer. Wickard Forest was drawing to a close, the dense canopy thinning, but even its ancient woods couldn't shelter the unwitting peddlers they had discovered. Their fate was sealed.

Alena, however, had her own thoughts, whirling restlessly in her glass prison. The closer they drew to the travelers, the more frigid her vial became, the glass coated in a thin layer of frost. It hung securely from Ivar's belt, nestled in a leather pocket, but the icy reaction to the proximity of innocent blood was unsettling. Ivar wasn't sure what to make of it. *Not all are innocent*, Alena whispered in his mind, her voice a cold caress. *There is power among them. They travel with shades.* Her tone, even though the mental link, dripped with disdain.

Shades. Ivar had heard of them, but never encountered one

in person. He assumed they were like any other magic-wielder—a good foe, still capable of bleeding. An even more satisfying kill. The thought of slitting the throat of a shade, of watching their blood spill, filled him with a dark anticipation.

Aldo stood at Ivar's side. Clad in his gleaming armor, he was always ready, one hand resting on the hilt of his broadsword. "The men are ready. The travelers have stopped," he reported, his voice a rumble of anticipation.

"They must know we're here," Ivar replied, a dry smile curling his lips. "We should give them a proper welcome."

"Welcome them, we shall." Aldo's grin was feral. This was what marauders lived for—to die in battle was the highest honor, a tradition passed down through generations. Dying of old age meant either being the fiercest of fighters or the deepest of cowards, and Ivar wasn't sure which was more likely.

"Ready the archers," Ivar commanded. "We'll send the arrows first to clear a path for us."

"Archers, first assault!" Aldo roared. "Ready!"

The archers stepped forward, their movements fluid and silent, like shadows creeping toward their prey. Bows were strapped across their broad shoulders, the polished wood gleaming in the dim light that filtered through the trees. Quivers, brimming with slender arrows, jostled with each step, the light wood of the shafts a stark contrast to the darkened forest around them. Each arrow was meticulously crafted, tipped with barbed stone heads designed to tear through flesh and bone, while the falcon feathers at the ends promised both speed and deadly accuracy.

With a practiced ease born from countless battles, they unslung their bows and fitted the arrows to the strings. Muscles coiled and ready, they moved in perfect unison, every motion precise and deliberate. As they drew back their strings, the tension in the air was palpable, the archers poised like coiled vipers, ready to strike.

The glass vial at Ivar's belt began to warm, the frost melting away as Alena's pleasure grew.

The forest, once serene, erupted in sudden chaos as birds, startled from their perches, took to the sky in a frenzy that echoed through the trees like a thousand panicked heartbeats. Leaves rustled in the wake of their flight, swirling in erratic patterns before settling back into the uneasy stillness. The forest held its breath, the usual hum of life stilled by an instinctive fear. Even the very earth beneath their feet seemed to tense, awaiting the inevitable with grim resignation.

"The very pets of Mother Earth cannot stand to be near us," Aldo muttered to Ivar, his eyes scanning the treetops. "We are dominant over all."

Ivar nodded, the weight of his own power settling on his shoulders. "Indeed."

"Archers, AIM!" Aldo's voice boomed once more, his presence commanding as he drew his sword and hoisted his shield.

The wind fell silent. The air grew heavy, a blanket of pressure that caused sweat to bead on Ivar's forehead. He wiped it away and nodded to Aldo.

"Away!" Aldo struck his sword against his shield, the metallic clang ringing out like a death knell.

The archers loosed their arrows, the wooden shafts slicing through the sky. They arced high above, darkening the sun, before plummeting toward their unsuspecting targets below.

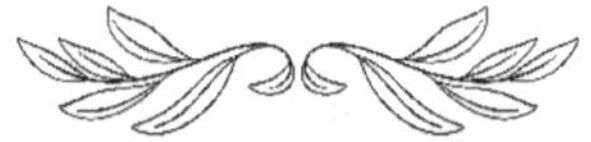

It had been two days since Melaney told Fiona about mirrors, and the thought of bringing doom to them weighed heavily on Fiona's mind still. Dax's efforts to cheer her up fell flat as they had every morning since, and Julian's warmth left her feeling colder as soon as he left her proximity to help get the wagon on the road. Fiona sent tendrils of air around the camp to wake up stragglers for breakfast.

They made good time getting back on the road, Fiona settled in to her usual quiet walking, Julian in his usual place beside her.

"Marauders!" The cry went up.

The travelers scattered, seeking shelter like they had the last time the marauders had nearly encountered them on the road. Fiona's heart leaped into her throat as the wagon creaked into a ditch and they worked to conceal it.

Crouching in the dirt was a torment. The slick leaves from the morning dew clung mercilessly to Fiona's hands, their cold wetness seeping into her skin. Ants, undeterred by her presence, swarmed her ankles, their tiny legs tickling as they explored the unfamiliar terrain. Granules of sand dug into the smooth skin of her knees, embedding themselves with a stubborn persistence that left a temporary imprint.

Those who remained standing on the road were the figures of men, their faces pale but set with grim determination. There was no turning back, no escaping the fate that awaited them. The marauders were close—too close.

Julian stood at the front of the pack of men, shoulders squared and tunic flapping in the breeze. His dark hair tossed in his face, and his tense jaw reminded Fiona of her father's look when he was hunting. The thought turned her stomach. Julian faced the same foe her father had.

Melaney was nowhere to be found. The shade had given her orders— where to go, what to do, when to tuck tail and flee— but had vanished shortly afterward. She had made no pretense about their situation, never sugarcoated the grim reality they faced. No one had asked her to.

It was this understanding that enabled some fifty men to stand on the path they had traveled, brandishing what they could find and waiting for the first onslaught of marauders. Fiona couldn't help but wonder where Melaney had gone. And what had she expected Fiona to do? The only instruction she'd received was "Stay alive. Keep with the wagon." Hardly useful in the face of impending doom.

Fiona curled her fingers into the gritty dirt, digging her nails into the earth. A pool of sand collected in her palm, and she instinctively squeezed it, feeling the tension flow out of her and into the ground.

As her gaze returned to the line of men on the road, she fixed her eyes on Julian's lean, muscled figure. He gripped a homemade club, a chunk of wagon axle reinforced with metal stakes driven into its tip. The spikes gleamed in the sunlight, and Fiona swallowed the lump forming in her throat.

But then, something caught her eye. Brannon and his friend Darry each brandished a pair of short, gleaming swords, the metal wickedly sharp and polished to a sheen. Their movements were precise, their stances practiced—nothing like the fearful, haphazard grips of the other men. Fiona's breath caught. These were no ordinary peddlers; they moved like seasoned warriors.

Her eyes widened as she realized that other peddlers in the group were similarly armed. What she had thought were simple makeshift weapons were actually spears, their tips glinting in the sunlight. A few of them even had small crossbows strapped to their backs, weapons that no traveling merchant should have possessed.

Fiona's mind raced. Had they always been this well-armed? The realization that she had underestimated them sent a shiver down her spine.

As she puzzled, a whistle pierced the air, sharp and sudden. The sound multiplied quickly, a dozen and then a hundred high-pitched shrieks twisting together into a cacophony that sent a jolt of fear through her. The men remained still, but Fiona flinched, tasting dirt as she ducked instinctively, her mouth pressed into the sand she had clutched moments ago. She spat in disgust. "Ew."

"Quiet," Lia hissed beside her, stretched out in the dirt, her voice tense. "It's the first attack."

"What could make that kind of noise?" Fiona whispered, her heart pounding.

Lia silenced her with a sharp gesture, a finger pressed to her lips as she closed her eyes.

The shriek grew louder, the sky darkening as the sun drifted behind clouds—or what she thought were clouds. Fiona squinted upward, her heart skipping a beat. Those weren't clouds. They moved, shifting in the air like dark slits with shards of the sky visible between them.

"Arrows!" The cry went up, and Fiona's blood ran cold.

Without thinking, she, Lia, and Natalie turned and dove

under the wagon, the world outside narrowing to a terrifyingly small view through the spokes of the wheel. Somehow, mud rose from the ground, covering the large gaps. Arrows sank into them, rendering harmless. Protecting them.

The shriek of the arrows became a hiss as they rained down, embedding themselves in trees, the ground, and anything—or anyone—in their path. Fiona waited, bracing herself for the inevitable cries of those struck down, for surely not everyone had made it under cover. But there was nothing. No screams, no shouts of pain. Only the relentless rain of arrows.

Curiosity got the better of her, and Fiona risked a glance through the wagon wheel. Her heart stopped as she saw an arrow hurtle toward her face, only for Natalie to yank her back just in time. The arrow wedged itself into the wheel where Fiona's head had been seconds before.

Her breath caught in her chest. "Thanks."

Natalie's grip on her leg loosened as she shot Fiona a stern glare. "Stay where you are!"

Fiona shrank back, scowling. Natalie had never spoken to her so harshly before. She curled up into a ball, willing the seconds to pass, each one more agonizing than the last, as the deluge of arrows continued. When the assault finally ceased, the silence that followed was deafening, pounding in her ears.

Then, thumping broke through the reticence—a strange slapping sound, leather against leather. Fiona raised her head slowly, almost too afraid to see the carnage on the road. She inched forward to peer around the arrow embedded in the wagon wheel.

The sight that met her eyes was worse than she had imagined. The men were scattered across the road, their bodies lifeless, like discarded dolls. Julian lay on his side at the front, his club rolled a foot away from his limp hand. Brannon and Darry were just beyond him, face down in the dirt, their swords still clenched in their hands, their once-vibrant bodies now lifeless.

"Don't move," Natalie's voice trembled behind her. "Just. Don't. Move."

CHAPTER 12

Fiona turned her eyes toward the chopping sound, her breath hitching as a goat lumbered down the path toward the men. A crude leather blanket was slung across its back, the rough fabric clouting the poor animal with each weary stride. Its head bowed low, curly horns resting parallel to its neck.

Lia swore softly.

"What does that mean?" Fiona asked, pulling back slightly.

"It means I don't like this," Lia murmured.

"I meant the goat," Fiona clarified, confusion knitting her brow.

"Goats are the marauders' symbol of lust and greed. They are coming to claim what they believe is now theirs."

As if punctuating Natalie's ominous words, several figures began to march into view. From a distance, their plated armor caught the sunlight, reflecting sharp glints that hinted at deadly intent. Drawn swords and ready spears. The marauders had arrived, and their presence exuded a chilling confidence. One's lips curled into a sneer, his throat shielded by thick fur, one fist gripping a broadsword while the other caressed something concealed by his belt—a movement that Fiona couldn't quite decipher.

They advanced, their pace steady and deliberate, radiating the triumph of men accustomed to victory. Within minutes, they closed the distance between themselves and the fallen men on the road. Fiona's eyes welled up with hot tears that streamed down her cheeks, the sting of loss sharp in her heart.

"Come out, the rest of you!" the leader's companion snarled, stepping in front of the larger man. "Make this quick and easy!"

Fiona's hands twitched involuntarily, the wind beginning to pick up around her. "They killed our friends," she muttered to no one in particular. "What have we got to lose?""

"Fiona, wait!" Lia called desperately, but it was too late. Fiona had already pushed through the mud and scrambled around the wooden wheel, her legs propelling her to her feet with a surge of adrenaline.

The larger of the two marauder leaders tilted his massive head to the side, the motion slow and deliberate, as if savoring the moment. His beady eyes, glinting with malice, locked onto Fiona, the corners of his mouth twitching into a sneer that sent a shiver down her spine. Those eyes— small, dark, and filled with a cruel humor— seemed to drink in her fear.

Without a second thought, she pushed off the ground, her feet pounding against the dirt as she sprinted toward him, her scream tearing through the air like a war cry. She had no plan, no strategy—only a raw, burning need to inflict pain, to make him feel even a sliver of the agony he had wrought upon her and her friends. Every fiber of her being surged with a singular focus: to hurt him, to make him suffer. The sound of her own fury echoed in her ears, drowning out all rational thought as she hurtled toward him, fists clenched and heart pounding with reckless determination.

He opened his mouth, first in surprise, then bursting into laughter that reverberated from his belly. Fiona's anger flared, fueling her determination. She lunged at him, small fists flailing wildly in front of her. All she wanted was to land one solid punch, just one. When her fist connected, it was with his belt buckle, the impact sending a hot, searing pain shooting up her arm. She staggered back, the world tilting around her.

Before she could recover, something heavy collided with her forehead, and exploding stars radiated across her vision. "Do you not know who I am?" the man raged, red dripping from the hilt of his sword. Fiona touched her forehead, feeling the sticky heat of blood. Her hand came away stained burgundy, her vision spinning in a disorienting haze.

A loud cry erupted all around them, deafening Fiona. She dropped to the ground, clamping blood-soaked hands over her burning ears. Panic surged through her as she wondered if the marauders had discovered the women and children hiding among the trees and behind the wagon. But then, she realized the sound was distinct—a chorus of men and women shouting not in pain, but in retaliation. The tone was powerful, different from the brutish shouts of the marauders.

Lifting her aching head, Fiona opened her eyes to an astonishing sight: the people of the caravan were on their feet, alive and fierce. How was that possible? She pushed herself onto her elbows, searching for Julian. The marauders were all around her now, momentarily pushed back.

How could she have been so foolish? Fiona's mind raced as she realized her mistake. The fallen men hadn't been dead— they had been pretending. They were drawing the enemy in, allowing the marauders to believe the arrows had penetrated their defenses. She looked around, bewildered. How had the arrows missed?

Where was Julian? Panic seized Fiona as she spun around, her eyes darting wildly in search of him. Her muscles screamed in protest, joints popping with every desperate movement. The towering forms of marauders, all rippling muscles and menacing boots, enclosed her like a living cage. She wasn't safe here—not in this deadly maze of flesh and steel.

Her mind raced. Running for the wagon would be a reckless move that would reveal its hiding place and doom everyone sheltering there. She cursed herself for her own foolishness, realizing too late that she had trapped herself. The weight of her mistake bore down on her, but there was no time for regret— only survival.

Scrambling to her feet, Fiona launched herself toward the men, who now stood with arms uplifted and palms skyward—a sign of truce or preparation for battle. A roar sounded behind her, but she dared not look. Rough hands grabbed her, yanking her to the side. She landed on a fallen limb, a nub grinding into her side with painful force.

"Are you okay?" Julian was sprawled next to her, his chest heaving as he panted for air. His arms still tightly gripped her, his knuckles white with the effort.

"I thought you were dead!" she gasped, her voice raw with fear and frustration.

"Melaney shielded us from the arrows," Julian said. "She hid past the tree line to hold the shield in place."

Fiona's body refused to move, so she lay there as Julian strained to his feet. "It's working," he mumbled, scanning the battlefield.

"What's working?"

"They're backing away."

Fiona rolled over, flinching at each spasm of her body protesting the movement. "Ah," she groaned aloud, wincing.

"Don't move," Julian instructed. "You'll make it worse. You look terrible."

"Gee, thanks." Fiona scowled.

Julian ignored her. She followed his gaze and her eyes widened in disbelief.

The men and women of the caravan had taken to battle with a ferocity she hadn't anticipated. They slashed through the marauders' front lines, their hidden weapons revealing themselves in the heat of combat. Julian's companions, once mistaken for simple peddlers, wielded finely crafted blades and concealed crossbows, their movements precise and deadly. The big leader of the marauders had vanished—no doubt to save his own skin.

"None of you were just peddlers, were you?" Fiona demanded, her voice edged with accusation.

He looked back at her, his blue eyes dark and apprehensive. "No."

"Figures," Fiona muttered, her voice laced with bitter

resignation. She stared at the fighting men, the fierce determination in their eyes now a cruel reminder of the deception she had been blind to. Her trust lay in ruins, shattered like glass, as she watched them strike with precision and skill.

"Fiona." His tone was strained. "It was for a purpose."

"Yeah?"

Fiona lurched to her feet despite her body's protests, her senses on high alert. She sensed a movement to her right and stepped to the side just in time. Julian, grasping for her hand, caught only air. He gaped at her like a fish out of water. "Fiona!"

She was about to open her mouth and laugh—laugh in the face of the deception she had been subjected to, laugh at his absurdity, and her own stupidity. But before she could, she felt herself lifted into the air. Beefy arms wrapped around her, squeezing the life from her lungs. She struggled, but in vain. Her arms were locked down, and her kicking feet found only air.

"Fiona!" Julian's voice sounded distant, as if carried from a mountaintop or through rushing waters.

Then, darkness overtook her, and she sank into the deep void, her world fading to black.

"When will she wake up?" The voice was rough, impatient.

"Ivar hit her pretty hard." Another voice, this one more measured.

"That doesn't answer my question." The impatience was growing, a sharp edge cutting through the words.

"Niklaos, have some patience. At least she's not awake to fight you." There was a hint of a smirk in the tone at the idea of Fiona awake and combative against them.

"That's true," Niklaos conceded. "I just hate having to carry her."

"Weakling." The insult was casual, thrown out without much

thought, but it hit its mark.

Fiona's eyelids felt as though they were weighed down by a vast garden of dirt. She tried to pry them open, but the effort was too much, so she settled on listening instead.

"I'm not a weakling," Niklaos shot back defensively. His voice was raspy, with a lilt that sounded almost Saxon—if such a place existed in Orthea.

"Shut your traps, lads," came a new voice, deeper and dripping with authority. "You're both dead if you mess this up."

"Yes, sir." Both men instantly turned sheepish, their tones changing. Fiona wondered who this man was to command such a response.

"I saw her twitch! I think she's coming awake!"

Fiona mentally cursed as she realized her thumb had betrayed her, moving involuntarily. The sound of footsteps rushing toward her filled the air, and she knew she had to act quickly. Summoning every ounce of willpower, Fiona forced her eyes open and tried to leap to her feet.

But her body wasn't ready. She misjudged her surroundings, and instead of a swift escape, she crashed to the ground, her shoulder hitting the earth with the force of a four-horse carriage. "Ummf," she groaned, panic surging as she tried to push herself up. Her head pounded, bringing back the memory of being struck by the hilt of a sword.

Strong arms grabbed her, lifting her roughly to her feet. On either side of her stood a grim-faced marauder. The one on the left was a bright blonde who would be pleasant to look at if he wasn't the enemy. The other had dark hair and a baby face that belied his mean demeanor. She froze, taking in their cold, calculating gazes.

"Good evening," purred the man who had spoken last. Fiona blinked, focusing on him. He was shorter than the other marauders, but there was an unmistakable command in his posture. His voice had an accent of clipped precision. She pursed her lips and looked away, refusing to give him the satisfaction of a response.

"Not in a talking mood today? That's fine. You'll have plenty of time to reconsider your behavior while you're our guest," the man sneered, his tone dripping with condescension.

The blonde marauder snorted, but a sharp rebuke from the shorter man silenced him. "Niklaos, that's enough."

"Sorry, Aldo," Niklaos muttered, his eyes dropping to the floor like a chastised child.

Fiona's gaze hardened as she stared at Aldo. She said nothing as he turned back to her, his expression unreadable.

"Tell Ivar she's awake," Aldo directed, his voice cool and commanding. The men holding her arms tightened their grip, lifting her back onto the bed with bruising force. "You shouldn't go anywhere," Aldo sneered, his words more of a threat than a suggestion.

Tenderly, Fiona rubbed at her aching arms, her mind racing. As her head continued to pound, she reached up and felt a bandage wound around her temples. She caught herself wishing for Julian to appear, sword in hand, to rescue her from this nightmare. But she quickly dismissed the thought. Julian wasn't coming. Why would he?

Aldo turned away, his stocky frame filling the bottom half of the doorway. Fiona's eyes fell to the sword that hung at his side, the hilt forever covered by one thick hand. If only she could reach it, grab it, run it through him, and run to freedom. But she had no training, no real chance. She would inevitably stumble and be knocked out, or worse.

Then, Fiona remembered the wind.

The breeze nudged at the door, lightly tossing the tent flaps back and forth, teasing the dark brown hair poking above Aldo's head. Leaning forward, Fiona called to the wind with her mind, urging it to her aid. It swirled harder, more insistently, but never breached the entrance to the tent. Aldo turned back around, a grin splitting his face from ear to ear.

""Good luck using magic in here, witch." His tone was mocking, a clear sign he knew more than she had anticipated.

Fiona frowned, confusion clouding her mind as Aldo left the tent, followed by two of his guards. Niklaos remained behind, his slender features twisted in seething anger. He shoved his hands deep into his pockets and plopped down on an overturned box, stretching his long legs as far as they would go. A bleak air surrounded him, as if he had long since given up on caring about anything.

Despite herself, Fiona clucked. "You poor thing. You always get left on guard duty, don't you?"

Niklaos's head shot up, his expression sharp and full of resentment. "Shut up, girl."

"Oh, sorry. I shouldn't have mentioned it." Fiona laid down, curling on her side with her head resting on her hands. "Let me know if anything bad happens."

She closed her eyes, feigning sleep. For a moment, there was no movement, as if Niklaos was frozen in thought. Fiona almost peeked to see what was happening, but just as she gave in to the temptation, she heard a slight shuffle.

Niklaos was moving. The sound traveled, starting near the door of the tent and then growing closer until it was right beside her bed. His hot breath dusted her face, and against her intentions, Fiona's eyes flew open.

Large hazel eyes were inches from hers. Fiona gasped in surprise, flinching away. Niklaos lifted a finger to his lips. "Shh," he whispered. "I'm not going to hurt you. I can't touch you, unless I want to die like Pavlo did."

Fiona's chest heaved as she gulped for air. "Who's Pavlo?" she asked.

"He was an idiot who tried to sample the goods and got his throat cut." Niklaos didn't move away, his hazel eyes locked on hers.

"Sample the goods?" Panic flared in Fiona's chest, a hot, searing burn.

"Oh, don't worry," he waved a hand dismissively, straightening up. "It wasn't you."

Fiona processed this for a moment, her breathing returning to normal. "If not me, then who?"

Niklaos regarded her warily, as if weighing the risk of answering. "I don't know if I should tell you. Ivar isn't a man to be trifled with, and he's not exactly stable."

"Please, tell me," Fiona pressed, sitting up and scooting closer to him. What if it was Emma? What if she could still be found in this place? Hope, fragile and desperate, welled up inside her, threatening to overwhelm her.

But Niklaos wasn't swayed. "You think you can persuade me? That I'm weak?" He laughed, a bitter, mirthless sound. "I'm sorry, but you're out of luck. I've already said too much. Ivar may have my head."

"If he does, it won't be much of a loss," Fiona snapped, turning her back to him. She faced the blank wall of the tent, her heart pounding with frustration. She heard Niklaos suck in a breath, but she ignored him.

A rustling at the tent doorway caught her attention, followed by a deep, booming voice that made Fiona jump. "Ivar is entering, girl. Be on your feet!"

Slowly, Fiona obeyed, sliding off the bed and feeling the cool grass beneath her bare feet. She lifted her chin high as a large, hulking man ducked into the tent.

Ivar, himself.

CHAPTER 13

We can't leave her with them!" Julian's voice cracked through the morning air, sharp and unyielding. He paced back and forth in front of the cook's campfire, his movements frantic, almost feral. The sun had barely crested the horizon, yet Julian had been up for hours, wearing a path in the dirt like a caged tiger. Every few steps, he would spin on his heel, his eyes blazing with barely contained fury. Each turn was punctuated by another outburst, another protest against the caravan's decision.

Melaney watched him from a distance, her gaze steady, though her patience was wearing thin. She had seen Julian like this before, but never with such intensity. He was usually the most composed among them. But now, he was unraveling. "We're charged with a higher purpose," she reminded him, her voice calm but firm.

Julian stopped mid-step, his head snapping toward her, nostrils flaring as he shot her a glare that could have frozen the very flames of the fire. "A higher purpose than saving one of our own? Is she that disposable now?" His words were laced with accusation, each one striking Melaney with the weight of the guilt she had been trying to suppress.

She had failed to see the marauders coming until it was too late. By the time she realized, they were already upon them, and Fiona had been taken. The caravan's precious cargo had remained safe, a small mercy, but Fiona's capture gnawed at her conscience like a festering wound. The elders had tasked her with delivering the cargo to Shades Hollow, and that duty had to come before all else.

Julian's pacing halted as he kicked at the dirt near the fire, sending a spray of embers into the air. The glowing sparks floated lazily before falling back to the earth, and for a moment, Julian watched them with a scowl that etched deep lines into his face.

"It's time," Brannon's voice rumbled behind her. He appeared at her side, his eyes hidden beneath the shadow of his hood, but the tension in his posture was evident as he waited for her command.

Melaney nodded to him, then turned back to Julian. "We need to go," she said, her tone taking on a finality that left no room for argument.

But Julian wasn't having it. "No!" His refusal was sharp, like a blade slicing through the morning's stillness. His head whipped up, his eyes wild. "I won't!"

"You don't want to deal with the council if you stray," Melaney warned, her voice tightening. She knew the consequences, as did he, but Julian seemed willing to face them. "You know what they will do."

"I don't care." Julian shook his head, his hair falling around his face in disarray. "I'm going after her."

"If you go," Brannon cut in, his voice low and resolute, "I'll be going with you."

"You can't," Melaney said, exasperation seeping into her words. She didn't like this situation any more than Julian did, but they had a mission to complete, a duty that couldn't be ignored.

"I can. I'm his right-hand man," Brannon growled, his loyalty to Julian clear. "Where he goes, I go."

Julian turned to Melaney, his demeanor suddenly calm, almost businesslike. "Tell the council I ordered him to come.

They can take it out on me if they are angry." Without waiting for a response, he began gathering supplies—rations, tools, anything they might need for the journey ahead. The tension in his movements had dissipated, replaced by a sense of purpose.

"I don't like this," Melaney muttered, but she knew there was no stopping him now.

"I don't either, Melaney, but it's what I need to do."

"We need to do," Brannon corrected.

The sound of footsteps drew their attention. Darry appeared on the other side of the fire, his expression curious as he took in the scene. "We need to do what?"

Julian didn't hesitate. "Get Fiona." He slung his pack over his shoulder, pulling the hood of his cloak over his face.

A wide grin spread across Darry's face. "That's way better than transporting a bunch of serpents," he declared with a clap of his hands, earning him a fierce glare from Melaney.

"You should not say such things out loud," she hissed, her eyes narrowing dangerously.

Darry's grin faltered. "What? What did I say?"

"You never know who might hear when they shouldn't," she snapped, her voice low and harsh.

Darry ducked his head in apology. "Sorry, I'll be ready in five minutes." He dashed off to gather his own gear, leaving the others in tense silence.

Melaney stepped closer to Julian, her voice softening as she laid a hand on his shoulder. "Since you insist on going, I'll give you my blessing." She channeled her energy into him, warmth spreading from her hand, wrapping around his body like a protective shield.

Julian's tense posture eased slightly, a small smile tugging at the corners of his mouth. "A protection spell. Thank you."

"I don't know how long it will hold up, so speed along, Julian," she advised, nodding towards the horses that Darry had brought.

Julian turned to Melaney one last time, his expression solemn. "I look forward to seeing you at the Hollow." With a tap of the reins, he urged his horse forward, the roan's hooves striking the ground with purpose as they set off, following the deep, heavy footprints left by the marauders.

Julian wanted to push his horse into a gallop, to escape the frustration and uncertainty gnawing at him. He was still upset—at Fiona, at himself—over their last argument. Her arrival had thrown their journey into disarray, and he disliked the disruption she caused. But even amidst his turmoil, something within him compelled him to find her, to confront the man who had taken her. He couldn't fully understand it, and he wasn't sure he wanted to. Melaney would likely have a thoughtful explanation, but there was no turning to her now.

So, he rode in silence, maintaining a steady canter, his eyes scanning the road ahead for any sign of an ambush. The familiar sounds of birds chirping offered some comfort, a sign that marauders were likely far off—they tended to silence nature wherever they went. Still, he knew better than to let his guard down. The steady clop of hooves on the dirt path was almost hypnotic, a rhythm that kept him focused but did little to quell the storm brewing within.

"I wonder how far they've gotten," Darry mused aloud, breaking the tension.

"Farther than I'd like," Julian muttered, leaning to the side and spitting onto the ground. "It's hard to say."

"They had a full night's head start," Brannon noted from his position just behind and to the right of Julian, ever the loyal shadow. "They could have covered a lot of ground by now."

"And so will we," Darry replied, determination etched into his features, reflecting the same resolve Julian felt but couldn't yet fully understand.

The three men rode on in silence for another half hour before Brannon broke it again, his voice probing. "What is it about her?"

"What do you mean?" Julian replied, feigning ignorance.

"What is it about this girl that's making you ride off into the unknown to rescue her?" Brannon pressed, his tone serious.

Julian stiffened, avoiding the question. "I don't know if rescuing will be involved, but I certainly hope so."

Brannon wasn't deterred. "I'm serious, Julian. You've never been one to stray from orders before."

"Call it a change of heart," Julian growled, keeping his gaze fixed on the road ahead.

"Mighty fine change of heart, if I may say," Darry quipped with a grin.

"You may not," Julian snapped, narrowing his eyes. He couldn't shake the feeling gnawing at his insides—the unshakable need to keep Fiona safe, no matter the cost. He didn't understand it, but the thought of anything happening to her was unbearable.

They pressed on, the conversation dying away as the path stretched out before them. When the sun climbed high into the sky and the grumbling of their stomachs could no longer be ignored, they finally pulled off to the side and dismounted.

Julian's legs wobbled as he hit the ground, his muscles protesting the long ride. He grabbed the saddle horn for balance before leading his horse over to where the other two were tying theirs to a low-hanging branch.

"Please tell me you brought something good to eat," Julian said, trying to keep his tone light as he looked over at Darry.

Darry's grin widened, his carrot-colored hair ruffling in the breeze. Two cracked teeth glinted as he pulled a pack from his saddle. "To be sure," he said with a touch of pride.

He spread a blanket on the ground, carefully placing a leg of turkey on each corner like a royal offering. With an exaggerated flourish, he gestured for them to join him. "Come on, they're not getting any fresher."

Julian and Brannon didn't need any more prompting. They fell upon the food like starved wolves, tearing every last morsel of meat from the bones. The horses watched with mild interest, shifting their feet as the men ate.

"At least you had the sense to bring cooked meat," Brannon jabbed, finishing first and tossing his bone into the nearby brush. The horses startled, tossing their heads at the sudden movement.

"Oh, you think I'm stupid, do you?" Darry's eyes flashed, but his grin stayed firmly in place. "I'll show ya how smart I am. Just you wait."

"One of these days, eh?" Brannon chuckled, licking his fingers clean of turkey grease.

"Hurry up," Julian growled from where he stood, repacking their bags. The brief respite had done little to ease his tension. "We don't have all day."

"Fine, fine," Brannon and Darry muttered, quickly gathering their things and brushing dirt over their tracks. They hoisted their packs back onto the horses, who shifted and snorted, eager to continue.

Julian mounted first, his horse stepping forward onto the path, ears pricked and muscles coiled with anticipation. He glanced back at his companions, their horses catching up as they prepared to move out.

"I know, we're too slow," Darry said, reading the look on Julian's face. The three of them urged their horses into a trot, mindful not to push the animals too hard. They needed their endurance to last.

Julian stayed silent, letting Brannon and Darry's easy banter wash over him. His mind was elsewhere, haunted by the memory of Fiona's deep red curls, her flashing green eyes, and the vulnerability in her gaze when she had mistaken him for someone else. His heart ached at the thought of their last exchange, the sharp words that had cut too deep on both sides.

The road stretched on, but Julian's mind was fixed on Fiona. He couldn't shake the feeling that he had to reach her, to make things right—whatever that might mean.

CHAPTER 14

Fiona locked eyes with Ivar, neither of them blinking, neither uttering a word. The silence stretched, thick with tension, as they sized each other up. Fiona had leapt to her feet the moment Ivar entered the tent, and despite the towering figure before her, she refused to back down.

Ivar was hideous, she decided. His chestnut beard was unkempt, covering most of his face, with only a sharp, crooked nose sticking out. His piercing brown eyes glared at her with a mixture of curiosity and contempt. He was considerably taller than her, nearly twice as broad, his sheer size radiating the authority of a war master. Fiona felt a tremor of fear ripple through her, but she thrust her chin forward, masking her fear with indignation.

"What do you want?" Fiona broke the silence, growling through gritted teeth.

Ivar raised an eyebrow, surprised. He wasn't used to defiance, especially not from someone in her position. He straightened, but before he could respond, Fiona caught movement behind him. Niklaos stood there, covering his face with his hand, his shoulders shaking in silent laughter. The smugness in his posture infuriated her.

"That is a very complicated question," Ivar finally answered, his voice gravelly and low.

Fiona's eyes narrowed. "What's complicated is that you went through the trouble of kidnapping me and dragging me here." Her tone was icy, her patience wearing thin. She just wanted to be home, far away from this madness, back in her quiet life where she could plan her future with Jason.

"I have need of your... services," Ivar said, a hint of amusement dancing in his eyes as he twirled a strand of his beard around one meaty finger.

"I have no services to offer you," Fiona snapped, her voice rising. "I don't even belong in this world! I shouldn't be here!" Her throat tightened as hot tears threatened to spill, but she forced them back, channeling her frustration into anger.

"On the contrary, you're more useful than you realize," Ivar replied, crossing his arms and rocking back on his heels, looking far too comfortable for Fiona's liking.

"Then tell me what you want from me," Fiona demanded, sinking back onto the bed with a scowl. She crossed her arms, mirroring his stance, though her small frame made the gesture seem almost comical. Still, there was no mistaking the fire in her eyes.

Ivar couldn't quite shake the confusion bubbling up inside him. He had expected tears, pleas, maybe even outright panic. Instead, he was met with raw, unyielding anger. She wasn't afraid, at least not in the way he was used to. And that unsettled him. Fear was his weapon of choice, his iron grip over those beneath him. But this young lady stood before him, fearless—or so it seemed.

As if on cue, the glass vial tucked into his belt began to heat up, a familiar and unpleasant sensation. Alena. Her presence stirred within the vial, her impatience growing. But he wasn't ready for her interference, not yet. He subtly pushed the vial deeper into his belt, ignoring the searing heat that radiated from it.

Fiona's gaze flicked to the movement. What's he hiding? She kept her expression neutral, filing the detail away for later.

Perhaps there was something here she could use.

The heat from the vial became unbearable, and Ivar clenched his jaw against the pain. Alena's presence was relentless, pushing against the edges of his mind, demanding his attention. She wanted out, wanted to communicate. But it was too soon— far too dangerous. Not even his men knew the full extent of his plan, and he intended to keep it that way until the moment was right. Timing was everything.

Alena's presence retreated with a sigh, leaving the vial cold once more. Ivar exhaled slowly, his mind racing. He turned from Fiona, his large hand bracing against the tent's doorway as a wave of nausea hit him. The pain from the vial had left its mark, a dull throb in his waist. Alena's push for control was getting out of hand.

As he placed a large hand on the doorway to steady himself, he drew in a breath and glared around him. Aldo moved to his commander's side.

"We're done here," Aldo barked from the entrance. He had been standing by, watching the exchange with quiet interest. "Niklaos, you're in charge. Don't mess this up."

Ivar left the tent, his steps heavy, determined to conceal the slight limp that threatened to betray his pain. Alena was becoming more of a liability with every passing day. Her eagerness to return was pushing him to the brink, but soon, once they reached Oldgrange and the tomb, she would have her physical form again. Then, the power would be his.

As he exited, Ivar cast one last glance around. His eyes landed on a small figure hiding beneath a table in the corner of the tent. The girl they had kept hidden, unnoticed by Fiona. Just the tips of her fingers poked out from beneath the tablecloth. He doubted Fiona had any idea she was even there.

Not yet.

As Ivar stood in the tent, towering over her, Fiona felt a bubble of heat rise in her chest, threatening to burst. Panic pulsed beneath her skin, a thick, suffocating force that she fought to keep at bay. For a terrifying moment, she thought it would spill out, suffusing the room, exposing her fear to everyone. But when Ivar turned and left, that bubble began to dissipate. Still, the adrenaline coursing through her veins left her hands trembling despite her efforts to stay composed. She leaned back against the rough wood of the table, crossing her arms in a vain attempt to hide her shaking.

Niklaos had moved to the doorway, his back to her, watching Ivar disappear around the corner. He remained motionless.

At last, she looked away from him and studied the bed in the corner of the tent. It was little more than a crude wooden frame topped with straw and a scratchy blanket. A far cry from the soft bed she had at home, with its down-stuffed canvas, the pillow her mother had sewn from an old dress, and the quilt that wrapped her in comfort. How she longed for even a piece of that world, something familiar to ground her in this nightmare.

A faint scuttling sound broke the silence, pulling Fiona from her thoughts. She glanced around, confused. Niklaos hadn't moved from his place at the door, and no one else seemed to be inside. She shook her head. Probably a rat, she thought. They were everywhere, scavenging whatever scraps they could find.

She sank into a chair on the opposite side of the tent, refusing to go near the bed. The last thing she wanted was to fall asleep and let her guard down. Sitting stiffly, she pressed her feet against the legs of the chair and clasped her hands in her lap, trying to steady the trembling that refused to leave her.

The scuttling sound came again. This time, something flashed in the corner of her eye—a pale blur of movement. Fiona jerked her head to the side in time to see the edge of a cotton fabric disappearing beneath the table. Her heart skipped a beat.

Someone else was in the tent.

She kept her composure, though inside, a mix of excitement and urgency gripped her. A companion— another captive? She didn't want to scare them, so she remained still, her body trembling with anticipation now rather than fear. The quiet shuffle continued from under the bed, and then, a small hand appeared.

The hand was pale, almost translucent, with delicate bones and a frayed gray sleeve that had once been embroidered with lace but was now tattered and brown with dirt. Something about the fabric tugged at Fiona's memory. She edged closer, inching forward in her chair, trying to get a better look without startling the person hiding.

Then, a face appeared. A small, gaunt face framed by a curtain of dirty, matted hair. Wide blue eyes met Fiona's green ones, and recognition slammed into her.

"Emma!" Fiona gasped, unable to contain her astonishment. The name escaped her lips before she could stop it. Niklaos spun around at the sound, his face impassive but alert. Fiona didn't care what he did now. She leapt from her chair, scrambling across the dirt floor, her heart racing as she crawled to the edge of the bed.

Dirt kicked up into her mouth and nose, but she barely noticed. Desperation fueled her as she grabbed onto the girl's frail form, pulling her out from under the bed. Fiona hugged her tightly, tears streaming down her cheeks as she sobbed into the girl's filthy dress. At first, the girl didn't respond, her body limp and unresponsive in Fiona's arms.

And then, it hit Fiona. This wasn't Emma—not the Emma she had grown up with back in Hibernia. This girl was different. She was from Orthea.

Fiona pulled back, holding the girl at arm's length. Her heart ached as she took in the hollow eyes, the dirt-smeared cheeks, and the utter emptiness in her expression. This girl was a shell, a broken thing, and the light of recognition that Fiona had hoped for was nowhere to be found.

"What's your name?" Fiona asked softly, her voice trembling as she cupped the girl's face with gentle hands.

The girl jerked away, startled, and Fiona dropped her hands, not wanting to frighten her any further.

"I'm not going to hurt you," she said, her voice soothing. "They're holding me here too. You're not alone." Fiona shot a glare at Niklaos, who raised his palms in mock innocence before returning to his post by the door.

The girl remained silent, curling into herself, pulling her knees under the bed again as though it were her only safe place. Fiona's heart broke at the sight. She wanted nothing more than to scoop the girl into her arms and run far away from this horrible place.

Instead, Fiona slowly scooted closer, careful not to frighten her further. She reached out, gently entwining her fingers with the girl's.

"I'm Fiona," she whispered, offering a small, hopeful smile. "I'm so glad I'm not alone here."

The girl's head lifted slightly. For a moment, Fiona thought she might smile back, but instead, the girl's voice rasped out, quiet and broken, like it hadn't been used in far too long.

"Welcome to the death trail," she whispered, her words sending a chill down Fiona's spine. "That's all that awaits us."

Then the girl twitched, a sudden convulsion of laughter spilling from her lips. The sound was wrong—hollow and manic, filling the tent with an eerie echo. Fiona shivered, dread creeping up her spine as the girl's laughter rattled through the air.

CHAPTER 15

Fiona sat astride a donkey, the crude animal beneath her a source of amusement for the marauders surrounding her. Their mocking glances barely registered. She didn't care.

She'd already insisted on removing her bandage. Flexing her fingers, she tested the ropes binding her wrists. The rough fibers bit into her skin, but the knots held fast.

Behind her, Moirin clung to Fiona's waist. Her bony arms wrapped tightly around her like a vice. Moirin's wrists were bound as well, and their fates were intertwined by more than just the ropes that tied them together. If one fell, they would both fall. It didn't seem like the worst fate to Fiona, considering what lay ahead. They were being taken somewhere, but all she could gather from the men's gruff, low conversations was one name they kept repeating.

Oldgrange.

The word sent a chill down her spine. Fiona knew of Newgrange in her own world—an ancient site steeped in power and mystery, a place where the dead rested, royalty entombed beneath mounds of stone. And if this world's Oldgrange was anything like it, Fiona feared Ivar's plans reached far beyond simple bloodshed.

Niklaos rode to their left, his blond hair tousled by the wind. His sharp, unyielding gaze fixed on the girls, as though he expected them to sprout wings and fly away. Fiona caught his eye and couldn't resist. She made a ridiculous face—eyes crossed, tongue out, fingers wiggling beside her head. He didn't react, not outwardly. But when she turned away, she could feel his gaze lingering.

"Don't be silly," came a dry, muffled voice from behind her. Moirin's tone, though weak, carried a hint of sharpness. "He's the enemy."

"I know," Fiona muttered back. "I'm just sick of him watching us like that. Why does he do that?"

"The last man who didn't bled from his throat," Moirin rasped, a grim chuckle escaping her before it dissolved into a hacking cough. The sound was wet and crackly. She spat onto the ground, and the donkey flicked its ears back as if to check on them.

Niklaos, noticing the movement, edged his horse closer. "Quiet," he warned, his voice sharp but soft enough that no one else would hear.

The army marched on in relative silence. The heavy smell of sweat mingled with the earthy scent of horses and damp dirt. Fiona's back began to ache from Moirin's dead weight pressing against her. Though frail, the girl was heavy enough to make every bump and jolt agony. Fire skittered up Fiona's spine, tears prickling at the corners of her eyes as the sun dragged across the sky, relentless and unforgiving.

Niklaos, riding beside her, glanced over. "You alright?"

Fiona bit her lip. "Fine."

He frowned, his gaze drifting to Moirin's limp form. "I can take her if you need a break."

Fiona shook her head, though the temptation to agree gnawed at her. "No. She's lighter than she looks, just... awkward to hold."

A wry smile tugged at Niklaos' lips. "Let me know if you change your mind."

She raised an eyebrow, shifting uncomfortably. "Wow, you're

so generous."

He clamped his mouth shut.

Finally, as dusk approached, the army halted and the camp was set up. The silence of the day shattered as Aldo barked orders, the men shouting back and forth as they hammered tent pegs into the ground and dragged supplies from wagons.

Fiona and Moirin stopped beside a brown tent with a thick red stripe that ran up one side and down the other, like a scar. It felt like a warning, perhaps to their own soldiers.

Niklaos approached the donkey, his face set in a hard line, as he untied Moirin's wrists. He didn't meet Fiona's gaze as he worked, his expression unreadable. Once Moirin's bindings were undone, she slumped into his arms without a fight, resting her head weakly on his shoulder. He carried her to the tent like she weighed nothing.

Fiona let herself slump forward, her forehead resting against the donkey's neck. She considered, for a fleeting moment, urging the beast into a run and making a desperate bid for freedom. But when she looked up, a massive man with bulging muscles held the reins, his hand resting on the hilt of a sword. Any hope of escape fizzled out as quickly as it had sparked.

Hands gripped her arms, pulling her upright. Startled, Fiona let out a yelp and jerked back.

"Quiet," Niklaos hissed again, his grip firm but not painful.

"You keep telling me to be quiet," Fiona shot back, her voice sharp. "Don't startle me, and I will."

Niklaos's lips twitched, but he said nothing as he helped her down from the donkey. She shook off his hold and marched toward the tent, chin lifted and back straight, determined to maintain a shred of dignity. She shoved through the flap as if she had any control over the situation and collapsed onto the thin mattress inside.

Moirin lay curled on the far side of the mattress, knees tucked to her chest, soft snores barely audible through the humid evening air. Fiona wiped the sweat from her face, feeling sticky and grimy. She longed for the cool embrace of a stream to wash away the dirt and sweat clinging to her skin. She could almost hear the water bubbling over rocks as she and Lia waded out into its depths, the sun warming their faces.

The sound of heavy, angry footsteps interrupted her daydream. Niklaos stormed into the tent, clearly displeased.

"Are you trying to get my throat slit?" he snapped. "Or yours?"

Fiona shrugged, nonchalant. "Last I knew, they wanted me alive, regardless."

Niklaos's face darkened, and he turned away, muttering something under his breath.

"What do you care if they kill me, anyway?" she asked.

"It's not about you," he muttered. "It's about survival."

Fiona snorted. "I'm not going down without a fight."

"You're going to get us both killed."

"Maybe," Fiona replied, her voice steady. "But I'm not going to make it easy for them."

Just don't do anything stupid." Niklaos stepped to the front of the tent and stiffly turned his back to her, ending the conversation.

Fiona stripped off her outer frock, shook what filth out of it she could and folded it neatly. She couldn't help but wonder about Niklaos. He was confusing—sometimes indifferent, sometimes hostile, and then, just when she thought she had him figured out, he showed signs of concern. She rested her face in her hands, elbows propped on her knees, and sighed.

Niklaos wasn't loyal to Ivar out of devotion. That much was clear. Fear drove his actions, and Fiona saw a possible advantage in that. Maybe she could use it—use him.

Niklaos might be her way out.

Melaney had never been so relieved to see Shades Hollow as she was upon rounding the final bend in the road. The familiar sight of the town amidst the shadowed forest filled her with a mixture of nostalgia and urgency. It was here that the council resided, waiting with bated breath for the arrival of the precious cargo Melaney had spent days guarding with her life.

The caravan passed somberly through the towering iron gates, a structure as much art as defense. The sharp tines curled upwards, twisting into the sky, a symbol of both strength and beauty. The fence encircled the town in a protective embrace, and as Melaney entered, she allowed a small smile to break through her stern expression. Despite everything, despite the weight of the journey and the losses they'd suffered, she was home.

Shades Hollow had always been a place of wonder to her, even as a child. The buildings, made from rich red wood, seemed alive with energy, humming with the enchantments woven into their foundations. At the center of the town stood the council hall, the only building stark and silver among the sea of red, green and other color outlying buildings. It was here that the annual protection spell was cast, an ancient tradition that fortified the town against external threats. The ceremony was only days away, and Melaney was grateful she had arrived in time, despite the setbacks that had dogged their journey. Not just the council of Shades Hollow, but council members from other Shade territories had begun to converge, traveling long distances to be present.

But Fiona. The thought of the girl lingered in Melaney's mind like a thorn, a rare and unexpected discovery that had turned her mission upside down. Fiona had been more than a delay; she had been a revelation. Yet duty pulled Melaney forward, forcing her to leave the girl behind with Julian, Darry, and Brannon in pursuit. She had a task to complete, one that could not be ignored.

The air within the caravan had been heavy with unspoken tension. Lia and Natalie had kept their distance, muttering between themselves, their disappointment clear. Melaney knew they questioned her decision to continue without turning back for Fiona. While they hadn't openly defied her, their silence toward her was as loud as any protest.

As they reached the steps of the council hall, Melaney paused, her toe resting on the first of five stone steps leading up to the wide wooden door, whitewashed like the rest of the building. Two open windows flanked the entrance, their burlap curtains fluttering in the breeze. The hall stood quiet, as if holding its breath in anticipation of her arrival.

The door creaked open before she could knock, and Melaney squinted into the dark interior. A skeletal hand emerged from the shadows, curling a long finger in a silent summons. Her stomach twisted with unease. It was rare to be called inside the council's inner sanctum, a place few were ever allowed to see. She had only been here twice before, and the gravity of the moment weighed on her as she stepped into the darkness.

The door slammed shut behind her, the sound echoing like a death knell. The world outside seemed to disappear, muffled and distant. Melaney stood still, her senses adjusting to the thick, muted atmosphere of the hall. There was a sudden spark of flint and steel, and a small flame flickered to life at the far end of the room.

Pale blue eyes gleamed over the candle's flame, their intensity piercing through the darkness. Melaney shifted as the man seated in the corner— Councilman Cleary— watched her approach.

"Come here, child," he croaked, his voice stretched and frail, like an ancient wind howling through a cracked window.

Melaney stepped forward, her movements deliberate. Cleary, with his stark white hood and long goatee, was a figure of power in the shade world. His presence hummed with an energy that prickled her skin. She stopped at the edge of the table, bowing her head in a gesture of respect. "Good day, Councilman Cleary."

Cleary set down the candle and extended a hand, the skin thin and rubbery like old parchment. "Melaney," he rasped, "you have brought us the snake?"

She clasped his hand, ignoring the cold, clammy feel of his touch. "Yes, Councilman. It's here."

Cleary's eyes lit with a mixture of delight and greed. He stood, wobbling slightly on his gnarled cane as he hobbled to the door. "Bring it in," he whispered, his breath quickening.

Melaney called to the men outside, and they moved swiftly,

lifting the wooden crate from the wagon with the reverence one would give to a coffin bearing a general. As they entered, Cleary hovered over the box, his bony fingers twitching with anticipation. His eyes gleamed unnaturally bright in the flickering candlelight they placed the crate on the table before him.

"It is time for the ceremony," Cleary murmured, almost to himself. His hands caressed the rough wood of the crate as if it held the answer to all the world's secrets.

Melaney hesitated. "Councilman Cleary," she ventured carefully, "I must ask leave of the ceremony this year."

Cleary's eyes snapped to her, sharp and questioning. "Why?"

"I need to aid a new shade," Melaney said. "She was taken by marauders, and I must go help Julian and the others retrieve her. It is my duty as Overseer."

Cleary's expression darkened, his eyes narrowing. "A new shade? From where?"

"She is a mirror," Melaney replied, knowing full well the weight of her words.

Cleary's expression shifted, surprise mixing with something darker, intrigued. "A mirror?" His voice softened. "That hasn't happened in decades."

"Yes," Melaney confirmed. "She needs the council's protection. Your blessing."

Cleary's blue eyes flickered with renewed intensity. He stepped closer, his frail form glowing with power. "A mirror... this changes everything," he whispered. His gaze drifted toward the box, then back to Melaney. "We must delay the ceremony."

Melaney's breath caught in her throat. "Delay the ceremony? Councilman, the other members have already begun to arrive from the distant territories. And the people need access to their--"

"Precisely," Cleary said, his voice gaining strength. "The arrival of a mirror is no mere chance. The ceremony must not proceed as planned until we understand the full scope of what her presence means. The convergence of the council will now serve a greater purpose. This mirror—she is something that we cannot ignore."

Cleary turned away from the table, his eyes glowing with the fire of new determination. "Go, Melaney," he commanded. "Bring her back."

Melaney bowed, relief washing over her. Without another word, she turned and left the hall, her thoughts already on Fiona.

Time was running out.

CHAPTER 16

ulian had pushed himself beyond his limits. They'd ridden hard through most of the night, stopping only for two brief hours of restless sleep, before tearing into cold jerk and saddling back up again. Anxiety pulsed through his chest like a hot, searing brand, every thought of Fiona tightening the knots in his stomach. His fingers had long since gone numb from gripping the reins too tightly. He slowed his horse to a walk, flexing his hands to ease the burning ache in each joint. Every movement sent a stab of pain through his knuckles.

"Look, their camp!" Brannon's voice cut through the quiet as he pointed toward the horizon, his gloved finger outstretched.

Julian perked up, scanning the landscape until he spotted what Brannon had seen. Old, blackened campfires dotted the ground like scars, stretching across the plains in a wide, half-mile radius. Scraps of wood— broken furniture, maybe— were piled haphazardly on one side of the perimeter. It was a ghost camp, abandoned for at least a day.

Julian dismounted without hesitation, crouching next to one of the fire pits. He thrust his fingers into the ashes, feeling them crumble under his touch. Cold. "They've been gone for a while," he muttered, rising to his feet.

Brannon and Darry also dismounted, their faces grim. The three of them picked their way through the desolate campsite, eyes sharp for any signs of a recent trail. As they reached the edge, a pile of bones caught the light, gleaming in the afternoon sun. Flies buzzed in dense, swarming clouds around what was left of the animals. Rabbits, pigs, rats—whatever the marauders had been able to feast on.

Julian crinkled his nose against the stench, forcing himself to keep moving. His horse followed as they pressed forward, but the skin along his neck prickled with unease. The thought of Fiona held by these men made his blood boil. His mind raced with images of her standing her ground, but he knew her sharp tongue might only make things worse. If nothing else, he knew Fiona wouldn't make anything easy on them. Perhaps they would throw her aside just to be rid of her.

He pushed the thought aside, nodding to Brannon and Darry. "Let's keep moving. I don't want to camp anywhere near this place." They all silently agreed, an unspoken tension hanging heavy between them. Their horses trotted forward, eager to leave the stench of death and decay behind.

"What's the rescue plan, anyway?" Darry asked, breaking the uneasy silence. His orange-colored hair bounced in the breeze, a stark contrast to the tense mood.

"Plan?" Julian frowned, the word sounding foreign. "I didn't really think that part through."

Brannon shook his head in disbelief. "We're chasing after marauders, and you don't have a plan? Brilliant."

Julian's shoulders sagged. "I've been... a little preoccupied."

"You might want to start thinking about it now," Brannon grumbled. His horse tossed its head as if agreeing with him.

Julian clenched his jaw, the weight of his rash decisions pressing down on him. He had charged into this mission on instinct, driven by a burning need to find Fiona, but now reality was setting in. He was leading his two best friends into what could very well be a death trap. The marauders were ruthless and well-trained, but retreating wasn't an option. Not now.

"We'll sneak in at night," Julian finally said, the beginnings of a plan forming in his mind. "We'll find where they're keeping her, cut her loose, and make a run for it. We can outmaneuver them in the dark."

Brannon snorted. "That's the plan? Sneak in and run?"

"I didn't say it was perfect," Julian shot back. "But it's better than marching up to their front door and asking nicely."

Darry chuckled, the sound laced with nervous energy. "Don't worry, mate. We'll make it work. Whatever comes, we'll figure it out."

The trees slowly gave way to the wide expanse of the Iridescent Plains. The grass thinned, turning to tufts of lime-colored blades scattered across the dry, chestnut dirt, the tips dotted with incandescent colors from the rainbow that gave it its name. The occasional tree was slender and young, offering little in the way of shade.

The sun beat down on them mercilessly, the heat rising in shimmering waves off the earth. Sweat dripped from Julian's brow, running down his temples in steady rivulets. His shirt stuck to his skin, and he wiped at his face with his sleeve, though it did little good. The fabric was already soaked through.

"Damn this weather," he muttered, the oppressive heat pressing down on him like a weight. It was supposed to be starting on winter.

"It's cursed, the heat," Darry remarked, his voice unusually serious. "I can feel it. Like someone's trying to slow us down."

Julian's hand tightened around his water skin, taking a quick swig before passing it to Darry. "We're not going to let the heat beat us. Drink up, boys. Stay sharp."

He tugged his hood up over his head, shielding his face from the sun's relentless glare. Brannon and Darry followed suit, both men pulling their hoods low as they continued to push their horses forward. The road stretched ahead, Julian's thoughts fixed on Fiona. On the moment he'd see her again.

On the moment he'd make things right.

"You're sick."

"No, I'm not."

"I hear you coughing."

"You hear nothing."

"Look at your eyes!"

Moirin gave a weak, bitter laugh. "How am I supposed to do that?"

Fiona paused. The marauders didn't exactly keep mirrors lying around. They had stopped for water, and the girls stood beside their donkey, finally untied and free to face one another. Moirin's condition had visibly worsened. Her eyes were sunken into her skull, her skin pallid and drawn. Fiona could see it in every movement Moirin made—the sickness was taking its toll. Her stubbornness, however, had only grown with her weakness.

"You look sick," Fiona pressed, her frustration mounting.

"Why tell them? It wouldn't do any good," Moirin said, stifling another hacking cough with the edge of her oversized sleeve. The wheeze that followed was harsher, louder than before. "They'd probably kill me."

"I thought they needed you."

"They have you now." Moirin shrugged her bony shoulders, the motion causing her tattered shirt to slip off one side. She snatched it back into place with a trembling hand. She was wasting away before Fiona's eyes, and it hadn't gone unnoticed. "I figured they'd have slit my throat by now."

"Stop talking about slitting throats all the time!" Fiona barked, the words rushing out in a sharp burst. "I can't take it anymore!"

"It's the truth," Moirin said with a faint raise of an eyebrow, her skeletal frame somehow still managing a bit of sass.

"Doesn't mean you have to remind me every few minutes that they have a throat-slitting problem." Fiona let out a frustrated sigh, resting her chin on her knees and closing her eyes. "It isn't helping anything."

Moirin's gaze flicked upward, past Fiona's shoulder. Fiona felt it before she saw it—a firm hand gripped her shoulder.

"She's right," Niklaos's low voice cut through the tension as he stepped between the girls. He released Fiona's shoulder and turned his cold gaze on them both. "It's time to go."

Fiona lifted her chin in defiance, her green eyes locking with Niklaos's. "What if I run?"

"You can't outrun arrows." Niklaos nodded toward the archers stationed around the perimeter, their bows drawn, ever watchful.

"I can try." The fire in Fiona's voice betrayed the anxiety twisting inside her.

"You can," Niklaos agreed. "But you won't."

"And why not?" Fiona challenged, her gaze blazing with determination.

Niklaos's eyes didn't waver. "Because you'd never leave her."

Moirin dropped her eyes. "So that's why you keep me alive," she muttered, her voice barely audible over the wind.

Niklaos glanced away, squinting into the distance, his expression unreadable. "I just follow orders. You should too."

Fiona clenched her fists, frustration boiling inside her. She turned her back on Niklaos, the anger she had been holding in threatening to explode. Her breath quickened, and she felt the familiar burn of panic rising in her chest. She shut her eyes tightly, willing it to disappear. But something else stirred within her—the wind. It began to pick up, a gentle caress at first, but then stronger, wrapping itself around her wrists, lifting her hair into the air like playful fingers.

Fiona opened her eyes and gasped. She was no longer on the ground. She was soaring high in the sky, the earth far below her, every tree and blade of grass vivid and distinct. She saw a doe grazing beside a fawn, their hearts pounding like drums, the rhythm echoing in her ears as she swooped closer. The sound was like a hammer to anvil.

"What are you doing?" Moirin's voice snapped her back to reality.

Fiona blinked, disoriented. "Huh?"

Moirin's suspicious glare burned into her, while Niklaos stood behind her, arms crossed, staring at Fiona with a mixture of shock and wonder. His hair whipped in the breeze that suddenly felt stronger, wilder.

When had it gotten so windy?

Fiona smiled at the feeling of the wind swirling around her, teasing her hair, grazing her skin. But Moirin and Niklaos didn't share her joy. They watched her warily, their expressions dark.

Aldo's harsh voice ripped through the air. "Mount up!"

Niklaos lifted Fiona onto the donkey with a surprising gentleness, his fingers working swiftly to tie her wrists. The ropes bit into her skin, and she winced.

"Is that really necessary?" Fiona whispered, glancing around nervously. "I'm not going anywhere, and these hurt."

For a moment, Niklaos's face softened, a flash of guilt passing over his features before being replaced with a frown. "Why should I care what hurts you?" he growled, his voice harsh, but the words didn't match his eyes.

"Because you do," Fiona said quietly, her gaze meeting his. "You're not like them." Play into his head.

Niklaos's expression flickered, uncertainty creeping into his eyes. It was working. But he shook his head, as if dismissing the thought. "No, I'm not," he muttered. Still, with a swift movement, he loosened the ropes. His hand lingered for just a moment before he reached up to help Moirin mount behind Fiona, tying her wrists securely around Fiona's waist.

"What about her?" Fiona protested, glancing back at Moirin, whose head lolled against her back.

"Don't push it," Niklaos warned under his breath, his eyes narrowing. "Stay next to me, or I'll have the archers shoot you."

Fiona raised an eyebrow, but she didn't argue. She knew she had won a small victory. The ropes were loose. It was a start. And she would need every advantage she could get.

CHAPTER 17

Niklaos was testing his boundaries. Ivar watched from a distance, eyes narrowed as the girls' donkey trudged forward, falling in line with their guard. Niklaos rode beside them, his actions a subtle defiance that hadn't gone unnoticed. Water dripped from Ivar's wild beard as he downed a swig from his waterskin, replacing the metal cap with a quiet click. His burn throbbed—a constant reminder of Alena's growing impatience, the searing pain now a part of him as much as any of his scarred flesh. The vial clipped to his belt glowed faintly, and he could feel Alena's presence simmering with unspoken rage. She had singed him once, a warning, and while Ivar had no intention of letting her do it again, he knew that once she was free, there would be a reckoning.

Aldo approached on horseback, his face a stony mask. "Should we replace him?" His voice was low, but the tension between the words was palpable. He tipped his head toward Niklaos.

Ivar took a long pause, his mind weighing each possibility. "No. Not for now," he answered, the words drawn out, as if each syllable had its own gravity.

Aldo gave a curt nod. "As you wish." Without another word, he spurred his horse forward, taking his place at the front of the line.

Ivar followed a moment later, pressing his heels into the horse's sides. As they reached the front of the army, Ivar turned in his saddle, surveying the expanse of men beneath him. It was a sight that never failed to stir something dark within him—a sea of iron and steel, armor gleaming under the sunlight, weapons ready, and every man facing forward like an unblinking predator. It was power, tangible and intoxicating, and it belonged to him.

His lips curled into a cold smile. If only his father could see him now. Though, in truth, he preferred the old man dead, buried beneath the surface of the earth where he belonged. These men were his to command, an army of faceless soldiers, each one waiting for his next word, his next command. He could make them tear apart the earth itself if he willed it.

"We're close to Oldgrange," Aldo muttered, pulling Ivar's attention back. "The men can feel it. They're ready."

"They're eager," Ivar finished for him. "So am I."

The procession lurched into motion, the sound of marching boots and clinking armor filling the air. It was a symphony of conquest, a melody Ivar had come to know well. Each step, each clang of metal, was a reminder of the power he held, the dominion he would soon claim.

In the quiet hum of his mind, Alena stirred. *At last, we are close. It is nearly time for me… and for you, Ivar.* Her voice slithered through his thoughts, warm and seductive. The wind picked up, carrying with it the promise of winter. *The winds favor us,* she continued, *her tone laced with delight. We are on time.*

Ivar clenched his jaw, trying to shake her presence. He didn't need her distraction now. Her eagerness for freedom was growing, and though he had bound her to the vial, it was clear she felt the power rising as they neared Oldgrange. He couldn't afford to show any weakness, not now.

Aldo shot him a glance, suspicion creeping into his sharp eyes. Ivar caught the look and hardened his expression, his gaze locking on the road ahead. *Go away, Alena,* he thought, willing her to recede into the glass prison.

But even as she quieted, Ivar felt her displeasure. A wave of insolence rolled over him—her irritation a tangible thing, simmering beneath his skin. She giggled faintly, a sound that grated against his nerves. It was as if she reveled in his internal struggle, taunting him with the inevitability of their bond.

He blinked, disoriented, his vision momentarily blurred. For a fleeting moment, he was lost in the landscape of his mind—a vision of Alena's pale hands lacing with his, a smile on her face, her eyes devouring him, consuming his very soul.

"Ivar?" Aldo's voice sliced through the haze, pulling him back to reality. Ivar flinched before quickly composing himself. He straightened in his saddle, squaring his shoulders, the sneer already curling back on his lips.

"I'm fine," he said, cutting off any further comment from his second-in-command.

Aldo nodded, his gaze lingering a moment longer before returning to the path ahead. But Ivar knew better. The moment of weakness had not gone unnoticed.

As the army pressed forward, Ivar clenched his reins, the leather biting into his palms.

In her glass vial, Alena giggled.

"This is a stupid plan."

Darry, Brannon, and Julian crouched in the brush lining the narrow, well-worn path, watching the marauders make camp. The sun was sinking low, streaks of pink, orange, and blue painting the horizon in long tendrils as twilight crept in. Dark clouds gathered, roiling in the distance like some foreboding creature, the maple trees trembling with anticipation, their pale green underbellies turning upward as they waited for the coming rain.

"This is a really idiotic plan," Darry repeated.

"Quiet." Julian's jaw was set, small blue veins rising out of his forehead and neck.

"It's about to rain," Brannon whispered, his eyes darting up to the blackening sky. "We should move to better cover before it hits."

Julian didn't take his eyes off the camp. "I'm not losing sight of Fiona."

She was there, in plain view. Fiona sat astride a small donkey, her figure slouched with exhaustion. The frail girl behind her, Moirin, clung to her like a vine, her bony arms wrapped around Fiona's waist, barely moving. Even from a distance, the other girl looked as if she were at death's door—her sunken cheeks and hollow eyes made her seem more ghost than human.

A white-haired man stood near the girls, his arms crossed over his armored chest, scowl fixed in place. He was clearly unhappy, probably stuck on guard duty—a dull, miserable task, especially for a marauder. Julian could feel the boredom radiating from him. But boredom had a tendency to breed carelessness, and Julian was ready to exploit that.

"It's about to rain, mate," Darry repeated once more, scratching his nose with his little finger, sniffing as he surveyed the sky.

"You said that already." Brannon rolled his eyes as he adjusted the grip on his crossbow. The weapon was loaded with a hand-crafted arrow—its slender, brown shaft adorned with roughly tufted tan feathers. It was worn from use but remained Brannon's favored weapon, one he never traveled without.

"That's how much I mean it," Darry grumbled.

"That's enough," Julian snapped, his voice low but laced with authority. "They'll hear us."

"That's not what I'm afraid of," Darry muttered, his eyes flicking toward the darkening sky. The clouds had thickened black and heavy, swirling above them. Lightning crackled across the sky, jagged lines of blue, white, and gold illuminating the storm's fury. The answering thunder was no less intimidating, a deep, grumbling roar.

"This could be a problem," Julian admitted, pulling back to reassess.

Darry and Brannon exchanged glances, then followed Julian deeper into the trees, taking cover beneath the thick branches of a towering tree.

"I already said that, too," Darry huffed, leaning against the tree trunk.

"I believe what you really said," Brannon corrected, "was that Julian's plan was stupid and it was going to rain. It hasn't rained yet."

As if on cue, the first heavy drops of water began to fall, pattering against the leaves like a thousand tiny drums. The rhythmic tapping grew louder, more insistent, as the rain intensified. Large droplets of water slipped through the thick canopy above, falling in erratic splashes that soaked their clothes, plastering fabric to skin and sending shivers down their spines.

The ground quickly became a slick mess, the once solid dirt path transforming into a treacherous mire of mud and water. Every step became a struggle as boots sank into the soft earth with a sickening squelch, and the rainwater mixed with the mud, turning it into a slippery quagmire that clung to their legs and feet. The earthy smell of wet soil rose into the air, heavy and pungent, as rivulets of water carved tiny rivers through the landscape.

The storm showed no sign of letting up. The wind picked up, howling through the trees and tossing the rain in sideways sheets, battering their faces and drenching them even further. Lightning flashed overhead, illuminating the darkened sky with bursts of white-hot light, followed by the deafening boom of thunder that rattled the ground beneath them.

Julian cursed under his breath as he wiped the rain from his eyes, the weight of the storm bearing down on them like a suffocating blanket. His clothes clung to him, water dripping from his hair and down his neck in cold streams. Every movement felt slower, more labored, the slick mud threatening to drag them down with every step they took.

"What now?" Brannon asked over the din, sitting down at

the base of the tree where the rain couldn't reach him as easily. His voice was calm, and his eyes were focused. He wasn't one to panic in the face of a challenge, but even he could see the situation was growing more complicated.

"We stick with the plan," Julian said, his voice firm. "This changes nothing."

"Except for the fact that now we might get struck by lightning," Darry intoned dryly, pulling his cloak tighter around him. "Two bolts, if we're lucky."

Julian shot him a glare that could've burned through stone. "You want to leave her with them?"

Darry's face remained impassive, but he held Julian's gaze for a long moment, tension crackling between them like the storm overhead. Finally, Brannon cleared his throat, shifting uncomfortably. The sound seemed to break the spell, and the three men sank back into the mud, crouching low as the rain beat down on them. The storm's fury had fully descended now, with lightning flashing above and thunder rolling across the sky.

The camp was still visible through the sheets of rain, the marauders unaware of their hidden watchers. Julian clenched his jaw, his heart thudding in his chest. He couldn't stand waiting, not with Fiona so close yet still so far out of his reach. But rushing in without a plan would get them all killed.

The minutes dragged on, the sky darkening further as night approached. They would wait for the deep of night, for the cover of darkness to shroud their approach. Fiona was depending on him, and Julian wasn't going to let her down.

Not this time.

CHAPTER 18

When the rain started, no one seemed to notice except Fiona, Moirin, and Niklaos. The downpour was steady, fat droplets cascading from the darkened sky, splattering against the ground and drumming on the tents. The prisoners' tent, as always, was the first constructed. While it was being erected, Fiona and Moirin slipped off the donkey and knelt on the ground beside it, using the animal's body as partial cover. Moirin let out a rattling cough, her frail form shivering violently despite the lukewarm air. Niklaos stayed close, his sharp eyes scanning their surroundings. His nervous energy was palpable, a tension that made Fiona uneasy.

A tall marauder ducked out of the tent's doorway, his voice rough and thick as he barked, "Let's go, ladies!" He waved them over with an impatient wave of his hand.

Fiona scrambled to her feet, pulling Moirin up with her. The two girls stumbled into the tent, their soaked clothing clinging to their skin as they collapsed in a heap on the damp floor beside the pallet that made for them.

"You need to change," Niklaos said as he entered the tent, holding a cloth bag under his arm. He handed it to Fiona, his face impassive. She took it, peeking inside to find two white cotton frocks, neatly folded. Surprised, she looked back at Niklaos, who only shrugged. "Had it on hand," he muttered before stepping back outside, leaving them to their privacy.

Fiona wasted no time. She knelt beside Moirin, whose skin had taken on a sickly blue hue, her thin frame trembling like a leaf. Fiona began unbuttoning Moirin's damp dress, the fabric clinging to her as if it didn't want to let go. Moirin batted at her hand at first, then gave up, too exhausted to resist. Fiona pulled the soaked garment over her head and helped her into the clean frock from the bag. It was far too large for Moirin's emaciated form, Fiona realized. The girl was wasting away.

After changing into her own dry frock, Fiona had barely finished pulling it down over her hips when Niklaos re-entered the tent. She spun around, hastily fastening the buttons at the front.

"Sorry," he muttered, his eyes flicking away. It was the first time she'd heard an apology from him.

"Thank you," Fiona said, smoothing the wrinkles from her dress. "It's nice to be in clean clothes for a change."

Niklaos nodded curtly. "You're welcome." He crossed the room and sat at the entrance of the tent, his frame filling the space. On impulse, Fiona followed and sat beside him, curiosity tugging at her mind.

"Are you even a marauder?" she asked quietly, her voice laced with skepticism. Niklaos looked startled, his brows drawing together in confusion.

"A what?"

"A marauder," she repeated, motioning to the camp outside with a flick of her hand. "You don't really fit the mold."

Niklaos's jaw tensed, and for a moment, Fiona thought she had pushed too far. "Why wouldn't I be?" he asked, his voice guarded.

"I don't know," she said, shrugging. "You don't seem as...ruthless as the others."

"Do I need to be?" His tone was sharp, defensive.

"No," she admitted, her voice softer now. "But you're different. I can tell."

"I wasn't always one of them." His voice was soft, distant. Fiona blinked, taken aback. "Aldo found me."

Fiona shifted closer, her curiosity piqued. "What do you mean?"

Niklaos let out a deep sigh. "I was a child, five years old, when the marauders came. My village... it wasn't a large place. We were farmers living quiet lives. My parents and my sister were good people. We didn't deserve what happened."

He paused, his jaw tightening as if debating what more to say. Fiona didn't push.

At last, he continued. "They came at dawn, burning everything. People were screaming, running... but there was no escape. I remember hiding in a cupboard, trembling, thinking if I stayed quiet enough, they wouldn't find me." His voice wavered for a moment. "But they did."

Fiona clenched her fists, feeling the tension in the air grow. Niklaos met her eyes, his expression darkening. "Aldo was leading them. I remember his face, how calm he was while everything burned around us. He found me, dragged me out. At the time, I didn't know why he didn't just kill me like the others."

"Why didn't he?" Fiona asked, her voice barely above a whisper.

Niklaos smiled bitterly. "I was young. Impressionable. He saw potential, I guess. He took me with him, raised me as one of his own, trained me to be a marauder. But I never quite fit in, no matter how hard I tried. The others could sense it, too. They called me 'The Stray,' like I didn't belong."

Fiona felt a pang of sympathy, imagining Niklaos as a boy, surrounded by violence and cruelty but never fully a part of it. "Did Aldo ever treat you like a son?" she asked.

Niklaos snorted, shaking his head. "He trained me, yes. Gave me a place among the marauders, but he never treated me as family. I was a tool. I couldn't rely on anyone but myself."

"But you stayed," Fiona said, her brow furrowing. "Even after all that."

"I didn't know anything else by the time I could've left," Niklaos admitted, his gaze dropping to the ground. "When you're raised in that kind of world, it warps you. You start to believe that maybe this is all you deserve, that you really are just a stray." He let out a bitter laugh. "I just... don't know how to leave."

Fiona's heart ached for him, for the boy who had lost everything, thrust into a life that wasn't his. "You're not a stray," she said softly.

Niklaos looked at her, his expression softening for a brief moment. "I don't know what I am," he murmured. He grabbed an extra blanket. "Make sure you bundle up tonight. It's going to be cold."

A cough broke the moment. Fiona could feel his gaze linger on her as she turned her attention back to Moirin, who lay curled on the pallet, her breathing shallow and labored.

"What's wrong with her?"

Fiona glanced over her shoulder, surprised by the question. "She's sick. I think there's fluid in her lungs. If she doesn't get treatment, she's going to die." She stood, moving closer to him, her eyes pleading. "Is there a camp doctor? Someone who can help?"

Niklaos's face hardened. "If Ivar wanted her treated, it would have happened by now."

Fiona's frustration boiled over, her voice rising. "If she dies, I'm leaving. I swear it."

Niklaos met her gaze, his expression conflicted. He should have laughed at her threat, mocked her for thinking she had any power in the situation, but instead, he only nodded. "I know."

"Then do something!" she snapped, her hands balling into fists. She could feel the burn of rage in her chest, the helplessness clawing at her insides.

Niklaos stepped closer, his face inches from hers, and placed his hands gently on her shoulders. "Don't you think I would, if I could?" he whispered.

Fiona blinked in surprise, the anger seeping out of her as quickly as it had risen. She stepped back, her heart pounding in her chest. Niklaos let his hands drop to his sides, looking at her with a mixture of helplessness and regret.

Without another word, Fiona turned away and knelt beside Moirin, brushing her feverish forehead with trembling fingers.

The girl's skin was cold and clammy, and her shallow breaths sent a wave of panic through Fiona's heart.

When she finally turned around, Niklaos was gone.

As the sun slipped behind a thick layer of clouds, casting the landscape in a dreary twilight, Melaney waded across the shallow river with Lia and Natalie at her side. The quiet between them was heavy, filled with unspoken worry that lined their faces in deep creases. No one dared break the silence yet; there was little to discuss until they got closer to the marauders and could assess the situation. Only then would they form a plan— no one would go in blind.

"They're not far now. We should reach them soon," one of the scouts reported to Melaney as he wrung out his drenched cloak. His horse pawed at the soggy ground, its breath visible in the cold, damp air.

"Thank you," Melaney replied, her teeth almost chattering. The wet fabric of her skirts clung to her legs, the weight of the soaked clothing dragging her down. A gust of wind swept across the river, making her shiver as the chill crept into her bones. She donned her robe to protect against the incoming bite of the air and glanced back at the shades still making their way across the water, the river's current tugging at their legs. This had been the calmest, shallowest crossing they could find, but it had still left them all drenched and uncomfortable.

"Should I go back and watch their movements?" the scout asked, adjusting his saddle with a quiet creak. The familiar scents of oiled leather and cold metal from his gear brought a small measure of comfort to Melaney.

"Yes," she nodded, sending him off with a wave of her hand. His horse trotted back through the forest, its hooves making soft, rhythmic thuds that faded into the distance.

The scout heeled his horse around and cantered back the

way he had come, his horse flicking its black tail around as it went. The pound of hooves receded with them.

A whiff of roses floated past her nose, and Melaney turned to see Dr. Stelios standing quietly behind her. His hunched figure appeared almost ghostly in the fog that had begun to roll in from the river.

"Doctor," she acknowledged him with a curt nod, her breath visible in the growing cold.

"Drink this," Dr. Stelios said, holding out a flask in his wrinkled hands. "It will protect you from the illness that lingers in these waters."

Without a word, Melaney accepted the flask, taking a long swig of the bitter liquid. She passed it to Lia, who did the same, and then to Natalie, who grimaced before swallowing it down. The doctor nodded approvingly as he took the flask back, slipping it into the folds of his robe.

"Carry on," he said, his voice as quiet as the fog that drifted around them.

"We need to start thinking about what we'll do once we reach the camp," Lia murmured as they resumed their trek.

"I've already thought of that," Melaney replied, her gaze sharpening. "We'll immobilize the marauders, then carry Fiona out of there, even if we have to fight our way through."

"Immobilize them? How do you plan to do that?" Lia asked, her brow furrowed with uncertainty.

Melaney's eyes flicked toward the wagon trailing behind them, its wooden wheels groaning with each bump in the road. "We'll figure that out," she said.

Natalie wiped her damp forehead with a cloth, her face glistening with sweat despite the cool, misty air. "Then let's get on with it," she suggested, tucking the cloth into her jacket pocket and striding ahead.

Melaney fell into step with her, the tension mounting with every step closer to the marauders' camp. Lia moved up beside her, her hands gripping the hilts of her short swords. Behind them, the wagon groaned and bounced, protesting the uneven terrain as if it, too, were eager to reach the destination.

The sky darkened further. Black clouds, thick and menacing,

rolled in from the horizon, and drops of rain began to fall. A drizzle turned into a steady downpour, and the rain plastered their hair to their heads, trickling down their faces in cold rivulets. The wind picked up, biting at their wet clothes, but they pushed forward.

Lightning flashed.

CHAPTER 19

Julian didn't mind the rain. In fact, he welcomed it. While it dulled most scents except for the earthy fragrance of soaked greenery, it muted the noises of the forest, masking even the slightest misstep. If he could sneak in under the cover of the storm, getting Fiona to safety would be far easier. He'd take her straight to Shades Hollow.

Kneeling in the mud, Julian traced intricate patterns with a fingertip. Lines curved and looped, connecting in a weaving design of circles, spirals, and symbols. Brannon and Darry watched, the tension between them palpable. This was not just a symbol, it was a mark of unity. At the center of the design, an array of snakes coiled around a single pole, slithering together as one. It represented the bond of the Shades: many acting as one.

Once finished, Julian sat back on his heels and admired the symbol, his fingers slick with mud. Brannon and Darry knelt beside him, the three forming a tight circle around the drawing. They clasped hands, their grip firm as the rain cascaded down their arms, trickling onto the damp earth. Closing their eyes, they began to chant, their voices low and fluid, the ancient words rolling off their tongues like the hum of distant thunder. The language was ancient, powerful, curling like white mist, invisible tendrils wrapping around them as it seeped into their very bones.

When the incantation faded into the rain, silence enveloped them like a heavy blanket. For a long moment, the air itself felt thick, charged with energy that hummed quietly beneath the surface. Julian opened his eyes first, a faint smile pulling at his lips as he met Brannon's and Darry's gazes.

They moved with a renewed sense of determination, standing and brushing the mud from their soaked clothes. Their gear was simple but effective—leather cufflets, leg guards, Shade garb that allowed for quick, silent movement. One by one, they assembled their weapons. Julian strapped a hunting dagger to his side, the leather sheath cool against his thigh. Brannon checked the tension on his crossbow, the dark wood glistening wet under the rain. Darry slipped a small throwing knife, sharpened to a deadly point, into the breast pocket of his tunic before tugging his gloves on.

In unison, they collected their things and carried them to the horses, securing everything to the saddles with practiced efficiency. Darry doused their small fire, the last puff of smoke curling up into the stormy sky as lightning flashed above them. The air rumbled with more thunder, although the rain lightened as if it was giving them a chance.

Julian and Brannon exchanged a glance. They handed their reins to Darry, who would stay back with the horses. Without a word, Julian and Brannon broke into a jog, their bodies low to the ground as they slipped into the shadows of the trees. Brannon's crossbow was loaded, the weapon held ready as they moved, while Julian remained empty-handed, his dagger still sheathed. Together, they circled around the western edge of the marauder camp, creeping through the cover of the forest.

The camp was quiet, with only a few marauders milling about. Most were likely hunkered down, waiting for the rain to pass. Julian's eyes scanned the perimeter, catching sight of a familiar figure. The white-haired man from earlier—the guard who had stood near Fiona—was pacing nearby, seemingly unaware of the danger that lurked beyond the tree line.

Brannon slowed his pace, raising his crossbow ever so slightly. His eyes flicked back to Julian, the message clear: Don't move. Stay low. But before Julian could react, the guard turned, and their eyes locked across the distance. For a heartbeat, the world stood still, the sound of the rain fading into the background. The guard froze, his expression unreadable.

Julian held his breath.

Niklaos's head spun. Fiona had gotten under his skin like a thorn. A beautiful, sharp thorn that he couldn't shake loose. She was everything he had never known in his life as a marauder—kind, compassionate, strong-willed. Qualities he was supposed to despise. But here he was, walking through the pouring rain, torn between duty and something he couldn't name. Something that made him want to protect her, even if it meant risking his life.

He wasn't sure why he was going to find one of the doctors for Moirin. Ivar hadn't ordered it, and seeking help would likely put him in danger. But Fiona had been clear—if Moirin died, she would try to escape. If that happened, Niklaos was as good as dead. They'd hunt her down, and him too. And the thought of Fiona being hunted, chased down like prey, filled him with dread he couldn't explain. He couldn't let them harm her.

So, he trudged through the camp, rain pelting his head and shoulders, soaking through his clothes as he wrestled with his decision. Each step toward the doctor's tent felt heavier. His soaked hair clung to his forehead, and the cold sting of rain dripped down his face, but he ignored it. The tent loomed ahead, a hulking shadow that seemed to mock him for his hesitation.

Just as Niklaos was about to turn back, reconsidering his decision, movement in the tree line caught his eye. He froze, heart thudding in his chest as he spotted a man standing there, half-hidden in the shadows. The figure was drenched, dark hair plastered to his skull, his eyes locked onto Niklaos's with unnerving intensity.

They stood there, staring at each other across the distance. Niklaos recognized the leather armor, the hood, the way the stranger held himself. This was no marauder. This man had come for the girls. There was no doubt. His instincts screamed at him to sound the alarm, to call for backup—but something stopped him. His heart pounded, as if uncertain whether to fight or flee.

Slowly, Niklaos raised his hands, a silent signal of surrender. He glanced around for any sign of marauder guards, but the camp was quiet. No one expected trouble in the rain. The stranger, the one Niklaos assumed was here for Fiona, mirrored his gesture, raising his hands in return. They were both soaked, rainwater dripping from their fingertips as they cautiously approached each other.

Thunder rumbled above them, and when they were close enough to see each other clearly, they stopped, an unspoken agreement hanging in the air. The dark-haired man spoke first, his voice low but confident.

"Who are you?" the man asked, his eyes glistening and sharp.

"Niklaos. Marauder guard," Niklaos replied, keeping his voice even. "And you?"

"I am Julian of the Shades."

Niklaos nodded, already knowing the answer to his next question. "What's your purpose here?"

Julian's gaze was steady. "You have a woman in your care. Red hair, a bit stubborn."

Niklaos couldn't help but crack a slight grin. "What of her?"

"I want her back," Julian said flatly.

The smile faded from Niklaos's face. He let out a breath, shaking his head. "I'm not sure I can help with that."

"The good news is, I'm not asking you to," Julian replied evenly.

Lightning flashed overhead, illuminating their faces for a brief second, followed by a deafening clap of thunder. Niklaos flinched, the tension building as the storm intensified. When the thunder rolled away, Julian's expression was hard. Niklaos pursed his lips. "The bad news is if I let you through here, I'm as good as dead."

Julian's face softened just slightly, a trace of regret in his eyes. "I'm sorry to hear that," he said. His accent was smooth, unfamiliar to Niklaos's ears, who was used to the rough, guttural accent of the marauders.

Fellow marauders. Men Niklaos had grown up with, fought alongside, laughed with. Men who trusted him. And yet, in this moment, he wanted to betray them. For Fiona. He could feel the weight of the decision pressing down on him, pulling at his conscience.

Fiona's face flashed in his mind—her fiery red hair, the way her green eyes had burned with anger when she'd told him Moirin was dying. She was fierce, unafraid to stand up to him, unafraid of the consequences. And that had drawn him to her in ways he hadn't expected. He knew what would happen if he didn't act. Ivar would kill him, sure as the rain was falling now. But if Fiona survived—if she escaped—then it would all be worth it. He'd die knowing she had a chance at freedom.

Niklaos clenched his jaw, the decision made. He gestured toward Julian, urgency in his movement. "Come with me."

Julian hesitated, surprised, but didn't argue. Together, they moved swiftly through the rain, shadows creeping around them as they made their way toward the tent where Fiona waited.

Fiona paced in her mind, her body still as stone while Moirin's damp head lay in her lap. Each breath the girl took sounded like twigs snapping in her chest, intertwining like branches that had blocked every bit of air she had left. Moirin's pale fingers had turned blue, her lips a sickly cobalt. Fiona had seen this before. The signs were all there—Moirin was slipping away, deeper into a raspy sleep that she might never wake from.

Outside, the storm raged. It mirrored the turmoil in Fiona's heart, the thunder booming in time with the wild beats of her pulse, and the lightning flashing like the firestorm coursing through her veins. She clenched her fists so tightly her knuckles turned white, the same pale hue as Moirin's skin. She was utterly powerless, forced to sit there and hold the girl as death crept closer with each passing breath.

Then came the thought that struck like a bolt of lightning. Julian. She could almost see his face, those mischievous eyes glittering with laughter as they had the last time they spoke. Was he out there somewhere, his journey finished, telling the tale of the red-haired girl he'd once known? The idea sent a pang of anger and longing through her. She wasn't supposed to care what Julian thought anymore, and yet...

Fiona shifted, lifting Moirin's frail body to the side and laying her gently down on the edge of the pallet. The space beside her was small but just enough for Fiona to curl up next to her, close enough to offer warmth, though Moirin was oblivious. Fiona kissed the girl's damp, dark hair and closed her eyes, exhaustion settling heavily upon her. It wasn't long before sleep began to pull her under.

"Fiona?"

The voice cut through her like a knife, sharp and startling. Julian. She bolted upright as if she'd been doused in cold water, eyes wide, searching. For a moment the world was nothing but a blur, spinning in disoriented confusion. Then, as she blinked, it sharpened into focus—Julian standing in front of her, rain-soaked, his face lined with weariness but lit with relief.

"Are you real?" she whispered, her voice trembling as she reached out.

His skin was rough with stubble, his clothes drenched and clinging to his lean frame. He looked like he hadn't slept in days. His hands found hers, and for a moment they just stood there, touching, confirming the other's existence. "You are real," Fiona breathed, her heart pounding.

Julian didn't answer with words. Instead, he brushed his lips against hers, a featherlight touch that sent a shiver through her. Then, with a sudden intensity, he was kissing her—urgent, desperate, like he was afraid she might disappear if he let go. Fiona melted into him, her fingers clutching at his shirt, which smelled of rain and earth. The world around them fell away, and for a heartbeat, nothing else existed.

"Alright, break it up, lovebirds." She pulled away from Julian, blinking up at Niklaos, who stood by the doorway with his arms crossed, looking displeased. "We don't have much time."

"We?" Fiona echoed, glancing between the two men.

"How do you think he got in here unnoticed?" Niklaos asked, raising an eyebrow.

Fiona lowered her eyes, avoiding the look in Niklaos's—sharp and full of resentment. "Thank you," she mumbled.

Julian's attention shifted to the bed, where Moirin lay still as stone, her labored breathing rattling in the quiet tent.

"Who is that?" he asked.

"That's Moirin," Fiona replied, her voice catching in her throat. "She's been with the marauders since before they found me."

"She's dying," Julian said. There was no emotion behind his words, only cold truth.

Fiona's heart squeezed. "Can we help her?" She couldn't bear to watch Moirin suffer like this any longer.

Julian shook his head. "I didn't come prepared for a sick girl, Fiona. I came for you."

"If I leave, she dies," Fiona insisted, her voice cracking.

Niklaos stepped forward, his voice low. "I'll carry her."

Julian turned sharply to face him, his eyes narrowing. "I appreciate your help, but you're not coming with us."

Niklaos's jaw clenched, a muscle in his temple twitching. "If I stay, Aldo will kill me. Ivar might even do it himself. Either way, I'm dead here. You take her—" he nodded toward Fiona—"and you take me, or I'm as good as gone."

Julian hesitated, torn. Fiona squeezed his hand, intertwining their fingers. "Let's go," she urged softly. "Let him come. Ivar kept me captive. Niklaos was just doing his job. He saved Moirin. He can help us."

There was a long, tense silence. The storm eased, the rain ceasing. Niklaos didn't wait for more discussion. He bent down and lifted Moirin's fragile body into his arms, her head lolling against his chest. "Let's go," he muttered, ducking out of the tent.

Julian shot a look at Fiona, who tugged on his hand. "You heard him," she whispered, her voice thick with urgency.

"I don't like this," Julian muttered as they hurried into the pouring rain, but he followed nonetheless.

Niklaos was already moving through the underbrush, rain soaking through his clothes. Moirin's limp body hung in his arms, her breaths shallow and uneven. Fiona and Julian ran past him, and Niklaos followed, the three of them pushing through the wet branches and brush.

They barely made it past the tree line when a voice hissed in Fiona's ear, causing her to jump. "Are you crazy?" Brannon appeared out of the darkness, his hood low over his face, scowling. "You're bringing a marauder with you?"

Julian kept moving, his face set with determination. "We don't have time to argue. Keep up."

The camp behind them was quiet, the tents glowing faintly with candlelight. A strange metallic taste lingered in the air, like something sinister was hanging just beyond the shadows. Fiona could feel it in her bones, the pull to run as far away from that camp as possible.

The storm began to subside as they pushed further into the woods, the rain slowing to a drizzle. A crashing noise from the north drew everyone's attention. Fiona's heart pounded as she squinted into the darkness, seeing only shadows shifting in the breeze.

"That would be Darry," Brannon said dryly, shaking his head. "Sneakiest man alive."

"Oh, hush it," Darry grumbled, stepping into view. His orange hair was plastered to his head, water dripping from his beard. He took one look at Niklaos, still carrying Moirin, and frowned. "You brought a marauder with you?"

"This is Niklaos. He helped me," Fiona explained. "He's with me."

"And who is that?" Darry pointed a long finger at Moirin.

"She's almost dead," Niklaos replied quietly. "Whatever you have in mind to do, Fiona, you should do it soon."

They put as much distance between themselves and the camp as they dared before they laid Moirin on the ground per Darry's orders, her frail body looking smaller and more fragile than ever. The horses tethered nearby snorted uneasily, sensing the tension radiating from the group as they gathered in a circle around her. Darry knelt beside Moirin and unrolled a small cloth from his pack, his movements precise and methodical. Fiona watched with a sinking feeling in her stomach, knowing something was about to happen but unsure if she was ready for it.

From the cloth, Darry removed five smooth, black stones, each one polished to a glassy sheen that reflected the dim light filtering through the clouds. He placed them around Moirin's body with the same careful precision—one stone by each of her hands, one at each foot, and the last on her chest, where her breathing was barely noticeable. Fiona's gaze flickered between Darry's hands and Moirin's pale blue face. The girl's fingers were cold, and her eyes had sunk into hollow shadows, as if death was already settling in.

The moon could be seen now, silver and shimmering through the translucent veil of the receding clouds. The dark knots across its surface seemed somehow a deeper contrast than normal. A clean, rustic smell swept through from the wet trees. On any other occasion Fiona would have relished it.

"Fiona, are you listening?" The sharpness of Darry's voice jolted Fiona from her thoughts. She blinked, realizing she'd been staring aimlessly into the sky.

"Sorry, what?"

"She doesn't need to do it," Julian protested.

Darry shrugged. "She's the closest to Moirin, the one who knows her best. That connection will strengthen the spell. It's the best way."

"What's best is not putting her at risk." Julian's voice was tight like an over tuned violin.

"What is it?" Fiona asked.

Julian opened his mouth to speak, but Darry interrupted him. "I can use a spell to bring your friend back from the edge of death, but everything has a cost. It'd take some of your energy to do it. You'd be weakened some for awhile."

Fiona avoided Julian's eyes. "I'll do it."

Darry gave her a grim smile, then motioned for her to kneel beside Moirin. "Place your hands over hers, on the stone."

Fiona knelt down beside her friend, her heart hammering in

her chest. The cool stone felt heavy and lifeless beneath her palms, but Moirin's faint, rattling breaths vibrated up through the rock. She bit her lip hard, tasting the metallic tang of blood. Darry placed his own hands over hers, his touch firm and warm.

"Don't move," he warned.

Julian shuffled his feet behind her, clearing his throat. Fiona glanced back and saw his face set evenly, careful not to show any emotions. He didn't like this, she knew that. But there was no other way.

Darry began to murmur in a low, fluid language that Fiona had never heard before. The words curled and twisted in the air, full of strange vowels and sounds that seemed to wrap around her, almost tangible. It felt ancient, older than anything she'd ever encountered.

The stone beneath her hands began to warm. At first, it was a gentle heat, like standing in the early morning sun, but it quickly grew hotter, radiating through her skin and up her arms. Fiona winced as a prickling sensation crawled up her fingers and wrists, like tiny needles stabbing her flesh. Sparks of energy darted between Darry's hands and hers, flickering into Moirin's chest and sinking into her body.

The pain intensified, but Fiona forced herself to stay still. She squeezed her eyes shut, trying to escape the sensation, trying to focus on anything else. Images of her home flickered in her mind—her small village with its modest buildings, the high gate that served little purpose, her parents' smiling faces, the safety and warmth of it all.

And then she saw King Rock.

It loomed before her, massive and imposing, casting a dark shadow across the land. Its surface was smooth and cold, grey like the storm clouds that had followed her here. Sunlight streamed from behind it, blinding her, forcing her to turn away. The murmurs around her grew louder, voices chanting, laughing, echoing in the air like a song she couldn't quite grasp.

One voice rose above the rest.

"He's here. He's here."

Fiona gasped, the words hitting her like a physical blow. She knew that voice—it was Julian's, but distorted, distant. Her heart raced as she searched the swirling shadows around her, trying to make sense of it all.

"Who's here?" she whispered, her voice trembling as dizziness washed over her. The world around her tilted, her stomach churning like a stormy sea. King Rock shimmered before her like a mirage, its edges blurring and shifting.

She reached out, desperate for something solid to hold on to, but her hand passed right through the rock. Instead of cold stone, her fingers sank into something warm and gelatinous, the scent of sulfur stinging her nose. She gagged, stumbling backward, her foot catching on a thick branch. She fell hard, her knees buckling as the ground rushed up to meet her.

Laughter erupted around her, loud and mocking, but she couldn't tell where it was coming from. The voices twisted together, overlapping, creating a cacophony of sound that echoed in her ears.

CHAPTER 21

var was not a man easily taken by surprise. His instincts were sharp, honed through years of brutal warfare and cunning survival. But now, hot breath washed over his face, and the rasping voice of Aldo, his most trusted man, dragged him from sleep like nails scraping over iron. The whisper of his name was enough to make him flinch, his hand instinctively clutching the hilt of his hunting knife. His eyes snapped open, the sharp point of the blade raised.

Aldo stood over him, his silhouette barely visible in the darkness, but the fear in his eyes was unmistakable. Fear was foreign to Aldo, a man who'd faced death countless times without blinking. Ivar sat up quickly, heart pounding, sensing that something was terribly wrong.

"What is it?"

"The girls are gone, sir." Aldo shrank back as he said the words.

Ivar's blood turned to ice. His body remained still, but inside, a storm brewed, violent and furious. "Where is Niklaos?"

Aldo shrugged his shoulders. "The bastard is gone, too. Nowhere to be found. I discovered their tent empty minutes ago and came straight to you."

"Niklaos was your find all those years ago, was he not?" Ivar's anger rose in hot waves from the pit of his stomach to the roof of his mouth, searing all the way.

Aldo bowed his head. "He was."

"Then you are responsible for him," Ivar growled, his voice like the thunder rumbling in the distance from the receding storm. He rose to his full height, closing the space between them in a single, swift movement. His breath was hot with rage. "You will find him. And you will bring the girls back, or you will lose your head."

Aldo's face drained of color. Ivar had never seen him frightened before, but now, beads of sweat formed on his brow. It was almost gratifying to Ivar. His anger seethed, bubbling up as he stared down at his second-in-command. Aldo had never failed him—until now.

"I will find them," Aldo promised, bowing his head, and then hurried from the tent, his footsteps quick and desperate.

Outside, the camp erupted into chaos. Men shouted orders, Aldo's voice rising above the din, his tone laced with urgency. Horses whinnied in protest as they were saddled, the sounds of leather and metal echoing in the cool night air. Riders galloped into the darkness, their mission clear—find the girls and Niklaos, no matter the cost.

Ivar sat alone in the tent, his thoughts a torrent of dark possibilities. The weight of the situation pressed down on him, threatening to crush his resolve. Reaching for Alena's vial, he clenched the glass in his hand. The once-frigid glass now burned against his skin, hot with her fury. He knew what she wanted. She wanted blood.

Stepping out into the night, he took a deep breath, inhaling the crisp air in an attempt to quell the rising panic. Panic wasn't something he allowed himself to feel, but this—this was a disaster. If the girls weren't found soon, everything would fall apart. The red-haired girl was the key to the plan, and without her, they were lost. Aldo would search relentlessly; Ivar had no doubt about that. He always did his job—because he knew it was the only thing keeping him alive.

But now, the stakes had changed. Ivar hated the thought of killing his oldest friend, but failure was not an option. He tasted bitterness on his tongue, revolted by the prospect. The idea of it lingered like a poison, and yet, he would do what was necessary.

No matter. Straightening, Ivar clenched his fists, the muscles in his arms bulging as his fury simmered beneath the surface. The guards nearby instinctively stepped back, their gazes averted as he passed.

The camp bustled with activity, the search parties preparing to head out in every direction. But for Ivar, the waiting was torture.

Inside his belt, Alena's vial pulsed with heat, the glass scorching his skin, though he barely noticed. Her rage was palpable, an inferno trapped within the glass. She wanted vengeance, she wanted blood, and Ivar would give it to her. Soon.

But first, he had to find the girl.

Alena was enraged. The glass vial scorched Ivar's skin. He didn't notice.

"Fiona?"

Julian's voice cut through the thick fog of Fiona's mind, pulling her from the dark void where she drifted. She stirred, testing her limbs to see if they would cooperate. They did, but each movement came with a dull ache, her muscles protesting the effort.

"Ow," she muttered, blinking her eyes open. White light invaded her vision and she flinched.

"Brannon put that thing away!" Julian hissed.

The light disappeared.

Fiona's vision cleared slowly. At first, all she saw was a dark blur, but then Julian's face came into focus—his beloved, handsome face. Without thinking, she reached up, her hand hot against his cool cheek. Julian's expression darkened for a moment, and he gently clasped her hand in his.

"What happened?" Fiona tried to push away the clouds looming in her mind.

Brannon's voice sounded from nearby, distant but steady. "We used some of your life force to help Moirin. She'll be okay until we get her to Stelios, but it drained you."

"I hate to break it up," Darry interrupted, his voice tense, "but we've got to move. Ivar's men will be searching for her soon if they're not already."

Julian nodded grimly and helped Fiona to her feet. Her legs wobbled beneath her, the ground swaying she stood on water. Pain shot through her feet, and she instinctively dug her nails into Julian's cloak, clinging to him to stay upright. His arm wrapped around her waist, steadying her.

"I've got you," he murmured.

Brannon took the lead, his bow at the ready, eyes scanning the trees for danger. Darry followed close behind, carrying their supplies. Niklaos walked in the rear, cradling Moirin's frail body in his arms as the girl slept, her breathing shallow and labored but improved. Fiona and Julian brought up the rear, their footsteps muffled by the damp earth beneath them.

Julian was warm. Fiona gritted her teeth. The pressure from his fingers wrapped around her side made her skin tingle. She snuggled her head into his embrace and he squeezed gently. Then, to Fiona's surprise, he brushed his lips on the top of her head.

Fiona glanced up, catching a crooked smile on his face. The sight of it, the brightness of his teeth against the darkness, made her heart flutter despite everything.

Their moment was cut short when Brannon stopped. Darry nearly collided with him, and Niklaos staggered, shifting Moirin in his arms to regain his balance.

"What the—?" Darry began, but Brannon hissed, silencing him.

"Quiet."

Brannon's knuckles whitened around the grip of his

crossbow. His eyes narrowed, scanning the woods. The thick foliage seemed to close in on them, the branches twisting and looming overhead like sinister shadows. Fiona shrank back, pressing herself against Julian's solid frame.

"Don't panic," Julian muttered, though the tension in his voice betrayed him. Fiona wasn't sure if he was trying to reassure her or himself.

A high-pitched screech ripped through the dense air, causing Fiona to jump. Her fingers dug into Julian's arm as he pushed her back against a tree. The bark bit into her skin, rough and unyielding, but she barely noticed. All her attention was on the noise—the predator that was approaching. Julian raised his dagger, the silver blade catching the pale light of the moon. Fiona's heart pounded in her chest, fear twisting her insides into knots.

"What was that?" Niklaos whispered from beside them.

The group instinctively formed a protective circle, pressing their backs to one another, with Fiona huddled close to the tree. Moirin still slept, oblivious to the danger, cradled in Niklaos's arms.

"Have you never heard a wild cat before?" Darry muttered. "What kind of training have you had, son?"

"I'm not your son." Niklaos raised his voice in derision.

"Both of you, shut it!" Julian growled.

Fiona was glad it wasn't because of her.

Silence fell again, but the tension was palpable. Fiona's heart raced as they listened intently, every creak of a branch or rustle of leaves setting them on edge. Something was out there, moving closer. Footsteps—soft but deliberate—echoed through the stillness.

Then she saw them—yellow eyes, glowing like embers, cutting through the darkness. They locked onto her, sending a shiver of pure terror down her spine. Cold sweat broke out on her skin, and she barely managed to whisper, "Julian—"

"I see it," he replied in a low voice. "Stay quiet."

From the shadows emerged a slender, sinewy creature. Dark spots marred its golden fur, muscles rippling beneath its sleek coat. Its head was disproportionate to its body—large, heavy, and crowned with a snarl of vicious, spear-like teeth. A ridge of white formed a ring around its throat and over its head. Small, pointy ears peeked over the ridge. Fiona trembled as the wild cat inched closer, its hungry gaze fixed on her.

"Watch out!" Darry shouted.

A thunderous crash reverberated through the trees. The wild cat froze in its tracks, startled by the noise. A whirring sound, sharp and metallic, filled the air as something heavy landed beside the predator, forcing it to retreat.

"Julian, what is that?" Fiona gasped, the words slipping out in her panic.

Before her stood a towering figure, limbs thick and gnarled, as though it had been carved from the very trees around them. Its arms, long and powerful, held a spear that shimmered in the moonlight. The creature's face was a mask of ancient bark, cracked and furrowed, as if etched by centuries of age. A beard of tangled branches and leaves cascaded from its chin, curling and twitching like restless tendrils. Its eyes, glowing white orbs without pupils, shone like twin moons, casting an eerie, ethereal light on the ground before it. Ears like a deer poked from the sides of its head and massive antlers stretched towards the sky, beckoning.

As it stood still, the wind whistled through the cracks in its bark, and leaves swirled around its feet as though nature itself was drawn to the being. Even the forest seemed to bow in reverence, the trees leaning in, as if recognizing one of their own.

"By the gods," Brannon breathed in awe. "It's a Leshy."

CHAPTER 22

"What's a Leshy?" Fiona gasped, her eyes wide. The towering creature stared down the cat with an intensity that could melt stone. She shivered, her breath catching in her throat.

"Guardians of the forest," Julian replied, his voice low and urgent. "Come on." He grabbed her hand, pulling her to the side as Brannon, Darry, and Niklaos followed suit. They hurried through the dense foliage, distancing themselves from the Leshy and the cat.

Behind them, the Leshy raised its massive spear and brought it crashing down with such force that it drove halfway into the earth. The cat, swift and nimble, leaped to the side, pouncing onto the creature's gnarled beard, its powerful jaws crunching into the twisted branches and sending splinters flying.

The Leshy let out a roar, a sound that reverberated through the forest like a thunderclap. It whirled, flinging the cat into the trees with such power that the creature slammed into the very spot where Fiona and Julian had stood moments before. The Leshy's spear followed, plunging into the cat's ribcage with a sickening thud. The cat screeched, snarling and snapping in vain. The Leshy withdrew the spear, a wet sucking sound filling the air, and plunged it back into the cat's hide, over and over, until the predator's cries weakened to whimpers and then faded to silence.

With a bellow, the Leshy hoisted the bloodied carcass of the cat above its head, muscles bulging under its bark-like skin. It drove the blunt end of its spear into the ground, using it as a post to display the slain beast, its lifeless body slowly spinning, its tongue hanging limply from its mouth.

"What's the Leshy doing?" Fiona whispered.

"Making an example," Brannon replied, his voice hushed. "The Leshy doesn't tolerate animals hunting for sport or pleasure. They protect the balance of the forest."

As if hearing them, the Leshy turned its head, its glowing white eyes fixing on the group. Fiona's breath caught in her throat as the creature lumbered toward them, each step shaking the ground beneath its enormous feet. It stopped in front of Julian, towering over him, its massive form even more imposing up close. Its gaze was unreadable, its face a mask of ancient wood, gnarled and unyielding.

Without thinking, Fiona stepped forward. Her heart raced, but something deep within her urged her. She couldn't explain it, couldn't name the force that compelled her feet to move, but it was undeniable. She needed to get closer. Its breath, slow and deliberate, washed over her in a warm, earthy gust. It wasn't what she expected—not the rancid stench of decay or the sharp bite of predator's breath. Instead, it carried the soothing scent of damp earth after a fresh rain, of wildflowers blooming in hidden meadows, and of morning dew clinging to leaves in the quiet dawn. It was the scent of life, pure and untamed.

Fiona inhaled deeply, the aroma wrapping around her like a comforting embrace. There was something about it that calmed her racing heart, that soothed the edges of her fear.

The world around her seemed to fade away—the rain, the cold, even the others. It was just her and the Leshy now, standing on the edge of something ancient and powerful. She lifted a hand to reach out to the creature. The rough texture of its beard, made of twisted branches and delicate leaves, brushed against her skin.

She held her breath as she ran her fingers through the beard's twisted tendrils, feeling the life force pulsing beneath the bark. It was as though the entire forest moved through the creature, a constant ebb and flow of energy that connected everything in the world around them. The Leshy cocked its head, its expression almost inquisitive. A low, guttural sound rumbled from its chest, something like a contented purr.

"Thank you," she whispered, her voice barely a breath.

The Leshy stood motionless, as if considering her words. Then, with a deep bow, it turned and leapt into the shadows of the forest, vanishing into the trees as if it had never been there. Only the gruesome sight of the cat, skewered and lifeless, remained as proof of its presence.

"We should go," Darry's voice shattered the silence. He glanced around nervously, his eyes darting to the sky as if expecting the forest to come alive once more. "That thing gave us a chance to live. We should take it."

Julian nodded, wrapped his hand firmly around Fiona's, his face a mask of wonder. "He's right. Let's move." Darry slung the still-sleeping Moirin over his shoulder, and they pressed on through the forest, their steps muffled by the damp leaves beneath their feet.

The storm had quieted, leaving only the occasional drip of water falling from the tree canopy above. Fiona's feet ached with each step, and her eyes struggled to stay open, her exhaustion weighing her down like stones tied to her ankles. She leaned against Julian, grateful for the steady warmth of his body next to hers.

He glanced down at her, concern etched on his face. "You okay?"

"Yes," she murmured, though her words felt distant, as if they belonged to someone else. The exhaustion was seeping deeper into her bones, making her feel as though she was moving through water.

Without warning, her legs buckled. Julian caught her as she started to fall, his strong arms wrapping around her waist. "She's done for tonight," he said. "She's still weak from the healing spell."

Niklaos, walking just ahead, turned. "We can't stop now. The marauders could be right behind us." His voice was tense, the urgency in his tone undeniable.

Fiona wanted to agree, to tell them to keep going, but her body refused to cooperate. She couldn't even muster the strength to speak. The darkness swirling at the edges of her vision grew thicker, more insistent, until it swallowed her whole.

She felt herself lifted, cradled in strong arms. Julian's voice, soft and reassuring, whispered in her ear, "I've got you. Rest now, love."

And then, everything faded to blessed peace.

Melaney pushed her way through the damp foliage, the thick leaves heavy with morning dew dripping onto her skin as she moved. She wiped at her brow with a wool-clad sleeve and glanced back to check on her companions. Lia, Natalie, Dax, and several others paused to study her as she mulled briefly over direction. Unlike their traveling methods with the snake cargo, they now openly carried weapons of various forms. Lia and Natalie, master archers, held bows at the ready with quivers stuffed with arrows. Dax also carried a small bow that matched his frame, and an equal number of arrows. For his young age he was as good at hitting a bull's-eye as any of them. Maybe better.

For the first time since they'd left Shades Hollow, Lia and Natalie had finally begun talking to Melaney again, though the tension still simmered beneath the surface. Their coldness toward her had softened now that they were united in the goal of getting Fiona back. But even as they trudged forward, Melaney couldn't shake the nagging doubt that gnawed at her insides. Would things have been different if she had gone after Fiona from the start rather than prioritizing the ceremonial snake?

A sharp whistle pierced the air, cutting through the stillness like a dagger. Melaney's head snapped up as she scanned for the source, every nerve on edge. What hadn't she seen? The others froze behind her, bows drawn, arrows nocked and ready.

Her heart raced as a faint buzzing sounded by her ear, and then a searing pain shot through her forearm. She looked down in disbelief, her eyes wide as she stared at the arrow lodged deep in her flesh. Blood seeped from the wound, dark and fast, staining the grass beneath her feet.

A deafening roar filled the air, a war cry that vibrated through the forest. Everything felt slow, heavy, like the world was muffled beneath a thick wool blanket. Melaney tried to shout, to warn her companions, but her voice stuck in her throat. The others had already ducked for cover as marauders charged out from the trees, their swords gleaming in the dappled sunlight. They were too close, too fast.

She felt herself falling, the soft forest floor rising up to meet her. Her body crumpled to the ground, the damp earth cushioning her fall. She lay there, helpless, her vision blurring as long, wide boots stopped inches from her face.

A boot tapped her forehead lightly, almost curiously. "This one's still breathing. Let's take her."

"She's no redhead, but she'll do," another voice growled, rough and impatient.

Melaney struggled to lift her head, but her body refused to obey. Her limbs were leaden, unresponsive. Panic flared in her chest, but she couldn't move. She couldn't fight.

"All Ivar needs is a magic wielder."

Strong, dirty hands gripped her body, hoisting her up as if she weighed nothing, and threw her onto the back of a horse, her body hitting the animal's hide with a force that knocked the breath from her lungs. She gasped for air, her ribs aching from the impact, while the men around her laughed. Their cruel voices rang in her ears, but she was too disoriented to focus on their words.

"Let's get back to camp. Ivar's going to love this," one of the marauders barked, his voice filled with dark amusement.

The horse began to move, each jolt of its stride sending waves of pain through Melaney's body. She gagged, the taste of vomit rising in her throat, but no one paid her any mind. She was just cargo to them, another prize to bring back to their warlord.

But then something cut through her haze of pain and fear: I'm no redhead? Fiona. The thought struck her like lightning. Fiona must have escaped. Relief flooded her, chasing away the terror that had consumed her moments before. If Fiona had gotten away, that meant Melaney was the replacement—her sacrifice for Fiona's safety. Somehow, that didn't seem so bad anymore.

She allowed her body to relax, letting the rhythm of the horse's gait rock her as she rested her cheek against the rough hide. Her fear gave way to a strange sense of peace. This was okay. If Fiona was safe, that was all that mattered now.

A life for a life.

Melaney felt a flicker of hope, even as the regret gnawed at her. She had made a mistake—prioritizing the snakes over her friend—but now she had the chance to make things right. She would take Fiona's place. She would pay for her mistake.

Regret was an unforeseen and bitter companion.

CHAPTER 23

A warm gust of air stirred Fiona awake, gently caressing her arm and teasing through her tangled red curls. She could hear the cheerful chirping of birds in the canopy above and knew that dawn had broken, even before she opened her eyes. She lay still for a moment, savoring the quiet rustling of her companions as they began to stir. The air smelled of damp earth and fresh leaves, a comforting scent that reminded her of better days.

Finally, she opened her eyes. The sky overhead was still soft with the early morning light. Nearby, Julian squatted over a small pile of twigs, his brow furrowed in concentration. His hands moved in slow, precise circles, manipulating the air around them with a patience that only came with years of practice.

"What's he doing?" Fiona asked no one in particular.

"What else would he be doing?" Darry's voice was gruff and crusted with sleep. "Building a fire."

As if on cue, sparks flew from Julian's hands, and flames sprang up from the twigs, licking at the wood. The scent of burning kindling and fresh smoke filled the air, warming Fiona with its familiar comfort. The fire's crackle reminded her of home.

Fiona thought back to the night before. The stones that had shifted magic through her and Moirin. Questions swirled in her mind.

"Those stones you used to heal Moirin," Fiona began, "What were they?"

Darry gave her a sideways look, a faint smile tugging at the corners of his mouth. "Obsidian," he said. "It's formed from the raw energy of the earth. It absorbs and transforms negative energy, making it perfect for healing rituals."

Fiona furrowed her brow. "Absorbs negative energy? How does it work?"

"It's ancient magic," Darry explained, his voice dropping to a more reverent tone. "Obsidian pulls the harmful energy from the body, like venom from a wound, and transforms it into something neutral—something that won't harm. When we placed the stones on Moirin, they drew out the sickness and replaced it with the strength of the earth. You were the catalyst."

Fiona nodded thoughtfully, glancing down at her hands. "It felt… powerful. I didn't expect it to be so intense."

"It always is, when it's done right," Darry said with a wink. "But it's also dangerous. If the person performing the ritual doesn't have control, the stones can take more than just the illness. They can take a piece of your soul."

Fiona had more to ask, but she heard the horses stir as Brannon sauntered into camp with a satisfied grin, pulling three rabbits off the rope slung over his shoulder. He dropped them on the ground, kneeling down to skin them with practiced ease. "One shot for two of them," he boasted.

Darry shook his head, grinning. "Kill two deer with one shot, and then come talk to me, brother."

Brannon snorted, but the smugness never left his face. "Same to you… brother."

Julian ignored them, taking the first skinned rabbit and piercing it through the middle lengthwise with a stick and propping it over the fire. The smell of roasting meat soon filled the camp, making Fiona's stomach growl in anticipation.

A groan came from a nearby clump of grass. Fiona nearly jumped out of her skin as Moirin pushed herself up, blinking in confusion. She stretched her limbs, her movements sluggish but far less frail than before. Her skin had regained a healthy peach hue, her hair, though still dirty, no longer matted and lifeless. She looked over at Fiona with wide, bewildered eyes.

"What happened?" Moirin croaked.

"Well, for starters, we rescued you," Darry pitched in before Fiona could respond. "Fair maidens and all that."

"How are you feeling?" Niklaos approached from the trees behind Moirin.

Moirin turned and, upon seeing Niklaos, gasped in horror. Scrambling backward, she pressed herself against a tree, her eyes wild with fear. "Get away!" she shrieked.

Fiona rushed to her side, placing a calming hand on her shoulder. "It's okay! He helped us get you out."

"He's one of them," Moirin hissed, her eyes brimming with tears. "One of those monsters."

"It's okay," Fiona assured her, keeping her voice steady. "He's on our side now."

"I'm sorry for everything you went through," Niklaos murmured, his eyes downcast. "If I could undo it, I would."

"But you can't," Moirin spat bitterly. "You never will."

Fiona pulled Moirin closer, wrapping her arm protectively around the girl's thin shoulders. "It's over now," she whispered soothingly. "Come, eat something. You need your strength."

"I thought I was dead," Moirin gasped as she clung to Fiona.

"You would have been," Darry said as he stepped forward, offering her a hand. "If it weren't for Fiona. She saved your life."

Moirin hesitated. Though her face now had some color, the haunted look in her hollowed eyes hadn't faded. "Who are you people?" she asked, her voice trembling but laced with the remnants of defiance. Her thin fingers curled slightly, as if she still wasn't sure whether to trust them.

Darry smiled softly, his tone kind but firm. "We're friends of Fiona's. And you, Moirin, are lucky we found you when we did."

Moirin studied them all for a moment, then cautiously took Darry's hand, allowing herself to be led to the fire. She sat slowly, her eyes darting between the faces around her, as though still uncertain whether to trust them.

As the smell of cooked rabbit filled the air, they began to eat, the fire crackling warmly in front of them. The rabbit meat was tender and flavorful, far better than Fiona remembered it being. It was a small comfort, but one she welcomed after the past few days. No one spoke as they devoured the meal.

Once the last scraps were gone, Julian stood and began kicking dirt over the flames.

Brannon snorted. "Come on, brother. You can do better than that." He snapped his fingers and the fire vanished, leaving not even a wisp of smoke behind.

"There's no harm in doing things the old-fashioned way," Julian retorted, hoisting his pack over his shoulder.

They packed up quickly. Moirin stood frozen against the tree until they were ready to leave, her eyes still glinting like a wild animal as she studied those around her. Debated. Slipping her hand into Moirin's, Fiona smiled encouragingly. "Come." Moirin followed her and they fell into step with the others. Julian circled around the back of the group and planted himself on Fiona's left side.

They had been walking for several hours when a sudden crack echoed through the forest, followed by the unmistakable sound of snapping branches. The group froze. Julian immediately stepped in front of Fiona, pulling her behind him as Brannon crouched low, his crossbow ready.

Fiona's pulse quickened, her eyes narrowing as she strained to see through the underbrush. A strange sensation swept over her, a lightness in her limbs as though she were rising off the ground. She felt herself lift into the sky so smoothly she hardly knew she had moved. The grass shrank into invisibility and she realized with surprise that she not only saw Julian and Moirin but herself still crouching. They looked up in surprise, or rather Julian and Moirin did. Her body remained frozen.

Looking around them, her gaze locked onto a figure moving through the trees ahead. She squinted, focusing in as the world around her sharpened. The figure's shaggy brown hair and awkward, young movements were unmistakable.

Dax.

Ivar stood at the entrance of the tent, his thick arms crossed over his iron-clad chest. The wind whipped through the camp, tearing at the loose ends of his tunic and sending a biting chill across his skin. The vial swung at his waist, the glass cool and silent. They had doused the campfires earlier to avoid the risk of flames spreading in the gusts. He was not happy with cold meat but it was better than being burned alive.

He remembered the first time he had seen a human burn into fiery ash. He had been a boy, standing at the front of a crowd with the other village children, his mother gripping his arm tightly. The soldiers had dragged a woman accused of witchcraft down the cobbled street, her ankles bound in a thick rope. She had been screaming, a sound that grew louder the closer they came to the square. The soldiers ignored her pleas as they hauled her to the center of town, where a wooden post stood like a grim sentinel, waiting for her.

Her husband trailed behind her, muttering prayers, his eyes wide with the knowledge that his fate would soon be the same as hers. The witch, they had called her, though she had been nothing more than a healer practicing small magics that threatened the wrong people. Ivar had watched, wide-eyed, as they strung her up by her neck, her body convulsing, limbs thrashing in desperation.

The soldiers had been efficient, lighting her dress on fire with a torch. The flames crawled up her body like hungry serpents, devouring her flesh while her howls pierced the air. Even now, those screams reverberated in his mind, a memory seared into his very being. Irony walked with him now.

A scout had come in moments ago and now stood behind his commander with arms crossed and mouth turned up in a sneer. "They are headed back now."

"It won't be the power of the new shade," Ivar grumbled, "But it will suffice."

Alena seemed to be in agreement. The vial remained cool to the touch. She would take whatever shade she could get now that the redhead had escaped. The original girl had been the plan, but the redhead had triggered a thirst for a powerful body. If the scout was right and they had the leader of the Snake Run it would be almost as good as the new shade. She vainly hoped it was an attractive body. Something she could work with.

Ivar turned away from the tent opening and nodded to the scout. "You're dismissed."

The young man opened his mouth, hoping for a word of praise. But one look at the glint in Ivar's eyes snapped his jaw shut. He bowed and retreated, the ambition dying in his eyes as he made his exit.

Left alone, Ivar sat down, the wooden stool creaking under his weight. He placed the vial in front of him; his fingers traced the rough lines of his palms, calloused and cracked from years of battle. Blood, mud, and death—they had all stained his hands.

"It is almost time," he murmured, his voice more tender than anyone had ever heard from him.

A familiar presence curled inside his mind, Alena's voice a sultry purr that sent a shiver through him. *We will be together in the flesh soon. I look forward to it,* she whispered into his thoughts, the promise laced with desire.

He grunted, his mind already turning to what would happen if Aldo failed. His friendship with the man meant little when weighed against his ambitions. If Aldo returned without the sorceress or worse, empty-handed, Ivar knew he'd be forced to do what needed to be done. Failure wasn't an option, not this close to the end.

Ivar's fist clenched as he imagined the cold steel of his blade sinking into Aldo's flesh. He would take no pleasure in it, but neither would he hesitate. "Soon," he whispered to himself. Alena's laughter echoed faintly in his mind.

CHAPTER 24

knew it!"

Fiona startled back into her body as Julian shook her shoulders none too gently.

"What is wrong with you?" Fiona stumbled back out of his grasp.

"Your familiar, Fiona! Don't you realize?" Julian's eyes blazed with excitement as he stepped closer.

"That's some eagle, if I do say so myself," Darry chimed in, leaning against a nearby tree, a smirk playing on his lips. Moirin stood rigidly next to him, silent but clearly on edge.

"Eagle?" Fiona asked, confused.

Julian's face lit up with a grin as wide as the horizon. "A beautiful golden eagle," he repeated, almost in awe. "You became part of it, Fiona. You became it." He tried to catch his excited breaths. "We all have familiars. Animals that bind themselves to us by magic. The moment you became a shade, your familiar found you... only your familiar is also part of your affinity. Your eagle is not just a bird—it's connected to the wind itself. I've never seen anything like it. I've only heard stories."

Fiona's mind swirled, trying to process his words. She

remembered Melaney mentioning a familiar before. But she'd become an eagle? But before she could fully wrap her thoughts around it, a small body barreled through the underbrush and Dax was on Julian. He knocked him to the ground with sheer velocity and, raising a small white-knuckled fist, hit Julian in the nose. Hard. Blood spattered onto his hand and he raised it again just as Brannon and Darry rushed forward, pulling him back.

"What the hell?" Julian spat blood onto the grass, glaring up at the boy as he wiped his face on his sleeve. "What is your problem?"

"Melaney is gone because of you!" Dax's voice cracked with the weight of his fury as he struggled against the iron grips of Brannon and Darry. "You left us! Now the marauders have her!"

Julian's face paled. "What?"

"They're going to hurt her!" Dax's voice reached a fever pitch, trembling with both fear and anger. "It's all your fault!"

"Okay, calm down!" Brannon barked, his grip on Dax tightening as the boy stopped struggling, but the fire in his eyes didn't dim. His glare remained locked on Julian, searing with blame and grief.

"We need to go back to the elders," Darry said. "Assemble an army. It's clear we can't handle this on our own."

Fiona tilted her head. "You think they'll help us?"

"They have to," Dax replied, desperation thick in his voice. "If we don't go now, it'll be too late for her."

Julian, now wiping the last of the blood from his nose, stood up, his expression hardening. "Then let's stop wasting time fighting amongst ourselves," he said gruffly.

"We'll get her back."

Dax ignored him.

"Don't you forget who I am, what I've done for you," Julian scowled. He slung his pack over his shoulder and turned east. "Are you alone?"

Before Dax could respond, more figures came out of the brush. Lia and Natalie, both scratched and bruised, limped into their arms. Lia cried, but Natalie remained as stoic as ever, scowling as she leaned against Brannon's supportive arm. "We were attacked on our way to get you," she said to Fiona. "They took Melaney, destroyed the wagon, and just the three of us escaped."

"You brought the wagon?"

"Just in case Fiona wasn't…fit to be walking home, yes."

"Well, this is a situation," Darry said. Behind him, Niklaos snorted.

"If you can walk okay, we can't waste time," Julian said to the two women, not unkindly.

"We can walk," Lia said. "We made it this far."

Ignoring Dax's venomous glare, Julian turned eastward, slinging his pack over his shoulder. "Let's go," he called back over his shoulder, starting down the path.

Fiona hurried to her place beside Julian. Her place? The thought startled her, lingering in the back of her mind like a whisper she hadn't meant to hear. Since when had she begun to think of him like that—like she belonged at his side. She couldn't pinpoint the exact moment, but now, with the steady rhythm of their footsteps in sync and the warmth of his presence beside her, she realized she didn't hate the idea.

Behind them, Brannon and Darry kept a careful watch on the rear, while Moirin drifted silently next to Darry, her eyes flicking nervously toward Niklaos, who followed at a distance, as though she feared he might strike at any moment. Dax, Lia, and Natalie brought up the rear, with Dax's eyes still locked on Julian like a predator.

"Think you can do it again?" Julian's voice broke the silence, pulling Fiona from her thoughts.

She blinked, startled by the question. "Do what again?"

"Call on your companion," Julian said with a grin. "Becoming it again with your mind. It was magnificent."

Fiona flushed, her cheeks warming under his praise. "Magnificent?" she echoed, unsure of how to take the compliment. "I don't know if that's the right word. I... don't even know how I did it."

"Or," Julian replied thoughtfully, "maybe you don't give yourself enough credit."

Her face grew even warmer, the blood rushing to her cheeks. "You give me too much credit," she murmured, keeping her eyes on the ground. "After all, I'm the reason for this mess in the first place. Whether anyone wants to admit it or not."

Julian's jaw tightened, his voice firm. "You are responsible for none of this."

"You can say that all you want," Fiona whispered, "but it doesn't make it true."

Dax's sharp voice sliced through the conversation. "Shut up! Someone might hear you!"

Fiona and Julian fell silent after that, both retreating into their thoughts. Fiona's mind wandered back to the feeling of the wind rushing through her hair, the sensation of flying with the eagle. Could she really do it again?

They moved on in silence, the forest growing darker as they pressed forward. Fiona stayed close to Julian, and she allowed herself to drift into deep thoughts. Notions involving flying and a golden eagle beneath her.

CHAPTER 25

var was not a patient man, and today his patience was at its breaking point. It had been an entire day since he'd dispatched Aldo, his right-hand man, along with several riders to retrieve his elusive prize. A shade who had escaped his grasp somehow.

Now, sitting in his tent, Ivar gripped a mug of bitter ale in one massive hand, his lips dry with irritation. He scowled as he drained the last of the drink, its taste more acrid than usual, no doubt reflecting his own foul mood. Was he getting soft? The thought gnawed at him. He was a warlord, feared and ruthless. This was nothing more than a nuisance. And yet, it gnawed at him.

The glass vial at his elbow heated, and with a grunt, he shifted it away. He was growing tired of Alena burning him every time she grew impatient. The delicate tinkling of glass filled the air, and his eyes shot down to the vial. The edge had cracked—a thin, lightning-shaped fracture spidering out in jagged lines. A warning. Alena was getting angry.

The sorceress without a body—without her full power. The reason Ivar even bothered to kidnap a girl in the first place and the source of his current irritation. Alena was a force even without a body, trapped in that cursed vial, her power limited without flesh to anchor her magic. Ivar had promised her a new body—preferably that of a powerful shade girl—and in exchange, she would help him conquer all he laid eyes upon. But their previous attempt had failed. The body of an ordinary girl hadn't been enough to sustain Alena's power, and it had nearly killed the girl before Alena returned to her vial. What he needed was a shade, alive and brimming with magic, and the power of Oldgrange, the old grave of kings to which they'd been traveling. He had thought he'd found the perfect candidate, but now it seemed his prize had slipped away, even taking a half-dead girl with her.

Despite the fact that he had an entire army at his back to achieve whatever he desired, Ivar could not believe the complications he now faced. It seemed that holding on to a girl was becoming difficult for an army of marauders. His teeth ground together as he rose to his feet, pushing the empty mug aside with a loud thud. The campfires had been doused, leaving the camp cloaked in a gray haze of ash and smoke. The horses whinnied in the distance as riders approached, and Ivar's jaw tightened. He strode toward the tent's entrance, ducking under the flap as Aldo and his men reined in their mounts.

Aldo rode at the front of the group, and Ivar's mood briefly lightened when he saw what they had brought. Draped over the back of a horse like a sack of grain was the limp figure of a woman, her dark hair hanging in loose waves. At last.

"I brought you a present, m'lord," Aldo called out, wiping sweat and dirt from his brow.

"Bring her inside," Ivar commanded, stepping aside as the men dismounted and gathered around the unconscious figure. Aldo hoisted her into his arms and carried her into the tent, laying her down on the ground before Ivar.

The moment Ivar saw her face, his smile vanished.

Dark brown hair—not red. The skin, though fair, wasn't pale enough. His hand clenched around the vial on his belt, its glass no longer hot but frozen, the stillness signaling Alena's sudden interest.

"This isn't the same girl," Ivar growled.

Aldo shifted nervously, licking his lips before replying, "No, sir. She's not. But she's better."

Ivar raised an eyebrow, unimpressed. "Better?" His voice dripped with disdain. "The other girl was a new shade."

Aldo straightened, though his hands fidgeted. "This is Melaney the Overseer."

The words hung in the air, thick and heavy. Ivar's eyes narrowed as he studied the unconscious woman at his feet. Melaney. The Overseer? The name rolled over his tongue like a foreign taste. He had heard of her before—the leader of the Serpent Ceremony, a figure of considerable power among the shades. But why did that name cause Alena's vial to freeze in his hand?

The air felt colder suddenly, as if the wind had shifted, the silence punctuated only by the distant whinny of horses. Ivar knelt beside the woman, lifting her chin with a single finger. Her face was peaceful, almost serene. Her chest rose and fell steadily in the deep, unknowing sleep of the drugged. Something about her face tugged at Ivar's memory.

Visions flooded his mind—a forest, sunlight filtering through leaves. Two women walking side by side, laughing. One of them he somehow knew was Alena, her dark hair catching the sunlight, her voice melodic and carefree. The other woman—Melaney—was beside her, their hands brushing as they walked together. The same dark hair, the same graceful movement. Sisters.

The realization hit Ivar like a blow to the chest. Of course. The same facial features, the same frame. Alena and Melaney were connected—by blood.

"They're sisters," Ivar murmured, the weight of his discovery settling into place.

"Sir?" Aldo asked, blinking in confusion.

Ivar stood, towering over Melaney's unconscious form. "Out," he barked at Aldo, the command leaving no room for argument.

The men fled the tent without a second thought, and Ivar stood in the dim light, staring down at the woman who was both a gift and a complication. Alena had shown him the truth, and now the path forward seemed clearer. Melaney would be the key to Alena's rebirth.

His hand drifted to the vial at his belt. Alena's presence in his mind was sharp, but satisfied. *Yes,* she whispered into his thoughts. *It is almost time, my love. Soon we will be together.*

The lake glimmered under the sun, the ripples catching the light with each passing breeze. It was beautiful, Fiona admitted, though in a rather wild and unkempt way. Julian had called it Wickard Lake, which, in her opinion, was a remarkably uninspired name. She told him so as they sat on a weathered log at the water's edge.

"I suppose I could rename it," Julian said with a smirk. "Would Lake of a Thousand Water Drops suit your refined tastes?"

Fiona rolled her eyes, brushing a strand of hair from her face. "You can't just rename things because their names are terrible. The world doesn't work like that."

Julian's grin widened, his eyes gleaming with mischief. "Sure, I can. I'm a shade, remember?"

"And I'm sure that has nothing to do with naming a landmark," she replied, shaking her head at his playfulness.

Their laughter faded as Fiona's attention drew to a figure crouched at the far edge of the lake. Dax stood at the water's edge, his hand submerged, stirring the surface in slow, deliberate movements. His face was set in a deep frown, the lines on his brow etched with a weight that hadn't been there before. He looked so much older than he had just days ago, and it made her uneasy.

Dax hadn't spoken much since finding them. His usual cheerfulness had vanished, replaced by a brooding silence. Lia and Natalie, who sat nearby, huddled close, their faces pale and gaunt, streaked with dirt and fatigue. Fiona couldn't help but feel a pang of guilt as she glanced back at Julian, remembering their banter while the others mourned. They had lost someone important— Melaney— and yet she had been laughing.

"Maybe we should get moving," Fiona said quietly, brushing off the dirt that clung to her smock. It was no longer white—closer to a muted gray—but it didn't matter.

Julian's face grew serious, sensing her shift in mood. He nodded. "I agree."

"I second that," came a voice from behind.

Fiona turned to see Brannon striding up to them, his steps light, but his face betraying a more serious intent.

"No one asked you, Brannon," Julian said, though the smile tugging at his lips softened the words.

"That, you see, is the entire problem," Brannon responded, dropping down onto the log where Fiona had been sitting. He picked up a twig and snapped it between his fingers. "If you had, I could have bestowed upon you a most intelligent suggestion." He lifted his chin.

Julian raised a brow. "Oh? And what profound wisdom would you have shared?"

"We should go to the Hollow."

Fiona crossed her arms. "The Hollow?"

"Shades Hollow," Julian answered. "The center of all things to do with shades. The very essence of our existence."

"The lifeblood of our existence," Brannon added, his tone almost reverential as well. "The holy ground where shades stand at their most potent."

"Dude," Julian rolled his eyes and clamped a hand over Brannon's mouth. "Shut up."

Before the conversation could go any further, Darry stomped up with an armful of wood, his face flushed from exertion. "Time for a fire."

"Who are you telling to shut up?" Brannon stood and punched Darry in the arm playfully.

"Well, let's see." Darry thought for a moment. "You."

The playful banter between the men erupted into a wrestling match, their laughter echoing through the quiet forest. Fiona shook her head, stepping away from the scuffle, wandering to the two quiet figures who had moved closer to the water.

Lia and Natalie barely glanced up as Fiona approached. Their eyes were hollow, distant, as though they were somewhere far from the fire and the laughter.

"They're talking about going to Shades Hollow," Fiona said as she sat beside them.

Lia sniffed, her voice soft. "Ah, yes. Home. That would be best. Perhaps the council will help."

"The council shouldn't have been necessary," Dax growled from where he crouched by the water, his hand still swirling in the cool lake. "This could have all been avoided."

Natalie sighed, her fingers nervously twisting the fabric of her worn dress. "It is what it is now. The Hollow may be our only chance."

"Do you think they've held the ceremony yet?" Lia asked, her voice laced with concern.

Natalie made a small gesture with her hand, shaking her head. "There's no way."

Fiona frowned, glancing between the two women. "What ceremony?"

"The cleansing," Natalie explained. "Each year, we cleanse our holy site, restoring the full force of our powers. Without it, our abilities dwindle."

Fiona's brow furrowed. "But Julian... He seemed fine. He's been using his power without any issue."

"We still have power," Lia clarified. "It's just not at full strength. He takes a moment to build a fire. We can't summon our familiars properly. That's why your abilities are... intriguing. You not only summoned your familiar, you embodied it. It's unheard of, especially near the time of the cleansing."

Fiona's cheeks flushed with heat. "I don't know why it happens. It just... does." She tilted her head at the two girls. "What are your powers?"

"Having power and having an affinity are different," Natalie said. "My affinity is water." She reached down and lightly trailed water droplets into the air, letting them fall one by one to the ground.

Fiona smiled. "It's lovely," she said, then looked at Lia. "And yours?"

"Mine's a bit unusual." Lia giggled despite herself.

A giant glob of wet dirt landed next to Fiona's foot, suctioning to it with a wet slurp, and she jumped, suppressing a shriek. "What was that?"

Lia smiled at her.

"Your affinity is mud?"

"Well, dirt, but yes."

Fiona remembered the mud that had formed a protective barrier around the wagon during the marauder attack. "The wagon. That was you."

Lia nodded. "Aye."

"Does everyone have something different?"

"You mean like do all powers not repeat themselves? Oh, if only we were that unique," Lia giggled. "Alas, there's only so many materials and elements to go around."

"Well, at least yours and Natalie's work together." Fiona wrinkled her nose.

Before Lia could respond, Julian jogged over, his chest heaving. Dax scowled at his approach and turned away, his face darkening.

"Dinner's ready," Julian announced, sweeping a hand toward the small campfire. "Let's eat while we still can."

As they gathered around the fire, Fiona felt a strange weight settle on her shoulders. The playful atmosphere had shifted. Brannon was staring at her, his eyes thoughtful. "Could you... do it again?"

Fiona blinked. "Do what?"

"The wind thing," Brannon clarified. "Can you do it again? Like before."

"I don't know," Fiona said, plucking at the berries in her hand. "I've only done it around my fingers on purpose."

"You should try," Brannon urged, his voice filled with an eager curiosity.

"Don't pressure her," Julian said, his tone protective.

Brannon smirked. "She can speak for herself."

Julian scowled.

Fiona hesitated, then lifted her hand. The wind responded immediately, twisting around her fingers in a chilled, playful dance. The tiny whirlwind spun in her palm, growing larger with each passing second. Leaves swirled into the air, caught in the rising wind, and the quiet ripples of the lake began to churn as the breeze intensified.

"Fiona, stop!" Julian's voice cut through the chaos, but the wind had a mind of its own now.

The whirlwind grew stronger, lifting her into the air along with the others, swirling them around in a tight, dizzying circle. Sticks, stones, and leaves whipped through the air as the wind roared in her ears. She squeezed her eyes shut, willing it to stop, willing the tornado to dissipate.

And then, as suddenly as it had begun, the wind ceased. Silence fell over the camp, thick and oppressive. Fiona crashed to the ground, her body slamming into the log, knocking the breath from her lungs. She groaned, clutching her side, her vision spinning.

"Was that really necessary?" Darry grunted, brushing dirt and leaves off his tunic as he staggered to his feet.

Fiona pushed herself up, cheeks burning with embarrassment. "I'm sorry... I didn't mean—"

Moirin's shriek pierced the air, drawing everyone's attention. She sat in the grass, eyes wide with terror as Niklaos approached her cautiously.

"I'm not going to hurt you," Niklaos said, holding his hands up in surrender. His voice was soft, pleading.

"Get away from me!" Moirin spat.

Niklaos backed away, pain flickering in his eyes. He stopped only when he stood on the other side of Fiona, his head bowed in defeat. "I didn't mean to upset you."

But it was clear to everyone—there was no peace between them. Moirin's hatred for Niklaos ran too deep. There would be no mending that.

CHAPTER 26

S o, she is your blood," Ivar thought aloud, alone in the dimly lit tent. The room was still empty, and Melaney still lay unconscious, her breaths shallow, her form slumped against the wall. The marauder sat in a nearby chair, twisting the vial in his hands, the glass catching what little light flickered from the dying fire. Inside the vial, Alena's essence stirred. "Should we go, then, and find another?" he asked, more to himself than to her.

The vial cooled in his palm as a voice, cold and calculating, echoed in his mind. *We go as planned.* Alena's presence rippled through his thoughts, commanding but calm. *This changes nothing.*

Despite her certainty, Ivar's thoughts wandered back to the vision that had plagued him for days—a vision of Melaney and Alena laughing together in the woods, their faces alight with joy and affection. In that fleeting moment, they looked like two halves of a whole, as though the darkness of the world had no place between them. Ivar couldn't help but wonder what had driven them apart, what had transformed that warmth into this festering hatred. How had two sisters, so close in their youth, ended up on opposite sides of a war?

"She's your sister."

It does not matter, Alena's voice snapped, sharp and devoid of emotion. *She stands against us. We will continue as planned.*

"As you wish." Ivar slid the vial back onto his belt, but a flicker of something—doubt? —remained in the back of his mind.

Are you getting soft? Alena's voice cut through again, though this time it was less a question and more a statement. Accusatory, probing.

Ivar's jaw clenched, anger surging. "Absolutely not," he growled. "You would do well to remember your place, sorceress."

Don't make me the enemy, Alena warned, her voice flattening into an icy calm that set Ivar on edge.

"I know who my enemy is," he snapped, his gaze shifting to the unconscious woman before him. "And I know my goal. That will never change."

Good. Alena's tone softened. *I will take you there—if you stay the course.*

"I know." His voice was gruff, his resolve hardened once again.

"Who are you talking to, sir?"

Ivar turned to see a baffled Aldo in the tent's entrance and shook his head. "No one," he replied curtly. "Myself."

Aldo stepped inside, fidgeting slightly under Ivar's cold gaze. "The men are settled back in," he reported, "and I've set up extra guards around the perimeter. We'll be prepared if the Shades come looking for her."

Ivar's eyes flicked to Melaney before settling back on Aldo. "Rest assured they will come. There is no 'if.'"

"We'll be ready."

"I hope so. I don't need to lose any more heads."

Aldo swallowed hard. He knew well enough that his leader's warning included him. "There will be no 'head losing,' sir. Not ours, anyway."

"See to it." Ivar waved him off, already growing impatient. "Now leave me. I have much to think about."

"Yes, sir." Aldo glanced at Melaney once more, his gaze lingering a moment longer than necessary before he exited the tent, the flap falling softly behind him.

"You don't need to worry," came a raspy voice from across the room.

Ivar whirled around, his dagger flashing into his hand in an instant. Melaney was awake, sitting up against the wall, her face pale and streaked with dirt. She looked as though she'd crawled through mud before arriving here, her once vibrant eyes now bloodshot and weary. Still, despite her appearance, she met Ivar's gaze without flinching.

He hesitated for a brief moment before lowering the dagger, though he didn't sheathe it. "I always worry," he snapped.

"I'm not going anywhere," Melaney said, her voice steadier now, though still hoarse.

"You're right. You aren't going anywhere."

"As myself, at least," she murmured, a faint, sad smile playing on her lips.

Ivar frowned. Melaney's lips upturned slightly.

"You thought I didn't know? I won't fight you. Not anymore."

The vial on Ivar's belt warmed, Alena's presence stirring once again. He sensed her irritation, her disappointment. No fight? she whispered, as if she craved the conflict.

"No?" Ivar sneered. "You'd just give in so easily? Play the martyr for your friends?"

"I owe it to them," Melaney said sadly. "I've already caused enough harm. I won't drag them further into this mess."

Ivar's eyes narrowed. "You think this will save them? You think we'll just let them live after we're done with you?"

"I will live for a while within my shell of a body," Melaney said, "You know that as well as I do."

"You won't be in charge, though. She will."

"She has much ambition. That is true." Melaney's face fell. "I wish it had never come to this."

"Speak for yourself," Ivar muttered. He turned away.

"Did she tell you why I'm so willing to do this?"

"You think you can save your friends," Ivar replied, his voice dismissive.

"It isn't just that, you know."

Ivar stopped, something in her tone catching him off guard. He turned slightly, catching a glimpse of her face—pale, trembling, her eyes filled with a pain she had never voiced. The vial on his belt grew warmer, almost uncomfortably so. Alena was growing angry, perhaps sensing something he had missed.

He shook his head, pinching the bridge of his nose. "You talk too much. Either out with it or shut up and go back to sleep."

"Since you put it that way," she said with a bitter smile, "I am a bit tired."

Ivar stormed out of the tent without another word, nearly knocking over one of the guards stationed outside. "Watch her," he barked, before stomping into the woods, frustration burning in his chest.

The morning following Fiona's tornado, Lia, Natalie, and Dax announced their plans to break off from the group.

"Is that really a smart thing to do?" Julian asked, crossing his arms, his eyes narrowing on the trio.

Dax scowled. "Yes."

"I understand you're upset with me," Julian said, "but that doesn't mean you have to split from the group."

"It's not about you," Lia interjected, stepping forward. "We want to scout the marauder army, plan the attack."

Julian chewed on the thought for a moment, his fingers tapping against his bicep. "It makes sense to know what we're dealing with," he said carefully, "but I don't like the idea of you three going off on your own."

"Yeah, we're so much safer here with you," Dax growled, "and her." He looked pointedly at Fiona. She swallowed hard, her stomach twisting.

Julian's eyes darkened. "Fine. Go then." Brannon and Darry stood behind him, silent and tense, their expressions unreadable.

Lia and Natalie exchanged quick, quiet goodbyes. Fiona clung to Natalie, her heart heavy with an unshakable sense of foreboding. "Please be safe," she whispered.

Natalie squeezed her tighter. "Always," she promised, a determined glint in her eye. "We'll meet again, and next time, we'll have the Shade army at our backs. We'll get Melaney."

"I know," Fiona said, although she didn't. She stood watching until the three figures disappeared from view, a growing ache settling in her chest. Julian's warm hand slid into hers, and he gently pulled her to him.

The remaining shades traveled quickly, managing to recover the horses sometime later that day. The three horses were unharmed from the tornado and still saddled so Julian swung Fiona onto his and then jumped on behind her and wrapped his arms around her to hold the reins.

"I know how to ride," she muttered, her cheeks flushing.

"I know." Julian's lips curved into a smile as he pulled her closer, his chest pressed against her back, his breath warm on her ear.

Darry and Moirin took another horse, and Brannon and Niklaos—the latter rather reluctant—took the third. The horses moved easily through the forest, dodging fallen limbs and angling around trees. They knew the forest as well as their riders, and even more so the route which they must take to get to the council.

Fiona watched the ground blur by, found herself dizzy, and focused up front on the trees coming towards and then passing them. They rode in silence, the forest blurring past them, leaves and branches whispering in the breeze. The horses moved gracefully, dodging fallen limbs and navigating around trees with an almost instinctual knowledge of the path ahead. Fiona found herself swaying with the horse's rhythm, her initial discomfort fading. She leaned back against Julian, her tension melting away as his arms tightened around her.

After hours of riding, the sun now hanging low in the sky, Julian reined in the horse, bringing them to an abrupt halt. Fiona, still half-drowsy from the ride, blinked in confusion. "Why are we stopping?"

"The horses need a break," Julian replied, dismounting. He reached up, offering his hand to help her down. Her legs trembled as they hit the ground, a reminder of the long hours spent in the saddle.

"You need one too," he added, a teasing smile playing at his lips.

"I'm fine," Fiona mumbled, embarrassed by her wobbling legs.

Julian chuckled, his gaze softening. "It's a rough ride. No shame in it."

Brannon, Darry, and Julian wasted no time unsaddling the horses, letting the animals rest after the grueling journey. White foam flecked their necks and flanks. Fiona winced, feeling guilty for questioning the break.

Nearby, Niklaos sat quietly, his posture tense as Moirin shot him dark, suspicious glances from across the clearing. Fiona teetered her way to join him.

"I think she wants to kill me," he muttered.

Fiona shrugged, keeping her tone light, though unease twisted her insides. "Can you blame her? You were one of her captors."

"No, I can't," he admitted, his expression grim. "But I do enjoy living."

"Give her time. Maybe she'll come around. And if not," Fiona added with a teasing grin, "keep one eye open at night."

Niklaos let out a dry laugh, though his eyes shuttered with worry. Fiona gave his leg a reassuring pat. "For what it's worth, I hope you survive this."

His lips quirked into a faint smile. "I appreciate that."

Julian returned from tending to the horses, catching the tail end of the conversation. "What's so funny?" he asked, sitting beside Fiona with an easy grace.

"Nothing," Fiona replied, her laughter dying as she sobered under his watchful gaze.

Julian studied them for a moment, then shrugged. "The horses will be ready in half an hour."

"Good," Fiona said. "The sooner we reach Shades Hollow, the

better."

From across the clearing, Moirin's voice cut through the quiet. "What will they do with him?"

All eyes turned to Niklaos. He shifted uncomfortably, his levity evaporating.

Brannon was the first to speak. "They'll put him on trial for his crimes."

Fiona shot to her feet, her hands balling into fists. "You can't be serious."

Brannon didn't flinch. "He's still a marauder. That makes him a war criminal."

"Maybe to the shades, but not to me," Fiona snapped.

Brannon held his ground, his voice careful. "The council won't care what you think of him. They'll listen, but it won't erase his past."

Niklaos looked pale. "And if they find me guilty?"

Brannon's silence was answer enough.

Fiona stepped forward, anger blazing in her eyes. "What will they do?"

Julian intervened. "Fiona, we don't know what they'll decide. Helping us escape might earn him some leniency."

"There better be leniency," Fiona muttered, her voice tight with frustration. She turned on her heel, her skirts swishing as she stormed down the hill, needing space to think, to breathe. At the bottom, she sank to the grass, staring out at the horizon, her heart heavy with uncertainty.

CHAPTER 27

"I t is time," Ivar said. To his right, Aldo dipped his head. The vial in Ivar's hand began to warm, but only to a pleasant, soothing temperature. Alena approved, he noted. More than approved, he thought darkly. Ever since his conversation with Melaney had been interrupted by the prisoner's insolence and his own loss of temper, Alena had remained quiet—relieved, even.

No matter, he mused. They were finally beginning the binding process, and soon Alena's spirit would be ready to possess Melaney's body. The first stages would paralyze her, dulling her senses and mind until she became a passive vessel. It wasn't strictly necessary, but Ivar knew better than to leave room for resistance. Melaney was a shade of considerable power, and the last thing they needed was her fighting off Alena's possession once they left the tent.

At Aldo's acknowledgment, the soldier waiting by the door turned and rolled it open, allowing a cool gust of air inside. The seasons were bringing a chill, and the days were getting longer. Winter was upon them.

Melaney walked into the tent, her arms bound in front of her and her face set in a stony, rigid gaze that locked immediately on Ivar. Something in the intensity of her stare made him take an involuntary step back. The woman was intimidating, even he admitted. No wonder she held such a position with the shades.

It will be better when her power is mine, Alena's voice hissed inside his mind, triumphant. *This body will be a better vessel than the last.*

"We're not there yet," Ivar muttered under his breath.

He could have sworn that Melaney's lips curled into the faintest smirk, mocking him. It was as though she knew something he didn't, as if she believed she still had the upper hand. A wave of unease washed over him. Was she trying to play with his mind?

Don't let her get inside your head, Alena snarled, sensing his faltering resolve.

What do you think you've *been doing all this time?* Melaney's voice rang out within his thoughts, clear as a bell. Ivar jumped, startled despite himself.

Sir?" Aldo's concerned voice cut through the tension.

Ivar straightened, trying to shake off the disorientation, but Melaney's voice continued to echo through his mind, cruel and taunting.

Of course he's not okay, Melaney laughed. *He's losing it,* she mocked. *He can't even keep his own thoughts straight.*

Ivar clenched his fists, fighting the urge to shout her down, but it was pointless. He was caught in the crossfire between two powerful women, each fighting for dominance within his own mind. He had never felt so helpless, so utterly out of control.

Go away, sister, Alena's voice slithered through his thoughts, cold and venomous. *Let fate run its course.*

Fate? Melaney's laugh echoed, cutting through Ivar's mind like a blade. *Fate is what brought you here, what cursed you. You'll never win this.*

My fate is mine to command, Alena whispered, her tone chilling. Ivar shuddered, feeling the weight of her malice.

You sealed your fate a long ago, Melaney countered, her voice like ice.

Alena seemed to sneer, even if just in Ivar's mind. *Don't*

forget who caused that fate. Who did this to me.

Melaney had no answer for that. There was silence for a moment, leaving Ivar grateful. A weight pressed against his chest and he looked down to realize he was crossing his arms too tightly.

Melaney's voice erupted once more, her words like a shriek of madness: *YOU ARE BOTH INSANE!*

Ivar snapped. "STOP!" he roared, clutching his head as if he could physically wrench them out of his mind. His outburst startled everyone in the tent. Aldo exchanged a wary glance with the other soldiers, all whom were now shifting uneasily, their eyes darting between Ivar and the prisoner.

Melaney's eyes remained narrowed, her focus unbroken. Aldo saw it—the connection. She was doing something to Ivar, something none of them could see. He had to act.

With a swift, decisive movement, Aldo stepped forward and swung his fist, connecting with Melaney's temple. Her eyes rolled back, and she crumpled to the ground, unconscious. Her head hit the floor with a sickening thud. He stood over her for a moment, his hand still clenched.

Ivar looked up at Aldo, his expression conflicted. Aldo waited for a reprimand, expecting his general to lash out, but it didn't come. Instead, Ivar nodded—a silent acknowledgment and a rare gesture of gratitude. The weight of exhaustion settled deeper into Ivar's features, his eyes hollow and his face sagging with relief.

"Out. Now," Aldo barked, motioning toward the open door. A few stray snowflakes had blown in, already melting on the floor. The soldiers wasted no time, practically tripping over each other in their haste to leave the oppressive atmosphere of the tent.

As the last soldier disappeared through the door, Ivar sank onto a nearby stool, rubbing his temples. "Mind-reading witches," he muttered bitterly. Aldo, standing close enough, caught the words but chose to say nothing.

The shades were back on the trail. Fiona's thoughts drifted as the horses covered ground at a steady pace, the rhythm of hooves lulling her into a state of near sleep. She leaned back, resting against Julian's solid chest, grateful for his arms securing her. Though the world around her blurred in the twilight, the safety of his embrace kept her anchored.

As her eyes fluttered closed, her stomach flipped, jolting her back to alertness. She shifted her position, shaking her head to clear the dizziness. Julian noticed immediately and leaned in, his breath warm against her ear.

"Are you okay?" he murmured, his voice sending a shiver through her. The sensation was distracting. Lightning fired down her center.

"Yes," she managed with a shudder.

"If you need us to stop, say so."

"We shouldn't stop until we reach the Council," she said, her tone firm. "Not until they agree to help us."

Julian's arms tightened around her, a tension creeping into his voice. "You expect them to pardon Niklaos?"

Fiona hesitated. "Yes. Without a doubt. He saved my life—and Moirin's, even if she won't admit it. He's not a bad person."

Julian snorted. "He's a marauder, Fiona. Who knows how many villages he's burned."

"Earlier, you almost defended him," she pointed out, her brow furrowing. "Now you've changed your mind?"

"I'm not defending him," Julian said, his voice cold. "I only care about getting Melaney back. Alive."

Fiona sighed, knowing there was no changing his mind. They fell into silence, the horses picking their way over logs and through shallow rivers. The landscape darkened, and soon the sky blazed with a blood-red sunset that streaked across the horizon like fire, casting the world in hues of crimson and gold.

When they finally stopped, Fiona's legs felt like jelly as she dismounted. Her feet hit the ground too soon, and she stumbled. Julian's hands caught her under the arms, steadying her before she could fall. She offered him a grateful smile, though she knew she couldn't hide the weariness in her eyes.

Brannon, crouched nearby, weaved twigs together to start a fire, then Julian started it with a flick of his wrist. Fiona settled down, pulling her knees to her chest. Her body ached in protest, begging for sleep, but her hunger gnawed at her too, rumbling in the silence.

Moirin sat down beside her, predictably avoiding Niklaos. Fiona followed her gaze, watching as the marauder gathered more wood for the fire. His movements were fluid and efficient, though his blond hair fell into his eyes. When he pushed it back, Moirin flinched, her body stiff with tension.

Fiona frowned. Despite Niklaos's clear intentions to help, Moirin couldn't shake her fear of him. Fiona understood—trust didn't come easily, especially with someone like Niklaos, whose past loomed like a shadow. Still, Fiona knew he wasn't evil.

As the fire crackled to life, its warmth wrapping around them like a blanket, Fiona rested her head on her knees. Sleep tugged at her, pulling her into its embrace. The sounds of the camp— Brannon and Darry in quiet conversation, the horses snorting, the fire hissing—lulled her into a half-dreaming state.

Something stirred her from the edges of sleep, something not quite right. Her eyes snapped open, and she took in her surroundings. The fire was burning brightly now, casting a golden glow over the clearing. Brannon, Julian, and Darry roasted skewered squirrels, while Moirin softly snored beside her.

Fiona's gaze drew to the woods beyond. The trees parted just enough to allow her a glimpse of a small creek, its waters gurgling. But what caught her eye wasn't the creek—it was the shadow near it.

A figure stood at the edge of the tree line, barely visible in the dim light. As Fiona stood, her heart quickened. She strained her eyes, trying to bring it into focus. The figure morphed into something more than a shadow—twisted limbs, a large braided beard made of twigs, and glowing white eyes.

The Leshy.

It watched her, unmoving, its long spear stretching from its hand to the ground like a silent sentinel and its twisted limbs melding with the shadows of the trees. For reasons she couldn't explain, Fiona wasn't afraid. A creature that looked as if it had been shaped by some ancient force of nature should have sent her heart racing, but its silent watchfulness felt less like a threat and more like a protective gaze; a guardian rather than a threat.

It didn't stir, didn't advance. Fiona took in the details: the moss growing in patches across its bark-like skin, the way its massive, gnarled hands gripped the spear with ease. The antlers that stretched into the sky, making the Leshy look twice as tall. Each movement—or lack thereof—was deliberate, measured, almost respectful. It was as though the creature had been waiting for her, watching over them from the safety of the shadows.

"Fiona?" The sudden call drew her attention away.

Julian appeared beside her, his eyes scanning the darkness. "What is it?" he asked, his voice low. He followed her gaze into the woods, but there was nothing there now. The Leshy had vanished, as if it had never been.

Fiona leaned against Julian, her breath escaping in a slow, relieved sigh. "Nothing," she whispered. "Just the wind."

Snowflakes began to fall lightly around them.

CHAPTER 28

Alena pulsed in the vial, radiating a sense of satisfaction that warmed her glass prison. Melaney's eyes fluttered closed, her body going limp against the bedframe. The silence that filled Ivar's mind was almost deafening—a sudden, unexpected relief from the relentless tension that had gripped the tent for hours. He exhaled and slouched back on the stool, a crude wooden frame stretched with deerskin, yet sturdy enough to support his weight. He had been sitting there quietly observing the mental struggle between Melaney and Alena, watching as the shade clawed her way back to the surface each time Alena nearly overtook her. It had been an exhausting battle of wills, but when Melaney showed no signs of yielding, he'd finally grown tired of the spectacle. One swift backhand was all it took to knock her unconscious and silence the fight—for now.

All was quiet at last.

"Now what?" Ivar's deep voice echoed in the stillness, startling even himself. His brows furrowed in irritation. It was unlike him to be flustered by anything, much less by this strange ordeal.

We continue our journey. Alena's voice fluttered through his mind, her presence shifting within the vial like a bird trapped behind glass. *Melaney's body is frozen now. She will no longer require food or drink, and she won't fight against us.*

Ivar stood and pulled the tent flap aside, his eyes immediately locking on Aldo, who lingered near the entrance, awaiting orders. "I want a guard on her all night. A reliable one."

Aldo straightened. "Yes, sir."

Ivar retired to his tent, shedding his armor piece by piece, tossing it aside until only his belt remained, securing the vial to his side. The vial was neither hot nor cold, Alena simply existed for the moment. He tucked his dagger under the pillow and closed his eyes, listening to the crickets. It was odd hearing them so far into the chilly season. He wondered if their noise was intentional or if it was from shivering in the cold. The thought brought a chuckle.

They were close now. Only a few more days, and they would reach Oldgrange. Alena's long-awaited chance at a new body—and power—would finally be within her grasp. Yet as he lay there, the same nagging question resurfaced in his mind: what had caused the rift between her and Melaney? He'd always assumed it was related to Alena's near-demise, but there was something deeper there, something personal.

The vial suddenly grew cold, an icy shiver running through his side. Why do you pry? Alena's voice snapped, sharp and venomous. Leave it alone.

Ivar smirked, imagining her snarling inside the glass. He tried to picture what her voice would sound like if she weren't trapped in his head. Maybe a high-pitched, shrill screech—like a falcon. The thought amused him again, and he chuckled under his breath. Just like a woman, he thought.

A sudden jolt of pain shot through him, brief but biting, as Alena sent a spark of electricity from her vial. He flinched, rubbing his side.

"I'll find out someday," Ivar said aloud, his voice cutting through the quiet.

Alena's laugh echoed in his mind, mocking and dark. *If you say so.*

Ivar fell silent, the outside sounds dulling his mind and his fingers twitching as he drifted to sleep. He would rest before the journey. Their victory was close.

When he awoke, pale morning light filtered through the tent flap, and his right-hand man's face loomed inches from his own. Ivar jolted upright, cursing under his breath as he swatted at the man.

"Dammit, Aldo!"

"Sorry, sir." Aldo stepped back, looking sheepish. "I've never had trouble rousing you before. Are you alright?"

Ivar groaned, sitting up and rubbing his temples. "I'm fine. Is Melaney secure?"

"Yes, sir. The camp's packed and ready to move out."

Ivar straightened. "What time is it?"

"A bit past sunrise, sir. Halfway to noon."

Cursing under his breath, Ivar threw on his gear and smoothed his thick, dark hair. He exited the tent and stopped next to a guard. "Ready my things," he snarled.

The guard scrambled away without a word.

The wind stirred the trees around them, flipping the leaves over like a bad omen. Ivar sniffed the air, catching the unmistakable scent of snow. Good. More snow would make it harder for anyone to follow their tracks, especially if Melaney's companions were foolish enough to mount a rescue mission. He could already imagine the scent of Shade blood in the air, his fists clenching in anticipation. If they came for her, they'd regret it.

And he hoped they were stupid enough to try.

The shades rode through the biting snow for what felt like eternity, Fiona's fingers and toes numb from the cold. Her once-tidy hair had become a hopeless mass of tangled fiery strands matted against her neck. She'd given up on conversation hours ago, settling into a grim silence alongside her comrades. Julian mirrored her example, though the others were not so quiet.

"Your hair, mate," Brannon called out to Darry.

"What about it?" Darry leveled a steely gaze at his friend.

"It's sticking up all over the place."

Darry's eyes narrowed. "So?"

"So, how d'you expect to snag you a woman with hair like that?" Brannon jabbed, smirking.

Darry snorted, "It's fashionable. Makes me look taller."

Brannon rolled his eyes. "You look like an idiot."

Moirin giggled softly from her place in front of Darry, the first lighthearted noise she'd made. "I like it," she said, casting an appraising glance up at Darry's hair.

"Don't encourage him," Brannon grumbled.

Darry grinned. "You'll think it's ridiculous until I'm using my mighty spiky hair to skewer marauders." He winked at Moirin.

Fiona laughed, but also found her gaze drifting toward Niklaos, seated tensely behind Brannon. His face was drawn, lines of worry etched into his brow. It pierced her heart to see him like this, clearly terrified. She wondered what was running through his mind—if he feared what awaited him at the council. She would have been scared too. All she could do was hope they showed him mercy.

A sudden shout from Brannon grabbed everyone's attention. Up ahead, black iron gates loomed, locked tight with shiny chains that glowed faintly in the dim light. As they approached, Fiona heard it—a murmur of voices from beyond the gate, mingling together like a distant hum.

Shades Hollow.

The group urged their horses into a gallop, the pounding hooves kicking up flurries of snow as they closed in on the gates. Fiona's heart quickened, her eyes fixed on the iron monstrosity. Its design twisted and coiled like a serpent, menacing and beautiful at the same time. Julian dismounted, walking toward the gate with a determined stride, his fingers moving in a subtle, commanding gesture as he murmured something she couldn't quite hear.

The gate rattled, chains clanging, and for a brief moment, Fiona thought it might not let them through. But with a flash of white light, the chains vanished, and the gates groaned open. Julian stepped aside and took the reins of his horse, leading them forward into Shades Hollow. The rest of the group followed, and Fiona glanced back at Niklaos. Terror had painted itself across his face, his grip tightening on Brannon as if he might slip from the saddle. His knuckles whitened, and Fiona's chest tightened in sympathy.

As Fiona and her group passed through the gates, a light dusting of snow fell gently around them, swirling in the air before settling on the ground like a delicate blanket. The village looked peaceful, the fresh snow softening the edges of the wooden huts lining the path. Their thatched roofs were lightly powdered, just enough to glisten under the fading light of the overcast sky.

The trees surrounding the village stood tall, their bare branches catching the snowflakes as they drifted down, the occasional twig bending under the modest weight. It wasn't a heavy storm—just enough to coat the landscape in a quiet shimmer. Every crunch of the horses' hooves magnified in the stillness of the hollow, the air crisp but not biting.

Fiona's breath fogged in front of her as she took everything in, the village quiet yet alive. The snow wasn't thick enough to cover the paths completely, leaving patches of muddy earth visible beneath the white dusting. Villagers peeked out from their doorways, their cloaks drawn tight around them, their eyes curious but cautious. A child ran between huts, leaving faint tracks behind before disappearing into one of the homes.

A larger wooden building up ahead loomed quietly, its weathered exterior softened by the thin layer of snow that clung to it. The windows, dark and shadowed, gave no hint of warmth or welcome, and the faint sound of the wind carried a distant whisper through the village. Despite the peaceful snowfall, an undercurrent of something powerful prickled at Fiona's skin as they approached.

Her pulse quickened as they approached the building. This is where I belong, she reminded herself, though nothing about it felt familiar. The unease gnawed at her. She wished her hair were anything but red. Brown, black, anything that didn't make her stand out like a beacon. I belong here.

The silence that followed their group was unnerving, broken only by the creak of saddles and the snort of horses. Julian, sensing her unease, dropped the reins and walked back to her. He stopped just shy of touching her, leaving a careful distance between them. Fiona held her breath, waiting, hoping for a brief connection. When none came, disappointment stabbed through her.

The door of the building creaked open, revealing an elderly man clad in a hooded cloak. His frail frame and whispery voice added to the growing tension. "Councilman Cleary," Julian greeted him with a respectful bow, echoed by Brannon and Darry. Fiona and Moirin stared, while Niklaos shifted uneasily in his saddle.

"Come inside. I have lit a candle for each of you," Cleary beckoned, his dark eyes flicking to Niklaos. "All of you, except that one."

Niklaos blinked in surprise. "Do I need to stay out here?" he muttered to Brannon, gesturing toward his horse.

"I wouldn't recommend it," Brannon replied without turning around, already stepping toward the door. Niklaos sighed, dismounted, and fell into step behind him.

Fiona brushed against Niklaos's muscled arm as they reached the steps. She offered a small, reassuring smile. "It'll be okay," she whispered, though his tight-lipped expression told her he didn't believe her. She averted her eyes, focusing instead on Julian's lean back as they entered the darkened building.

Inside, the air was heavy with an ancient energy. A row of candles flickered in the center of the room, casting long shadows on the walls. Councilman Cleary raised a hand, gesturing for them to take a candle. Fiona followed Julian's lead, reaching for the nearest one. She cupped her hand around the flame, mesmerized by the way it flickered and danced.

Cleary moved to the far wall, pulling aside a panel and revealing something small and writhing. Fiona's heart froze—a snake. Its black body coiled around Cleary's arm, its head resting near his shoulder as if watching her. She shuddered, the hair on her neck standing on end.

"Snakes are sacred to Shades," Cleary explained, catching her expression as the black serpent coiled itself tighter around his arm. Its sleek, onyx scales glinted faintly in the dim light of the hall. "You'd do well to get used to it. You must be Fiona."

Fiona shot a look at Julian, who stood beside her, his eyes twinkling with amusement. He could have warned her. She narrowed her eyes at him before returning her focus to Cleary.

The elder councilman didn't miss the exchange and smiled faintly, though his eyes remained shadowed. "I see you're unfamiliar with our customs." He gently stroked the snake's head as it settled, its tongue flicking out in rhythm with Cleary's slow, deliberate movements. "But in time, you'll understand. These creatures are more than just animals to us—they are symbols of wisdom, protection, and rebirth. They carry the history of our people."

Cleary turned his attention fully to Fiona now, his posture still but his words resonating with a weight of history. "The Shades were once a wandering people, without a home or sanctuary. It was our connection with the land, and the creatures who inhabit it, that helped us survive. The snake, in particular, is revered because as it sheds its skin to change, grow, adapt, so do we change, grow, and adapt. Much like you, I'd imagine."

Fiona felt a flicker of unease at his last comment but remained silent.

"Julian should've told you," Cleary added, casting a brief glance at the man beside her, his tone more pointed now. "But I suppose he prefers to let you experience things firsthand. After all, that's how we all learn."

Julian's smirk faltered slightly under Cleary's knowing look, but he shrugged it off, his expression still lighthearted. "We've been a little preoccupied, Councilman."

Cleary chuckled before continuing. "I wasn't always a councilman, you know. Once, I was like you—unsure, caught between the life I'd known and the path that awaited me. The Shades weren't always a unified people, either. We were scattered across Orthea for centuries."

His eyes softened with memory, and the serpent shifted

again, resting its head near his shoulder. "I was born to a family of healers. We traveled constantly, never staying in one place for long. We knew the land and its secrets, but we didn't have a place to call our own. When the time came for the Shades to gather, to form something permanent, my family was one of the first to join. I've been here since before the walls were raised, when the Hollow was nothing but trees and earth."

Cleary's gaze drifted over the room, as though seeing the past layered over the present. "The council formed to guide us, to ensure our people had a future. That taught us how to lead. To see beyond the immediate, to understand that survival means embracing change, even when it's uncomfortable."

He met Fiona's eyes again, his voice gentle but firm. "You're on that same path now. You've been thrust into something larger than yourself, but that doesn't mean you're without control. Like the snake, you have the power to shed what was and embrace what will be. Whether you choose to do so, well, that's up to you."

Fiona swallowed hard, feeling the weight of his words settle over her like the snowfall outside. She hadn't expected to be confronted with such wisdom, not from an elderly man with a snake wrapped around his arm. But his words stirred something inside her, a faint echo of the uncertainty she had felt since being thrust into this world.

Cleary turned toward the snake, gently coaxing it to unwind from his arm. "Do not fear this world, Fiona."

"We came to ask for help," Fiona said, clearing her throat. She didn't like his focus on her.

"I know," Cleary said. "I'm the one who authorized Melaney to retrieve you from the marauders."

"You knew she was going?" Julian's voice was tense. "Why didn't you better equip her?"

"She was meant to go with who she did."

Brannon shook his head. "You're a seer. You could have changed the outcome."

"Should I?" Silence blanketed the room. Cleary chuckled, his face weary. "I have done this many years, and never have I steered my people from the path they are meant to take."

"You make it sound like we don't have a choice." Fiona's words were louder than she intended, angrier. "I thought we all decide our own fate."

"What do you think she did?" Cleary's voice sharpened. "She knew going to save you most likely ended in her own demise."

"So, she's going to die, then?"

"Perhaps."

Julian shifted. "I don't understand why you're letting this happen."

"I don't think you understand how being a seer works, Julian."

"I know you can tell the future."

Cleary's eyes gleamed. "To an extent, yes. But fate is not something you can avoid, Julian, nor are choices. If I had stopped her, she would have gone anyway. And if she hadn't, you," he pointed at Fiona, "would be gone."

Fiona swallowed hard. "Gone?"

Cleary nodded. "Taken over by the sorceress. Your mind wiped, her consciousness in its place. You would cease to exist."

"That's what they wanted me for?"

The room fell into a stunned silence, each of them grappling with the weight of his words. Darry ran a hand over his face. "So, what do we do now?"

Cleary's gaze was unreadable. "That depends on what outcome you desire."

Fiona's frustration boiled over. "Could you be any vaguer?" she snapped, earning a warning look from Julian.

Cleary sighed, his patience worn. "If you leave now, you will die. Wait until morning, and you have a chance."

Brannon nodded. "We'll wait."

Cleary's attention shifted to Niklaos, who looked pale and on the verge of collapsing. Fiona instinctively stepped forward, but Julian's firm hand on her elbow stopped her.

"What is your name, young man?"

"Niklaos."

CHAPTER 29

I don't think it will work." Aldo shook his head, disappointment evident as he and Ravi peered over the edge of the cliff. Below, jagged rocks and a river far beneath marked their unforgiving descent, framed by the Iron Wolf Mountains in the distance. "We need to slow down," Aldo added, his voice edged with concern. A few drifting snowflakes floated down, marking the official descent of winter. One step closer to the solstice and Alena's rising.

Ivar moved a hand over the vial beneath his cloak. He still wondered if she would keep her word or if he'd be forced to spill sorceress blood. The uneasy thought nagged at him, but he said nothing. Behind them lay the dense edge of Wickard Forest, its intertwined branches casting long, skeletal shadows over the dark-leaved ground. Before them stretched the gray and white expanse of the Iron Wolf Mountains, the sharp peaks cutting into the sky, their tips covered by low-hanging clouds.

A gust of icy wind swept across the cliff, pushing at the travelers, forcing them to pull their hoods low and wrap their cloaks tightly around their faces. The slender river below cut a path between them and the foot of the first rocky growth. They'd have to circle around and descend. Ivar stood at the invisible line where the forest gave way to the harsh, barren mountain range, shaking his head at the sight. He hated delays. "We'd better get to it, then," he muttered, turning on his heel. His officers followed without hesitation as he made his way back to the bulk of his army.

Melaney lay draped over the donkey that had previously carried Fiona. Her body was limp, her eyes open but glassy and unseeing, staring into nothing. No one dared look at her for long; her mere presence unnerved them, as if to meet her gaze was to stare into death itself. The rumors of her power had already spread like wildfire through the camp, and many viewed her captivity as an ill omen. Yet they marched on, driven by their fear of Ivar if not their loyalty.

The army moved eastward, following a barely visible trail that snaked around the edge of the mountains and disappeared into the wilderness. The path was faint, beaten down by travelers who had once braved the journey but lacked the courage to continue into the unforgiving Iron Wolf. Ivar's men, however, pressed forward. They rounded the first long bend just as the day began to fade into twilight.

The soldiers pitched camp quickly, eager to rest after the day's grueling march, and delivered Melaney to Ivar's tent.

A trio of archers returned from the forest just after sundown with a pile of rabbits. They skinned and skewered them, propping them over the fire. The rich smell of roasting meat soon filled the air, a welcome comfort against the cold.

Ivar and Aldo sat together by the fire, tearing into the roasted rabbit legs, their backs turned to the unconscious shade. Neither of them acknowledged her; it was as if pretending she wasn't there would make her presence less of a threat. As they ate, the vial containing Alena warmed against Ivar's chest. He glanced at Aldo, who was devouring his food with a quiet intensity. His leg was halfway gone within minutes, grease dripping down his chin.

Silence hung between them until both men had finished, licking the last traces of grease from their fingers. They tossed the stripped bones outside the tent, letting the wild dogs have what was left.

At last, Aldo said, "Ivar, may I speak freely?"

Ivar narrowed his eyes. "Yes."

Aldo hesitated, then squared his shoulders. "You told us that this body would be a sacrifice. You said we needed a girl to harness the power of Oldgrange. What you didn't specify is how."

Ivar's gaze hardened as Aldo spoke, though he remained silent, waiting. He'd wondered when Aldo would begin to question him more directly.

"There's more than what you've been telling us," Aldo pressed, crossing his arms as his courage built. "What are we doing, Ivar? What's this really about?"

For several long moments, Ivar said nothing. He stared at Aldo, taking in the man's stance, his growing defiance. Aldo had never confronted him like this before. The man had grit, Ivar admitted to himself. He waited longer than necessary to respond, drawing out the silence, watching Aldo shift under the weight of it.

"If I tell you," Ivar finally said, his voice low and measured, "you must believe me."

Aldo nodded, though his face lined with trepidation. He stood, rigid, while Ivar remained seated. Ivar waited, expecting some sign from Alena—a burn from the vial or a sudden warmth—but she remained silent, neutral, giving no sign of her preference.

And so, Ivar told Aldo everything. Every secret. Every lie. Every plan.

He watched his friend's face shift as the truth unraveled. Aldo's jaw tightened, his eyes widening as the depth of Ivar's deception came to light. The man had followed him for years, believed in him, fought beside him—but this was a lot.

When Ivar finished, the silence that followed was colder than the winter air outside the tent.

Aldo took a step back, his breath visible in the cold. "You've damned us all," he whispered, the weight of Ivar's revelations crashing down on him.

Ivar's expression didn't change. "Maybe. But we will rise,

Aldo. With her power, we will rise above them all."

Cleary stood in the doorway of the main building, his arms raised in greeting to the light dusting of snow falling around them. Snowflakes landed softly on his upturned palms, melting almost instantly, but his smile grew with each flake that touched his skin. To his right, Fiona scowled, trying to figure out what exactly there was to be happy about. Snow would only slow them down further, and her mentor, Melaney, might be lost forever. Her thoughts darkened further at the idea of a powerful sorceress attempting to rule the land, even with a legion of Shades to defend it.

The night before had been tense. Niklaos and Cleary stood toe to toe in a confrontation that Fiona didn't fully understand, but the air between the two had crackled with tension—Cleary's wizened calm facing Niklaos's youthful arrogance. Julian had swiftly ushered everyone, including Fiona, out of the building before she could witness what happened next. Afterward, she'd been led to a hall where hot rabbit stew and roasted potatoes filled her plate, but her mind stayed on Niklaos. Every time the door opened, she looked up, hoping to see him walk through. He never did.

Several women had taken her and Moirin under their care after dinner, guiding them to the living quarters for unwed ladies. Fiona bathed in near silence, slipping into a plain white gown afterward, her hair braided by one of the women. The shared quarters were humble, the women of the Shades sleeping together in joint rooms, rather than private chambers. Fiona and Moirin huddled under a single blanket as the last candle was extinguished, leaving them in near total darkness. Fiona missed Natalie and Lia fiercely. She closed her eyes and tried to call out to her eagle, hoping to see them in her mind's eye, but all that greeted her was silence.

Now, standing beside Cleary, Fiona waited as the light snow continued to fall. Below them, the Shades gathered in a quiet mass, their faces glowing with anticipation. Even the children stood still, their usual energy tempered by the sacredness of the moment. On her other side, Julian shifted uncomfortably, his gaze darting over the crowd. Fiona glanced at him and leaned closer.

"What's wrong?" she whispered.

Julian jumped, startled. "Eh? Oh." He glanced back toward the gathered Shades. "Just ready to get this done."

"Uh huh," Fiona said, her curiosity piqued. "What's going on?"

"The ceremony," Julian replied.

Cleary began to speak. "Greetings, Shades! Thank you all for gathering here for our annual cleansing." His voice echoed over the crowd, and he continued with a speech about the importance of the cleansing ceremony and the responsibility of those who bore the title of Shade. His words felt rehearsed, as if recited from the same script every year.

Julian muttered under his breath, just loud enough for Fiona to hear, "Like they had a choice."

Cleary raised his hands high. "To the sky!" he declared.

The crowd mimicked his motion, lifting their hands and repeating in unison, "To the sky!"

Cleary then lowered his hands, pointing toward the ground. "To the earth!" Again, the crowd followed suit. Fiona watched with a mixture of curiosity and skepticism as Cleary reached into a basket at his feet. From within, he pulled out the coiled black snake. It wrapped around his arm, its head resting on the back of his hand as it flicked its forked tongue toward the onlookers. The crowd gasped in delight, while Fiona wrinkled her nose in disgust. She'd never been a fan of serpents, and this one was no exception.

"May the serpent ever bless our way of life," Cleary intoned, his voice taking on an almost mystical quality. The snake began to glow, the light starting at the tip of its tail and cascading up its back until it encased its head, growing stronger as Cleary continued. "May we grow in all ways. May we honor the traditions of the Shades!"

The crowd erupted in cheers, and Cleary raised the glowing snake high above his head. Fiona half-expected it to sink its fangs into his flesh, but the snake remained still, coiled peacefully around his arm.

"To the Shades!" Cleary and the crowd shouted in unison, their arms raised once more. A bolt of white lightning shot up from the crowd, spiraling upward before descending in a high-pitched whine. It wound its way around the gathering, encircling them until it formed a shimmering bubble around the building. The sound intensified, piercing Fiona's ears, and she covered them with her hands. She squeezed her eyes shut against the blinding light, shuddering until the noise began to fade.

When she opened her eyes again, the bubble had vanished, leaving the building and its surrounding fence gleaming as if freshly washed. It looked like someone had given it a fresh coat of paint. Fiona's jaw dropped.

And then she felt it. The tingling of power that wrapped around her. She looked down at her hands, her arms. They glowed. She felt more alive than she had in days. She looked up to see Julian lit in a similar fashion, and then to the people around her. They all glowed like the snake. The crowd around her erupted in celebration, exchanging hugs and handshakes as the light beneath their skin faded and they began to look normal again.

Cleary lowered the snake back into its basket, his face beaming. He leaned in toward Fiona, his voice low beneath the noise of the crowd. "There you go, girl. Our power is now restored."

Fiona nodded, though she didn't fully understand. Why did the Shades need to replenish their power? If they were so strong, why did their energy fade over time? She gripped the railing in front of her, staring at her hands as they flexed, still buzzing with that strange energy. The others celebrated around her, but all she could think of was her lost mentor. Melaney was out there somewhere, unable to partake in the joy the Shades now felt. For all anyone knew, she might already be dead.

Julian appeared at her side, his expression relaxed but with an undertone of curiosity. Gone was the tenseness from before the ceremony. "Have you tried to call your familiar?" he asked.

Fiona shook her head. "I couldn't right before the ceremony."

Before Julian could respond, Cleary's voice cut in. "Just before the ceremony, all magical energies are blocked. I hope it didn't make you afraid."

"No," Fiona lied, swallowing hard.

Cleary smiled and spread his hands. "Bring it here, young one. Let's see yours."

Julian jumped in before Fiona could answer. "Perhaps she'd feel more comfortable practicing alone before presenting it to everyone," he suggested, earning a grateful glance from Fiona. "I remember how I felt before I got the hang of the two of mine."

Fiona snorted. "Two? You get more than one?"

Julian raised an eyebrow, a mischievous smile forming on his lips. Mine do travel in pairs."

Julian raised his arm and closed his eyes. Thunder rumbled in the distance, and a low growl echoed across the valley. Fiona turned, her breath catching in her throat as two ghostly white beasts with red eyes galloped down the path, their gaze locked on her.

CHAPTER 30

var set his cot beside Melaney's still body, her frailty more evident with each passing day. Though he had little patience for sentiment, he didn't want her to die from the bitter cold of the Iron Wood Mountains—not yet. He rolled a pillow beneath her head and draped another over her pale form. Her breath came in faint, shallow puffs, her nose and cheeks drained of color, nearly as white as the snow outside.

Put me under the blanket, Alena's voice slithered into his mind, her impeccable timing not failing to irritate him. Silence for days, and now here she was, offering to warm the sister she both despised and needed.

Ivar sighed and placed the vial that contained Alena's essence next to Melaney's chest, watching as it gently rose and fell. He climbed onto his cot, pulling his cloak tighter as the chill gnawed at him. Even with the campfires burning, the mountain cold was merciless, cutting through every layer.

Aldo's reaction to their earlier conversation kept replaying in his mind. The look of disappointment in his friend's eyes had unsettled him. Aldo wasn't angry about the plan itself, but rather that Ivar had kept so much from him. His questions had been relentless—about Alena, her past, and Melaney's involvement. Finally, after hours of interrogating his commander, Aldo had bid him goodnight and retreated to his tent.

Ivar could only hope Aldo's loyalty would remain intact.

Beyond these mountains lay Oldgrange, their destination, and the key to everything they had worked for. So close, and yet instead of relief, a knot of tension coiled tighter within Ivar's chest. Scouts had found no trace of the Shades, but that meant little. Anything could happen between now and their arrival to the grave. The redhead, crossed his mind—had she reached Oldgrange with reinforcements? Was his head start enough to prevent interference from the Shades?

He clenched his fists, trying to quell the unease creeping into his thoughts.

Have faith in me, Alena whispered, her voice laced with dark amusement. *They haven't met me yet.*

Ivar closed his eyes, trying to picture Oldgrange with Alena standing at its gates. But he didn't see her in Melaney's body. Instead, her old form flickered in his mind—dark hair, slender, but her face twisted with bitterness, her eyes cold and sallow. The smile that curved her lips was hollow, her teeth bared against the backdrop of a raging storm. A shiver ran down his spine, not from the cold, but from the darkness she exuded.

What happened to you? he asked, the question slipping out before he could stop himself. *Tell me.*

At first, silence greeted him. He thought she might ignore him entirely, as she often did when the subject of her past came up. But as he lay there, trying to rid his mind of her image, her voice returned—soft, almost fragile.

We were more than sisters, once. The words caught him off guard, his breath hitching. He hadn't expected her to open up, much less like this. He remained silent, waiting for her to continue.

We were best friends. We did everything together. But my true best friend was my familiar, Nissa. She was a fae—a mischievous one, always playing tricks on the Shades. Most of the time, it was harmless fun. But one day, Nissa took her pranks too far. She gave a child a nightmare so terrifying he wouldn't speak for days. I was warned there would be consequences, but I never imagined what Cleary, our magistrate, had in mind.

Ivar listened intently, his heart pounding in his chest as Alena's voice filled his mind with memories from a time long past.

One afternoon, my sister and I went into the woods to collect berries. Cleary found us at the edge of a ravine. Nissa was by my side, and when she saw him, she hissed. I knew then that something was terribly wrong. Nissa had never shown anger before, not even when people scolded us for her tricks. Cleary told me that Nissa had to go. And do you know what my sister did? Her voice broke, and Ivar could almost hear the tears she held back. *Melaney agreed with him. She did nothing. She stood there as Cleary captured my fae in a bubble of magic, as Nissa fought and screamed, and he dragged her away. I begged Melaney to help, but she stepped in front of me, telling me it was for the best. That Nissa had earned her punishment.*

Ivar clenched his fists as Alena's voice trembled with fury.

I lashed out, slapped her across the face, and she shoved me down the ravine. I fell hard. I don't remember much after that, except the feeling of my soul being ripped apart when Nissa was taken from me. My fae—my other half—was destroyed, and with her, a part of me died too. I didn't wake again until you came, so many moons later.

Ivar sat up, running his hands over his face, trying to process the weight of what Alena had shared. *I don't know what to say.*

Then don't, she replied, her tone cold and final. *There's nothing you can say that will fix what happened.*

Isn't there some way to get Nissa back? he asked, desperate to offer something, anything, to ease her pain.

Once an affinity is destroyed, there's no coming back. It's over. And so is Melaney, she added, the bitterness returning.

Ivar finally understood. He laid back down, staring into the blackness of the tent, wishing he could find a way to soothe her anguish.

Don't pity me, Ivar, Alena's voice cut through the silence. *Just keep helping me.*

He nodded to the darkness. *Consider it done.*

Fiona swallowed a scream and raised her arms to shield herself as dogs descended upon her. Her heart hammered in her chest, waiting for the bite of fangs, the punishment for doubting Cleary's power. The searing pain she expected didn't come. Barking filled the air, vibrating through her bones. Hot canine breath brushed against her skin, stirring the tiny hairs on her arms, their presence pressed in from either side. The thud of their paws pounded the earth close enough that the ground trembled beneath her. The sharp snap of teeth and the rush of their panting surrounded her, but no bite came. She winced, expecting an attack, but then—silence. A soft whine followed, almost... playful?

She peeked between her fingers and blinked in shock. The two ghostly beasts sat obediently at Julian's feet, their long black tongues lapping at his face and neck with an enthusiasm that softened their fearsome presence. Both hounds had short, sleek white fur that glistened like satin and bright red ears. They stood tall, their shoulders reaching Julian's waist, their faces slender and chiseled.

"Those are…" Fiona began, her voice shaky.

"My familiars," Julian confirmed, pushing the dogs off him as they attempted to lick him again. He stood, wiping the drool from his cheek. "They come when I call, or when they feel like it."

Fiona stared, awe mixing with a lingering fear. Their eyes, still glowing an unnatural red hue, locked onto her again. She shuddered, knowing they wouldn't hurt her, but the sheer size and power they exuded kept her cautious.

"They're harmless," Julian said, noticing her unease as he playfully scruffed the necks of the closest dog to him. The beast leaned into his touch. "At least, to us. Meet Blaze and Ember."

"Fire names," Fiona murmured. "They're beautiful." She rubbed her arms. "You can call them now."

"Our power is restored. So, yes. I can."

Fiona looked around at all the shades, at the variety of familiars that had begun to appear. Her breath caught as she saw Darry with his hand resting on the flank of a massive otter-wolf beast, its fur gleaming a wet, dark brown in the snow with fierce, predator's eyes that glowed amber. Its powerful paws scraped the ground, claws digging into the earth with anxious energy, its long, sleek tail twitching as if ready to let off pent-up energy. The end flattened, perfect for swimming, Fiona realized. Like an otter. It said on its haunches and let its front feet rest against its stomach, waiting.

"That's Tobar," Julian said, following her gaze. "He's far more comfortable in the water, but he'll stay on land as needed."

Brannon's familiar sent a chill down her spine. The creature prowled around him in slow, calculated circles on its sharp cloven feet, its lithe body tall and slender, exuding a sense of strength, cunning, and barely restrained violence that opposed Brannon's calm demeanor. Its fur was thick and course, goatlike, black as night, and its emerald eyes gleamed, locking on her before flicking back to Brannon.

"And that's Moss. I'd steer clear of him unless he approaches you."

She'd only heard of the dobhar-chu and the pooka in legend, but here they were. Real.

Fiona cast a glance toward Cleary, who was now deep in conversation with a group of Shades, his face alight with pride and authority. Something still felt... off. She couldn't shake the feeling, and it gnawed at her mind. "I wonder if I could call my eagle now..." she mused aloud, her thoughts drifting back to her earlier attempt when her connection had felt severed.

Julian caught her contemplative look. "Are you alright?"

Fiona forced a smile. "Perfect. What's next?"

"We need to discuss the rescue mission for Melaney," Julian said, his tone shifting to a more serious one. "Cleary should be willing to send the Shades now that the ceremony's over."

Without another word, Fiona marched over to Cleary, her nerves bristling with urgency. She cleared her throat, and Cleary paused, turning his gaze to her. His eyes, though calm, had an air of authority that made her feel like a small child interrupting her elders.

Fiona closed her eyes for a moment to steady herself. "I believe we have someone to rescue."

Cleary stared at her, his face blank.

"You know, from the grips of the marauders and all that. Before they take the strongest power in the world."

"Oh, right. Yes. Tell Julian to ring the bell."

"I'm right here," Julian said from Fiona's side. He stepped up to the large bronze bell hung above the door, and with a wave of his hand, the bell began to swing. The soft clang echoed through the air, growing louder with each pass, until it filled the entire village with its deafening chime. The crowd of Shades gathered, eyes somber and focused, their chatter silenced by the sound.

"Thank you for your attention," Cleary announced, his voice carrying a haughty tone that grated on Fiona's nerves. "We have a dire situation. Melaney has been taken by the marauders—by Ivar himself. We must retrieve her before they can use the power of Oldgrange against us."

A murmur rippled through the crowd, uncertainty written on their faces. Fiona couldn't tell if they were afraid of Ivar or simply hesitating in disbelief. How could they hesitate at a time like this?

"Cleary, we need to act now," Julian urged, stepping forward. "Time's running out."

"I need volunteers," Cleary called out. "If I get none, I'll assign you."

Julian stepped forward. "Fiona and I are going, of course."

Brannon and Darry appeared from the middle of the crowd. "We'll be going, as well."

Fiona gave them a small smile, feeling a spark of hope. Julian continued, "Lia, Natalie, and Dax are already scouting ahead. We need to meet up with them." He looked around him. "We're going to need more than just a handful of Shades to face Ivar, though. This is Melaney we're talking about!"

A surge of energy pulsed through the crowd, and one by one more Shades stepped forward, offering their help. By the time Fiona looked back, a hundred Shades stood ready, their expressions set with determination. She studied them, trying to remember how many marauders there had been. Would that be enough?

Cleary frowned at the gathered shades and said, "You should leave before sunset." His eyes turned to the noon sky. "Get what weapons you need and assemble quickly."

CHAPTER 31

"Where's Niklaos?" Fiona cornered Julian as soon as everyone dispersed. "What'd Cleary do with him?"

"What do you care?" Julian stared at her. "He's a marauder."

"I thought you'd care more than that," Fiona shot back, undeterred. "He helped you save me."

Julian shook his head, an edge creeping into his tone. "I owe him nothing. All he did was show us which tent you were in that night. I'd have figured it out on my own eventually."

Fiona swallowed hard, trying to push down the rising tide of frustration. The heat of angry tears threatened to spill over. "You don't think that's worth something? You think he left with us because he was a hostage? That he thought he'd end up in some kind of shade prison? He wasn't ever one of them, even when he was with them."

Julian's mouth tightened. "Did I do nothing?"

"I'm not saying that," Fiona's voice softened, but she couldn't let this go. "I wish you'd understand."

A heavy silence hung between them before Julian sighed, finally meeting her gaze. "Cleary has him in the main building, but I doubt he'll set him free anytime soon."

"What does he gain by keeping him locked up?" Fiona's frustration bubbled over.

"Justice," Julian said, stepping closer, his hounds flanking him, their red eyes flickering between him and Fiona, alert. "For all the shades who died at the hands of marauders. Think of Melaney."

"I am thinking of her." Fiona's fists clenched. "And I don't think she'd want someone punished for doing the right thing."

"You don't know what she'd want," Julian snapped, his patience fraying.

Tears finally spilled from Fiona's eyes, hot and furious. "If you won't help him, I'll do it myself."

"It's best to let Cleary handle things." Julian set his jaw stubbornly, looking away.

Fiona felt a cold knot forming in her stomach. "He should let the people have a say."

"That's not completely how it works."

Fiona closed her eyes for a moment, trying to compose herself. "I'll talk to Cleary. There has to be something we can do."

Julian shrugged, his tone indifferent. "Be my guest, but he's not the easiest to influence. Be prepared for things to not go as planned. Either way, we need to pack."

Fiona ignored him and stormed off.

Cleary stood like a sentinel on the porch of the main building, his presence regal and unyielding. He reminded her of a king on his throne, a thought that soured her stomach even more. Without hesitating, she marched up the steps until she stood toe to toe with him.

Cleary's expression remained impassive, though his eyes sparkled with quiet amusement. "You have something to say, Fiona?"

"I do," she said, standing tall. "I want to know what you plan to do with Niklaos."

Cleary waved a hand dismissively, as if brushing off a child. "He will be dealt with soon enough. You needn't worry about it."

"I am worried," Fiona snapped. "That's why I came to you."

Cleary's smile was patronizing, his eyes filled with condescension. "My dear, he's a marauder. One, I might add, who took part in the kidnapping of your beloved Melaney."

"You don't know that. I don't remember seeing him there."

"I don't imagine you would, what with being knocked out cold," Cleary replied smoothly, his smile widening.

Fiona's anger surged. "I can't believe you won't even give him a chance. He saved my life."

"I believe Julian has that honor, as well as Brannon and Darry," Cleary said coolly, his smile never wavering.

Fiona's hands balled into fists, the air around them thickening as the wind began to stir. "He helped."

"Fiona—" Cleary started, but she cut him off.

"Let him go," she demanded, her voice firm, the wind picking up and ruffling through Cleary's hair, as the air bent to her will. "Now."

Cleary's eyes widened slightly as the wind intensified, slamming the wooden door behind him with a sharp crack. He jumped, startled for the first time. "Now, young lady, you stop that this instant."

"They said you're a seer. Did you see that coming?" Fiona said, her chin raised defiantly. "Bring me Niklaos. I'll take responsibility for him."

Cleary studied her for a long moment, his calculating eyes tracing her face. Then, a slow grin spread across his features. "Fine. But if he does anything—anything at all—it's on you."

He turned to one of the shades standing behind him and muttered something under his breath. The man nodded and disappeared inside the building. Cleary returned his gaze to Fiona, his steely expression back in place.

"He'll join you when the portal opens," Cleary said. "I hope you know what you're doing, Fiona."

She did, too.

CHAPTER 32

The sight was magnificent. Ivar watched as his hot breath spiraled into the frigid air, rolling in white swirls that dissolved into the biting cold. His gaze shifted to the towering mountains before them, their jagged peaks piercing the heavy gray sky. They had long since left the flat, shimmering plains behind and were making impressive progress through the thick, untouched snow drifts that blanketed the landscape like a shroud.

Melaney's skin had taken on a bluish hue, the cold seeping into her flesh despite the meager fur skin thrown haphazardly over her limp form. She lay slumped across the back of a donkey, her breath shallow but steady. As long as she was alive, Ivar didn't care if she was half-frozen. He glanced at her, indifferent, and tugged his cloak tighter around himself. The vial at his waist radiated a steady heat, warming him from the inside out.

Alena, who had been silent for much of the journey, had transformed from irritable to almost pleasant after sharing her story. She had been pleased with Ivar's response, and his confidence in her loyalty grew with each passing day. Her quietness now gave him space to think—something he valued more than conversation.

"Thank you," a low voice rumbled beside him. Aldo spoke so softly that only Ivar could hear.

Ivar glanced at his friend, eyebrows raised. Sentiment wasn't something either of them indulged in, and Aldo's sudden expression of gratitude felt out of place.

"For confiding in me," Aldo added, his voice gruff, as if the words tasted foreign on his tongue.

Ivar's eyes narrowed. "Not all secrets can be held by one person." His tone was flat, practical. He turned his attention back to the mountains. "This way, if something happens to me, you'll see the plan through." The silence between them stretched out, taut and uncomfortable. After a pause, Ivar shot a sharp look at Aldo. "You will do that, right?"

Aldo didn't respond immediately. He seemed to mull over the question, as though the answer wasn't as simple as a yes or no.

"Yes."

Ivar said nothing in response, but his unease grew. Everything was going according to plan—a rare occurrence that only made him more cautious. He wasn't accustomed to things unfolding so smoothly, and the unsettling calm set his instincts on edge.

He flexed his gloved fingers around the reins of his horse. The truth was, if they could get Alena into her new body, she would handle whatever trouble found them in Oldgrange. But that was the plan—until it wasn't. The shades were coming. He could feel it in his bones, as though they were already on the edge of the horizon, hunting them, closing in with each passing hour. He could sense them in the air, and the faint cooling of Alena's vial only confirmed his fears.

They may reach us before we get there.

Ivar's lips pressed into a thin line as he spurred his horse forward, quickening the pace. Snow crunched beneath hooves as they raced against time and fate, and though the mountains loomed ever closer, the looming threat of what pursued them weighed heavily on his mind.

Julian led Fiona down the snowy road to his home, one of the small shacks on the outskirts of town where all the bachelors lived. His hounds remained outside, content to lay in the snow and snooze. The inside of the dwelling was modest and bare, save for a few practical belongings, but immaculately clean. He busied himself preparing a travel sack for his horse, stuffing it with dried meat, a flask of water, and a few sharp daggers, not saying a word.

Fiona wandered through the space, her curiosity piqued. Despite spending all this time with him, she realized she knew so little about Julian. She stepped into the only other room, taking in the sparse arrangement: a bed, a wash basin, a set of folded clothes, and an orderly collection of belongings.

A dagger called to her, jammed to the hilt inside the pages of one of the only books in the house, a thick one collecting dust on the bedside table. She carefully extracted it, looking around to see if Julian noticed, wiped the dust from it, then tucked it away in her cloak. As she did so, her gaze fell on a beat-up box in the far corner, barely visible beneath a worn quilt. Dust clung to the edges, as if it hadn't been touched in years, a forgotten relic of the past.

"Not much to see in there." Julian's voice startled her. He appeared in the doorway, his expression unreadable, jaw clenched. "You ready?"

Fiona's curiosity flared as she glanced back at the box.

"What's in there?"

"That's a memory box. Not much interesting there." His voice was casual, too casual, but the tightness in his shoulders told a different story. There was something in the way his eyes avoided the corner, a flicker of discomfort betraying the nonchalance.

She knew better than to press, but it gnawed at her all the

same. "Sorry if I pried," she muttered, watching as he shoved the last few things into the sack he'd been packing and yanked the drawstrings closed with more force than necessary.

He shrugged, brushing off her apology. "Doesn't matter. It's just old stuff." But his words, like his movements, seemed heavier than before.

She thought of the kiss between them at the marauder camp and moved closer to him. "I never said thank you. For saving me."

He paused. Stared at her as his blue eyes darkened. "Of course," he said. "We must hurry." He grasped her cold hand in his warm one.

Fiona bit her lip, and silence fell between them as he led the way outside and down the lane toward the village square. The shades were already gathering. Their arrival was faster than she'd expected, and the sight took her breath away—people and creatures of all shapes, sizes, and forms, each one a reminder of the myths she'd grown up with. Legends made flesh. She wondered what Erin would have made of it all.

The crowd felt much smaller than earlier that day. Fiona frowned, but she had a question to be answered.

She left Julian's side, weaving through the crowd to stand by Brannon and Darry, who hovered on the edge of the assembly chatting quietly. She threw a glance back at Julian as he stepped onto the porch, preparing to address the shades. Her curiosity nagged at her.

"Brannon, what's in Julian's memory box?"

Brannon's easy smile faded, his expression turning serious. "I don't think it's my place to talk about that."

"That's it?"

"He's like a brother to me, Fiona. If Julian wants to share, he will. It's not my business."

Fiona frowned but dropped the subject as Julian raised his arms to address the group. The chatter stopped, and a hush fell over the square. She scanned the crowd for Cleary but saw no sign of him.

"We must move quickly," Julian announced. "Bella has agreed to portal us to Oldgrange. Make sure you've dismissed your familiars."

There were murmurs of agreement, and Fiona watched as the crowd began to shrink. Creatures vanished, leaving only their human counterparts standing in their place. The shades were fewer in number than she'd thought. A knot tightened in her chest—would they be enough to face the marauder army? Alena?

She turned to Brannon, lowering her voice. "Why do they have to dismiss their familiars?"

"Portal magic doesn't agree with them. It messes with their essence, sometimes even kills them."

Her eyes widened. "Why?"

"Familiars are magic," Brannon explained, his voice grim. "The portal overloads them. They can only take so much magic before they break apart. But don't worry, they can recall them on the other side."

Fiona's gaze swept over the crowd again. "Where's Niklaos? They were supposed to bring him to me."

As if on cue, the door to Cleary's headquarters creaked open. Cleary stepped out, dragging Niklaos behind him. Fiona's heart sank. The young man was battered, his clothing torn and smeared with dirt, and his face was a mess of bruises and cuts. One eye was swollen. Cleary yanked him down the steps, barely giving him time to keep up.

"Here's your charge," Cleary said, his tone flat.

"What did you do to him?" Fiona rushed to Niklaos's side, gently lifting his face to look at her. His eyes were hollow as he stared into her eyes, his spirit crushed.

Cleary's regarded her coldly. "We had to ensure we gathered all possible information on the marauders. And on their treatment of you." He leveled a stern gaze at her. "You should be thankful we took such measures on your behalf."

She glared at him, fury bubbling up inside her. "And did you? Learn anything useful?"

Cleary shrugged. "No."

Fiona's temper flared. "He needs medical attention. He's in no condition to travel."

"You said you wanted him," Cleary replied with a dismissive

wave. "He's yours now. What happens to him is on you." His gaze shifted to Niklaos. "And him."

"What happened to all the people who volunteered to go?" Fiona pressed.

Cleary smiled, the gesture not reaching his eyes. "It seems not everyone was truly up to the challenge."

Julian's voice interrupted before she could respond. "Mount up!" He was already beside the horses, preparing for their departure, getting on his horse. Fiona's gaze shifted to the black gelding assigned to her, its dark eyes watching her.

Darry sidled up to her, grinning like a fool. "I hope you know how to ride," he teased, "because that one's yours. And you'll be taking marauder boy with you."

Fiona swallowed hard. She had grown up riding her father's old farm horse, but this was different. The gelding in front of her was young, powerful, and unfamiliar. Its muscles rippled beneath its sleek coat, and it snorted as she approached, its breath misting in the cool air.

Darry chuckled. "It's fine. Unless, of course, you need help."

Fiona shot him a glare. "I'll manage."

Julian's voice cut through Darry's teasing. "Leave her alone."

Without another word, Julian dismounted and crossed to her, lifting her by the waist as easily as if she weighed nothing. His hands were warm against her sides, sending an unexpected shiver down her spine. She sat atop the horse, trying to ignore the heat creeping into her cheeks. Niklaos climbed up behind her, his breath ragged, his hands shaking as he clung to her waist. Julian side-eyed him as he turned away.

"Sorry," Niklaos whispered in Fiona's ear.

Julian swung back onto his horse, his eyes scanning the crowd. "Bella!"

A woman with midnight-black hair that coiled over her shoulders glided forward, her doe-brown eyes gleaming. The chiseled planes of her face—high cheekbones, strong jaw—gave her an otherworldly beauty that captivated Fiona instantly. Her lips were set in concentration, and her entire presence radiated an inner power that went beyond mere physical strength. Muscled arms, toned from years of training, lifted and with a sharp flick of her wrist, the air crackled and sparked as though infused with raw energy.

The atmosphere shifted, electric with tension, as a shimmering oval of light burst into existence before them. It rippled like water disturbed by an unseen force, glowing with an iridescent hue that danced across its surface. The portal pulsed gently, a hum reverberating through the ground beneath their feet, as though the very fabric of reality had bent to her will. Every movement she made was precise, and the sheer command she held over magic left Fiona breathless.

"Hurry," Bella called. "I can't hold it for long."

Julian spurred his horse forward, disappearing into the portal, followed by other shades. Fiona nudged her gelding to follow, Niklaos still clinging to her, and as they passed through the shimmering light, a strange sensation washed over her, like liquid sliding across her skin. On the other side, they emerged into sudden biting cold, with a vast, open plain and mountains looming closely. She looked down, surprised to see her arms were dry.

"Move!" Brannon burst through the portal behind her, nearly knocking into her horse as it skittered sideways. More shades rode through the portal.

Fiona glared at him but said nothing, urging her horse forward until she caught up with Julian. He kept his eyes fixed ahead, his face hard as stone. She couldn't help but glance back at the portal as Bella joined them on the other side of the portal and it collapsed with a wet sucking sound, leaving no trace behind.

And with that, they were off, galloping toward Oldgrange.

CHAPTER 33

They were close—so close Ivar could feel the pulse of Oldgrange's ancient power. The air around them thickened with a fine mist of rain and snow, intertwined with magic, swirling around the army as they marched. Each droplet that touched his skin made it tingle, as if the very air was charged with energy. Alena, ever vigilant, kept the small vial warm in his grasp, its heat radiating outward, shielding him from the bitter cold that enveloped the mountains. Her magic was subtle but steady in the unforgiving weather. They had to keep moving. The winter solstice was drawing near.

The doorway would only be open for a short while—an hour at most. But that would be enough. If they reached it soon, Alena could complete the mission without interference, and by morning's light, Oldgrange would be theirs.

Don't worry, her voice slid into his thoughts, calm and teasing.

I'm not.

I can sense your feelings, remember?

Doesn't mean you should, he replied with a smirk.

Despite the mounting tension, Ivar caught himself smiling.

Soon, he'd be able to hold her, to feel the warmth of her skin beneath his hands, to kiss her. Tomorrow, when the sun illuminated the doorway of Oldgrange, everything would fall into place. With Alena by his side, their power would be unstoppable.

He placed a hand over the vial, feeling the gentle heat radiate through his fingers, spreading warmth through his chilled body. Alena's magic, always there, always steady. His sorceress, his weapon.

A rough clearing of a throat pulled Ivar from his thoughts. He turned to see Aldo, his second-in-command, watching him with a cautious gaze. "We're nearly there," Aldo said, "but we need to make camp soon."

"We'll stop at the edge of Oldgrange," Ivar said, his tone firm, unwilling to waste any more time than necessary.

"The men should rest before then," Aldo pressed, glancing at the weary soldiers trudging behind them.

"They will!" Ivar's voice rang out, echoing off the towering mountains surrounding them. His outburst sent a ripple of unease through the ranks as soldiers slowed to glance nervously in his direction. He cursed himself for the slip in control. He needed to focus—Alena, the mission, the men. He couldn't afford to let his mind wander.

Aldo stood silently, waiting. His weathered face betrayed no emotion, but the weight of his patience gnawed at Ivar.

"We'll make camp when the sun touches the tops of the trees," Ivar said, more calmly this time, steadying himself. He cast his gaze across the darkening horizon, calculating the distance remaining. "We'll resume before first light. That will give us time for what's needed tomorrow."

Aldo nodded, satisfied with the answer. "Yes, sir." He gave a short command, and the army resumed its march.

Ivar lingered for a moment, watching them. His men were tough, hardened by years of battles and survival in the wilderness. But they weren't machines. If he pushed too hard, they would break. And if he lost their respect now, it would all crumble. The solstice was coming, and Oldgrange rested over the next stretch of mountains. All this—the cold, the exhaustion, the waiting—would soon be over. Victory was within reach.

He fell back in line, weaving through the soldiers until he returned to the front. Every step brought them closer to Oldgrange, to his destiny. He clenched his fists, ignoring the cold bite of the wind against his face.

The shades rode close together, their brown hoods flapping in the biting mountain wind, faces hidden beneath the shadows. The cold was unforgiving, cutting through the thick fabric of their capes and settling deep into their bones. Fiona huddled close to her horse, her thighs aching as she gripped the saddle tightly. The last thing she wanted was to fall and give people something to laugh about. Behind her, Niklaos rested his head on her back, his body pressing into hers.

She tried to glance over her shoulder at him, but only caught a glimpse of his blonde hair whipping in the wind. Fiona looked around her at the others, the dozens of shades riding into the snow and wind. She couldn't help but wonder, not for the first time, if they had enough fighters to take on the marauder army. She'd seen how ruthless those men were—how much they relished battle. Where they thrived in the chaos of war, she just wanted to save Melaney and survive. Were the shades, despite their skill and powers, truly enough?

A sharp whistle cut through the air, snapping her from her thoughts. The horses' ears perked up, and the group slowed to a halt, gathering in a tight circle. Julian and Fiona moved to the front. Julian stood tall in his saddle, scanning the horizon. His blue eyes met Fiona's for the briefest moment before shifting back to the distance.

"What was that?" Fiona wrapped her frozen fingers around the reins, trying to keep her voice steady. Niklaos jerked straight with a start, but said nothing. His hot breath hit the top of

Fiona's back.

"Scouts," Julian replied.

As if on cue, three riders appeared over the horizon, galloping toward them at full speed. Time seemed to slow as they covered the ground, hooves thundering against the frozen earth. They came to an abrupt stop, spraying dirt and snow in their wake. The rider in the middle was young, maybe around Dax's age. Fiona blinked at him, surprised at how youthful he looked.

The boy caught her staring and narrowed his eyes. "You got a problem?"

Fiona shook her head, avoiding his gaze.

Julian ignored the exchange, his focus on the scouts. "How far are we from the marauder army?"

"A day's ride, if we keep this pace. Less, if we push it," the boy said, casting a look over the group.

Julian nodded. "Any sign of the others?"

The young scout shook his head. "No."

"Keep looking," Julian ordered.

Without another word, the scouts turned their horses and disappeared back into the distance, the sound of hooves fading quickly. Fiona leaned closer to Julian, her voice low as she asked, "Who are they looking for?"

Julian's jaw clenched. "Dax and the others."

An ebony-skinned woman trotted her horse up to Julian. She reached into her saddlebag and pulled out a piece of jerky, handing it to Julian before tossing a chunk at Fiona. Fiona caught it and passed a second piece to Niklaos. She rode through the group, distributing the jerky with quiet efficiency.

"Thanks, Dakara," Julian said, finishing his jerky quickly.

The meat was good, moist and flavorful. Fiona chewed thoughtfully, wondering if it was deer. Everything in this world seemed familiar, yet foreign. The animals might look the same, but for all she knew, they had different names. It was a stark reminder that she still didn't fully understand this world she found herself in.

As she licked her fingers clean, a sharp pain shot through her stomach, forcing a gasp. She held her belly. The meat must have disagreed with her--but the pain intensified, spreading like wildfire through her body. Her vision blurred, dark spots clouding her sight.

A scream. Her scream. Fingers on her face, feeling her frigid skin. Her fingers.

"Fiona!" Julian's voice reached her, but it sounded distant, muffled.

Niklaos shifted behind her, but then his weight vanished. He must have fallen off, she thought dimly. She tried to look for him, but her eyes wouldn't focus. The reins slipped from her grasp, and her horse reared. She was falling, helpless to stop it. The world tilted, and then she hit the cold, hard ground with a bone-jarring thud. Pain shot through her shoulder, stealing her breath. She gasped for air, willing it to push into her lungs.

Footsteps pounded toward her. Hands grabbed her, repositioning her body. She tried to move, but nothing cooperated, and she heard Niklaos's panicked voice a million years away, "Is she okay?"

"Shut up," Julian snapped, his tone sharp. He sounded closer. Above her.

"She needs Melaney or Stelios," Dakara said, her voice calm but urgent. "I'd wager she hasn't had the tea recently."

"It's been a while," Julian muttered. "I didn't think..."

"Melaney knows how to make the tea. I'm not that far in my training. However, I think I can bring Fiona around awhile longer."

Fiona groaned, trying to speak, but only a garbled sound came out. Her tongue betrayed her, refusing to move, trying to shift to the back of her throat.

"Please work faster."

"I'm trying, Julian. This takes a few minutes to work."

Julian didn't respond. Fiona worked her eyes open enough to see a blurry Dakara wrestling with a mortar and pestle, grinding something up. When it was to her satisfaction, she opened her water skin and poured straight into the mortar, then ground some more.

The world shifted. The snow swirled into a sinkhole writhing and alive, beckoning and pulling, as if ready to open up and swallow Fiona whole. She tried to scream, terror rising bile in her throat, but nothing came out anymore.

"Dakara!" Julian's voice toned desperate.

"It's ready."

Julian lifted Fiona into a sitting position, cradling her against him. "Drink this," he whispered into her ear, the cool rim of the mortar pressed against her lips. Fiona opened her mouth, letting the bitter liquid flow in, fighting the urge to gag. She swallowed as quickly as she could, but the liquid was too much, too fast, and she coughed, spilling some onto Dakara's hands.

"Don't drown her." Brannon sounded far away, his voice an echo.

"She'll be fine," Dakara said, but her voice seemed far away too, like the world was slipping out of focus. The noise around her grew louder, overwhelming, every sound blending together into an unbearable cacophony. Fiona pressed her hands over her ears, trying to block it out.

"Dakara, the noise," Julian's voice broke through the chaos.

Suddenly, everything went silent. Fiona opened her eyes and found herself surrounded by a glowing bubble of magic. It rippled around her, Julian, and Dakara, separating them from the outside world. Everything beyond the bubble was a blur, muted and distant. The sinkhole was no more.

Dakara looked as old as Melaney up close. Lines crisscrossed at the corners of her eyes, telling of a woman who loved to laugh. She didn't smile as she leaned in to examine Fiona's face.

"Feeling better?"

Fiona nodded, though her body still felt weak. "A little. What happened?"

Dakara exchanged a glance with Julian before speaking. "You're a mirror in this world. You weren't born here—you crossed through. That makes you an unborn."

"Unborn?" Fiona frowned. "What does that even mean?"

Dakara's expression softened. "The world doesn't recognize you, so it tries to reject you. The tea is magic. It helps keep you anchored, connected to this world so it doesn't... kill you."

Fiona shivered at the thought. "How often do I need to drink it?"

"Once a month, at least for now. The longer you are here, the longer you can go. One day, you may not need it." Dakara handed her a small, black pouch. "Guard this. Your life depends on it. Make more of the tea when the time comes." She looked Fiona up and down. "Before all this happens."

The bubble vanished, and the cold mountain air rushed back in. Fiona staggered as she stood, Julian steadying her arm. His hand lingered, sending a rush of warmth through her, and she leaned into him.

Niklaos stood nearby, his face tight with concern, and he looked steadier despite his injured face. "Are you alright?"

"I'm fine," Fiona said, brushing off his worry and moving her arm from Julian's grip.

"That didn't look like fine," Niklaos muttered. Julian opened his mouth as if to say something, then clamped it shut and walked away. Fiona tried to hide her shakiness as she started to pull herself onto her horse. Niklaos's hands grabbed her waist and pushed upwards, allowing her to fling a leg over the horse's back. She slid herself forward to give him room to climb up behind her.

"I know you still feel weak," he murmured in her ear. She hoped he wouldn't say anything, not that the shades had any interest in him. He was only here because of her.

She wrapped the reins around her hands, not trusting herself to hang on otherwise. Niklaos wrapped his arms around her, this time less to steady himself—she knew—and more to steady her. They moved together as the gelding stepped forward.

Julian whistled and the group began to turn. The cold grew more bitter as they moved down the slope and further into the mountains.

"Why so few shades?" Niklaos spoke low so the others couldn't hear.

"I don't know." Fiona had to turn her head to speak, thankful her horse seemed focused on staying with the others. She wouldn't have to attempt to steer him, something she wasn't sure she could handle in her condition.

"I thought Melaney was in a position of power." Niklaos's stubbled cheek brushed against her face. She faced the front again.

"Yes, but not like Cleary. He probably had a hand in our numbers."

Niklaos's brow furrowed. "Why wouldn't he want Melaney back?"

"Good question."

Fiona had no answer to the question that swirled relentlessly in her mind as her horse picked its way through the leafless shrubbery and thin sheets of snow. Cleary was a mystery, indeed.

CHAPTER 34

var allowed the men to make camp well after nightfall, the thick darkness settling over them like a shroud. They'd made good progress, and Oldgrange was not far now. A few hours of sleep would be enough before they readied themselves for the final push. Alena had been silent for hours, no doubt conserving her energy for what awaited them at dawn. Ivar could hardly contain his anticipation and wondered how he'd manage to sleep at all.

"Bird?" Aldo's voice broke the quiet, and Ivar glanced over to see him holding a stick skewered with tender meat. The rich scent of roasted game filled the air, the juices sizzling as they dripped into the campfire.

Ivar accepted the offer without a word, nodding his thanks as he bit into the savory meal. The taste was earthy, laced with salt and fat, and he tore into it hungrily, juices running down his chin, tangling in his beard.

Aldo lingered, watching him. "Are you ready for this?"

"Why wouldn't I be?"

"Just asking."

"I'm ready," Ivar said, his voice sharp as he wiped his mouth with the back of his hand.

Aldo nodded, looking as if he wanted to say more.

"Speak up."

Aldo looked thoughtful, as if weighing his next words. He hesitated, then spoke up. "Are you sure you know what you're doing? With this woman, I mean. What if she's not what you expect?"

Ivar's jaw tightened. "What if she is?"

Aldo shifted uncomfortably. "I don't mean to question you. I'd follow you into any fight, you know that. I just want to make sure this is the right move for us."

Ivar turned on him, his expression cold. "The only 'us' in this is me and Alena."

Aldo's face flushed with anger. "In case you didn't notice, you've got an entire army behind you. We're all in this, whether you like it or not."

Ivar's eyes narrowed, his voice dropping to a dangerous whisper. "Why are you questioning me?" His tone stiffened, laced with warning. Anyone else would have been dead for less, and Aldo knew it.

Aldo held his ground, but there was a flicker of unease in his eyes. "I have a bad feeling about this. About her."

Before Ivar could respond, the vial hidden beneath his tunic began to heat, its warmth creeping across his chest until it burned. He winced, his hand instinctively moving toward it. His nostrils flared with anger. "Do not question me!"

The men nearby fell silent, their gazes snapping toward the confrontation. The crackling fire was the only sound as Ivar dropped the empty stick into the grass, slowly wiping his fingers on the fur hide at his waist. His fists clenched and unclenched, a warning in the deliberate slowness of his movements.

Aldo stood his ground at first, his face unreadable, his loyalty battling with his concern. The tension stretched between them, taut and fragile, waiting for one of them to break, but it was Aldo who relented, his shoulders relaxing as he dropped his gaze. "Yes, sir."

Ivar's voice was barely a whisper, but every word dripped with menace. "Do not ever question me again, or your head will be on a spike. Understood?"

Aldo's jaw tightened, but he nodded, his eyes cold and hard. "Yes, sir."

As Aldo turned and walked away, the vial cooled against Ivar's chest, its heat fading as quickly as it had come. A whisper echoed in his mind. You'll have to kill him.

Ivar didn't flinch. *I know.*

The biting winds tore through Fiona's clothing, chilling her down to the bone despite her robe and hood offering some protection from the relentless elements of the mountains. Each gust seemed to carve deeper into her, and she hunkered down, trusting the horse to navigate the rocky terrain while keeping pace with Julian ahead. Niklaos leaned heavily against her back, his head resting on her shoulder, his chin lightly tapping her neck with every jolt from the horse. A knot of dread formed in her stomach and her anger towards Cleary surged—why had he forced Niklaos to come along in his weakened state, a state he'd put him in to begin with? His determination to feed his gathered strength into her had long since gone dry, and now he just held on.

After what felt like an eternity of harsh winds and rugged trails, the shades reached the top of a steep incline as the sun dipped below the horizon. The scouts had already scaled the other side, meeting them at the peak. The young boy dismounted from his horse, a cautious hand still gripping the reins. His horse, oblivious to the tension in the air, tugged at a scraggly patch of grass near a cluster of stones.

"The marauders made camp just outside Oldgrange," he reported. "They'll be moving at first light, so they won't stay there much longer. We should camp here and track their movements."

Dakara shifted eagerly in her saddle. "Why don't we just

attack now? Catch them while they're off guard."

Julian stroked his chin thoughtfully before responding, "We could. But have you ever fought in the dark?"

Dakara squared her shoulders. "Yes."

Julian nodded, his eyes narrowing. "Then you know how dangerous it can be. It's too easy to lose control of the fight."

"I still think it's worth the risk," Dakara insisted.

Julian closed his eyes, the weight of the decision hanging over him like the oppressive winds. The horses fidgeted, hooves scraping against rocks, and the only other sound was the whistling wind. Fiona, feeling the gusts lash against her face, instinctively raised her hand, pushing against the air. To her surprise, the wind stilled. Julian's eyes snapped open, his sharp gaze locking onto hers.

"Fiona," he said quietly, "It's time you tried using your familiar again. Can you embody the eagle and fly over the marauder camp? We need to know their positioning."

Dakara interjected, doubt clouding her features. "She might be too weak. Send your hounds instead."

But Julian ignored her, his focus still on Fiona. She took a breath, nodding even though her body trembled with exhaustion. "I can try, but I've never done it on command."

Sliding off her horse, her legs shook under her weight. She moved toward a flat rock and sat, drawing her knees close as she concentrated. She closed her eyes and visualized the eagle—its sleek wings, piercing eyes, soaring above the trees. But nothing happened. No shift. No connection to her familiar.

Again and again, she tried, each attempt leaving her more drained until her body gave out, and she collapsed off the rock. Julian rushed to catch her before she hit the ground, pulling her into his arms to steady her.

"It's okay," he murmured. "We'll try again later."

The shades set up a small camp, cold jerky passing as dinner, as they refrained from lighting a fire that could give away their position to the marauders. Julian helped Fiona lie down beneath a rock outcropping, sheltering her from the unforgiving wind. As he tucked a blanket around her, she managed a faint smile.

"Thanks."

"Don't mention it," Julian said, his tone casual. But he leaned closer, his face only inches from hers. In the dim light, she could see the lines etched in his face, the weight of unspoken burdens. Her stomach flipped.

"Julian?"

"Yes?" He paused.

"Why are you nice one second, and so... distant the next?"

He sat back, his brow furrowing. "I don't know. One minute you drive me mad, and the next... the next you pull me in. You remind me of..."

Fiona waited, but Julian didn't finish. Her thoughts drifted to the memory box she'd seen at his house. "That box you have... It belongs to someone else, doesn't it?"

His eyes darkened as he gave a single nod.

Fiona's heart softened. She placed a hand on his cheek, feeling the rough stubble against her palm. He didn't move away. "I shouldn't have pried. I'm sorry. Everyone has the right to their past."

Julian's voice was quiet, pained. "We've all lost someone."

Fiona's chest tightened. "And we choose to be strong or let it break us."

Julian's gaze shifted, flicking over her features. "You lost your fiancé. What did you choose?"

The mention of Jason hit her like a punch. "I chose to keep moving."

Niklaos appeared near them, laying down a few feet away. In the dark his bruises looked terrifying, and Fiona resisted the urge to reach out to him. His sorrow-filled gaze met hers for a brief moment before he closed his eyes, exhaustion taking him.

Julian noticed but said nothing. Instead, he lay down next to Fiona, pulling her close beneath the shared blanket. His body heat radiated into her, and though she considered resisting the comfort, she couldn't. As his warmth seeped into her, Fiona's mind swirled with conflicting thoughts. He was kind now, but would he retreat again tomorrow?

Sleep came eventually, and with it, Fiona's familiar.

Fiona felt herself rise into the air, her body dissolving and melding seamlessly with the eagle's form. The sensation was unlike anything she had ever experienced—her human flesh transforming into powerful wings, her heart synchronizing with the steady, rapid beat of the bird's. A warmth flooded through her, not the biting cold of the mountains but a comforting heat that coursed from her core and spread to every feather. The wind cradled her, lifting her higher and higher until the mountains stretched out beneath her like a jagged sea of shadows.

The world below opened up in sharp relief, her new eyes capable of perceiving even the tiniest details in the landscape. Every brittle branch of the leafless trees seemed to quiver as she passed overhead, every jagged rock casting long, creeping shadows in the fading light. Below her, a mountain goat grazed on a tuft of grass, its slow, methodical chewing seeming almost lazy in comparison to her swift flight. The goat looked up at her, unafraid, as though it recognized the predator above but knew no harm would come from her.

The eagle's capabilities were far beyond what her human senses could comprehend. In the dark of the night, she could see the fragile outline of a mouse scurrying for cover, each tiny footfall leaving a faint trail in the snow. A single snowflake spiraled lazily down into a ravine, and she could make out every delicate ridge along its edges as it floated through the air. Even the tiniest rustle of pine needles in the trees below was not lost to her new ears, their heightened sensitivity catching every sound of the nocturnal world coming to life.

Though darkness was closing in around her, it didn't hinder her. The eagle's eyes pierced through the night as if it were day, tracing the lines of the landscape, every rise and fall of the earth beneath her. She could sense movement in the distance, a subtle shifting of shadows that would have been invisible to her human eyes.

Fiona marveled at the raw power and grace of the eagle, feeling not only her newfound strength but also the wild freedom it possessed. She was no longer bound by the cold or fatigue of her human body. Here, in the skies, she was weightless, invincible. The wind was not her enemy, but a companion, lifting her ever higher, carrying her effortlessly over the mountains and valleys.

The marauder's camp was not far, and not hard to spot in the black of night. It spread across a blanket of white snow like a dark stain against the pristine snowy landscape, the tents anchored into the ground like claws. Fiona shuddered at the sight, remembering her time with them as a prisoner. She wondered how Melaney was faring, or if this was a vain fight and her mentor was already dead.

She couldn't be. Fiona shook her head and the eagle mimicked her movements. They needed her body desperately now that all other options had escaped. They'd keep her alive and protected at all costs. Fiona couldn't be sure, but she had to believe.

Fiona circled lower, her sharp eyes scanning every detail. The firepits were cold, no smoke rising from them, and the tents themselves seemed lifeless. Her heart began to race as she glided over the camp, searching for any sign of movement, but there was none. No figures huddled around campfires, no murmurs of men preparing for the morning march.

Then, it hit her—the camp was empty. The tents remained, but there were no horses, no scouts, no marauders.

They had already packed up and left.

Dawn was breaking soon, and they had moved out, abandoning the site in the dead of night. The army had vanished into the wilderness, leaving everything behind.

It was if they'd gone to war.

CHAPTER 35

Fiona snapped awake in the exact position she'd fallen asleep. For a moment, she was disoriented, her mind swimming with fragments of dreams. She blinked up at the black sky, feeling Julian's steady breath next to her ear. His warmth pressed against her, but she still shivered. Something was wrong—she could feel it in her bones.

A twig snapped in the distance, and she shot upright. The sound echoed in the quiet night, sharp and unnatural. Ivar. The thought hit her like a hammer. Her mind raced, memories flooding back of her flight with the eagle. The marauder camp had been empty. They were hunting the shades.

She had to warn them. Now.

"Julian!" Fiona hissed, shaking his shoulder frantically. "Julian, get up, now!"

He jerked awake and sat up. "What is it?"

"The marauders are coming," Fiona whispered, her voice tight with fear.

"How d'you know?" He frowned, glancing around.

"I flew over their camp," she admitted, tears welling up in her eyes. "It was abandoned. They're hunting us. We've got to warn the others."

"Fiona, wait—" But she had already scrambled to her feet, her legs moving faster than her thoughts. She ran past Niklaos's prone form, grabbing his arm as she darted by. "Marauders!" she shouted.

That word was all it took to get him to his feet. He groaned, rubbing sleep from his eyes, and followed her as she ran around the camp, shaking the others awake.

Julian and Dakara took up station with several others at the front, weapons drawn, eyes locked on the mountain. The faint blue of dawn stretched across the horizon, casting long shadows. Fiona returned to Julian's side, her chest heaving as she woke the last of the camp.

"Where are they?" Julian asked, scanning the dark ridges.

"I don't know," Fiona replied breathlessly, "but their camp was empty when I flew over it."

"They could be anywhere," Dakara muttered grimly.

The shades waited, tense and silent, for what felt like an eternity. Fiona's heart pounded in her ears, her body thrumming with dread. Her breath curled in front of her, swirling like smoke under the full moon, casting its cold light over the camp.

Doubt gnawed at Fiona, sinking its claws deep into her mind. What if she was wrong? The thought hit her with crushing force, her stomach twisting in knots. She could feel every heartbeat thudding in her chest, each one like a hammer driving her anxiety deeper.

Her mind raced, second-guessing the vision she'd had during her flight with the eagle. Had she really seen the empty marauder camp, or was it some fevered trick of her imagination? The night air bit at her skin, and the cold only sharpened the uncertainty. Her breath curled like smoke before her, dissipating into the void, and for a moment, the silence felt suffocating. What if her warning had stirred them all to arms for nothing?

Then, from the darkness, two figures stepped into view.

Fiona squinted, trying to make them out. A chill slid down her spine as recognition hit her. Ivar and Aldo.

They stood in the distance, weapons drawn. Ivar wore a sinister grin, but Aldo scowled, his eyes cold and hard. Silence hung heavy between the two groups as more marauders emerged from the shadows, flanking Ivar on either side. The army revealed itself slowly, deliberately.

As the moon began to sink, the sky brightened with the coming dawn. Ivar glanced at the horizon, his grin vanishing. His jaw clenched, and then he barked a command. The marauders charged, a thunderous war cry shaking the earth. Then, he and Aldo turned and mounted on horses, galloping away.

Fiona's blood ran cold. "Julian!" she gasped, stepping back. "They're coming!"

"I see that!" he growled, tossing her a dagger and drawing his sword. "Shades, call forth!"

The shades whistled a haunting melody, their harmonies nearly drowned by the marauders' roar. Familiars began to appear by their masters' sides. Blaze and Ember materialized beside Julian, their hackles raised, saliva dripping from their snarling jaws, their red ears flattened against their slender skulls. Darry stepped in front of Fiona, followed by Tobar, the ferocious Dobhar-chu, the otter-dog of legend, pawing at the ground in anticipation of the battle.

A hand grabbed Fiona's arm and pulled her back. She twisted around, clawing and scratching to free herself. "Stop!" Brannon protested. "Come with me!"

"I have to help!" Fiona protested, desperately producing the dagger from her cloak.

Brannon shook his head, his face grim. "Julian made me swear to keep you safe."

"Julian!" Fiona cried, trying to break free, but Brannon's hold tightened.

"Take her, Moss!" he ordered. Before Fiona could react, the pooka appeared and wrapped its arms around her. Its emerald eyes gleamed, with mischievousness or malice she couldn't be sure. She fought against its sinewy grip, but it held her easily, carrying her away from the front lines and into the cover of a shallow ravine.

Once there, the pooka set her down, but kept its iron grip,

shielding her as the battle raged above. Shadows twisted and clashed, the sound of steel and cries filling the night. Fiona strained to see through the chaos, her heart lurching as she failed to spot her friends.

Someone stumbled into the ravine. The pooka whirled, growling low in its throat, claws extended. But it was Niklaos, staggering toward them, blood staining his tunic. He collapsed to his knees, his face pale.

"No!" Fiona fell beside him, her hands trembling as she pulled him into her arms. "Niklaos, how bad is it?"

His chest heaved, his voice hoarse. "I don't know."

Fiona lifted his shirt, her breath catching at the sight of the gash across his abdomen. The rising sun illuminated the wound, the red staining her hands. She tore the edge of her skirt, wrapping it tightly around him. "This will have to do for now."

Niklaos gritted his teeth. "We need to get to Melaney."

Fiona nodded and turned to Moss. "Take us there," she pleaded. "Please."

The creature stood motionless, his eyes hard and unyielding.

"If you don't take us, I'll go alone," Fiona warned, stepping closer. "Brannon wouldn't like that, would he?"

The mention of Brannon made the pooka shift uneasily. It glanced at the battle before finally nodding. In one swift movement, it scooped Niklaos into its arms and began sprinting east.

Fiona didn't wait. She closed her eyes and whispered, "Come to me."

This time, she didn't become the eagle, but instead a predator's screech filled the air, echoing off the mountains. Fiona looked up to see an eagle swooping down toward her. Its feathers gleamed like burnished gold under the fading moonlight, its wingspan stretching wider than she was tall. Every powerful beat seemed to command the wind itself, as if the very air bent to its will. Its eyes, deep and piercing, glowed like molten amber, burning with an ancient intelligence.

Her golden eagle. It was a normal size, at first, but as it drew closer it grew as if stretching itself to become the size of a small dragon. To accommodate her.

The eagle's talons, sharp as daggers and glinting like steel, stretched out as it landed gracefully before her. It stared at her for a moment, and she knew what it wanted. As she climbed onto its back, she felt the strong muscled beneath its feathers ripple and tense. The bird's sharp, curved beak caught the light as it waited for her to secure herself. She grabbed hold of the feathers at its neck and clung tightly as the eagle lifted off the ground. She felt the air around her hum with its flight, a wild, primal energy filling her as they rose above the world. Each swoop, each tilt of the eagle's wings was so precise, so commanding, that it felt like she was not just riding it but becoming a part of the sky itself.

Fiona cast one last glance at the battlefield, desperate to spot Julian, but the faces blurred in the frenzy. Her heart clenched as she turned her gaze forward. Melaney was waiting—she could only hope they'd reach her in time.

The sun was rising, and time was running out.

Ivar and Aldo reached the camp just as the first blades of the sun pierced the horizon, casting faint orange light across the landscape. Time was running out. They rushed into Ivar's tent, and Aldo hoisted Melaney's limp form over his shoulder. Her skin was cold—so cold that it sent a shiver down his spine as her lifeless arm grazed his neck. For a moment, the icy weight of her body made him wonder if she was already dead. He quickly shoved the thought away, lifting her onto his horse before leaping up behind her.

The two marauders spurred their horses into a gallop, their breaths heavy in the crisp morning air as they raced toward Oldgrange. In mere minutes, the ancient tomb loomed ahead, rising like a stone sentinel guarding the burial place of countless kings and sorcerers. The tomb's domed structure defied the weight of centuries, solid and immovable against the encroaching light. At the entrance, the darkened doorway began to brighten as the first rays of the sun crept toward it, preparing to bathe the stones in golden light.

Placing the vial beside Melaney's head, Ivar stepped back. All they had to do now was wait. Alena's vial shimmered from clear to pale yellow, beginning to absorb the sun's energy.

"No!" A scream ripped through the still air, followed by the piercing shriek of a bird.

Ivar barely had time to react before a massive golden eagle swooped down from the sky, its talons gleaming like sharp daggers in the morning light. It dove straight for him, beak slashing through the air with deadly precision. He ducked just in time, feeling the rush of wind as the eagle's beak barely missed his face. The bird soared upwards, circling high above before angling back down for another attack. This time, Ivar was ready. He swung out, catching the eagle with the back of his hand. The bird spiraled down, crashing into a snowbank and vanishing beneath the white powder.

Panting, Ivar rushed toward the snowbank, intent on finishing the job, but the eagle had disappeared—only a deep hole remained where it had landed.

"Aldo!" he barked, scanning the skies. His comrade ran to his side, pale and shaken. "What was that?" Aldo gasped.

"An eagle. One of theirs." Ivar growled, eyes darting across the tree line. "Did you see where it went?"

"No." Aldo pointed to the doorway. "But the light—it's almost there."

The sun's rays climbed higher, brushing against Melaney's still form. Her pallor began to fade, her body absorbing the light as the vial turned a bright, blinding yellow. The transformation was beginning.

A sudden roar echoed through the valley, and both men turned to see a massive, goat-man creature leap into the air. It came down on Aldo with a terrifying force, its great claws slashing at his head. Aldo dropped to the ground, blood spurting as the pooka snarled, its eyes gleaming with a mischievous but lethal glint. It slashed again, this time silencing Aldo's screams.

Ivar froze, his heart pounding in his chest. He knew better than to face such a creature. The pooka's fanged grin was as wild as it was menacing. But then, Ivar's gaze shifted beyond the beast—to the figures approaching from the trees. Fiona and Niklaos. Both armed—though poorly. Fiona clutched a dagger, and Niklaos, barely standing, held a stick so large it required both hands to wield.

Ivar chuckled darkly. "I have to give you credit," he said, his voice dripping with sarcasm. "You are stubborn. Niklaos, I thought you were dead."

"Not yet," Niklaos rasped, his face battered and bruised. "Fiona saved me."

"To what end?" Ivar sneered. "So, you can die here together, traitors to your own blood?"

"No," Niklaos spat on the ground, his expression resolute. "To save my soul by doing the right thing. And you're not my blood."

Ivar's gaze dropped to the red-soaked shirt clinging to Niklaos' torso. "You can't fight me, boy."

"No," came a new voice from behind. "But I can!"

Ivar whirled, barely managing to deflect a sudden blow from a sword hilt. He stumbled back, surprise flashing across his face as a dark-haired young man stepped forward, his weapon raised and eyes blazing. Two white dogs with red ears scampered to his side, snarling and snapping warnings.

"Julian!" Fiona gasped, her eyes wide in disbelief.

In the distance a boom echoed across the mountain.

CHAPTER 36

Julian squared off against Ivar, his shoulders heaving, sweat dripping down his brow. He drew back his sword, daring the marauder to charge him again. Ivar obliged, leaping forward with a savage grunt. His fist swung in a wide arc, and Julian dodged, the blow whistling past his ear. Before he could recover, Ivar followed up with a brutal uppercut to Julian's jaw, sending him crashing to the snow-covered ground.

With a guttural growl, Julian raised his hand, calling on his flames. Fire crackled to life, searing heat snapping into the air as he lashed out at Ivar.

The marauder snarled, dodging the first strike, but Julian wasn't done. He whipped the flames again, the fiery tendril striking Ivar's arm and setting his sleeve ablaze. Ivar roared in frustration, batting at the fire as it singed his coat.

With a beastly snarl, he rushed forward, his massive frame moving with terrifying speed. Julian swung the flames again, but Ivar swatted the fire aside, lunging straight at the younger man and delivering a blow to his head that sent him sprawling backward, flames flickering out as he hit the ground hard.

Fiona cringed at the sharp crack of the blow and cried out.

"Stop!"

Ivar ignored her, raising a giant foot to crush his opponent's skull. Fiona's heart raced—Julian wasn't moving.

Fiona sprinted to his side, her legs shaking as she forced herself forward. She wished for the wind to come, to do her bidding, and it did. It snaked around her, forming an ethereal hand of swirling air. It slammed into Ivar, throwing the marauder to the ground. With another thought, Fiona shaped the wind into a barrier around Julian. The shimmering air pulsed with power, but each beat drained more from her. This was more than she had ever dared to summon before, but she held it in place as she held Julian's head.

"Wake up," she said. "Julian!"

The clanging of weapons filled the air, and Fiona's gaze snapped behind her. The remnants of the marauder army had descended upon them, followed by shades. The battle was moving towards them. Niklaos and the pooka fought, their weapons a blur as they fended off the attackers, but they were losing.

Fiona's strength ebbed as the last of her energy vanished and the barrier faltered. She dropped to her knees, barely catching herself with her hands, her vision dimming.

Ivar laughed, shaking her out of her daze. He rose, brushing the dirt and snow from his coat with slow deliberation, blood glistening on his knuckles and steam flowing from his mouth. "You really think you can win?"

"I will," Fiona managed between ragged breaths, though even she didn't believe it.

"You are mistaken." His voice was dark, gleeful. "Look."

Fiona followed his gaze, her heart sinking. The doorway at Oldgrange—its stones were glowing with an ominous green light. She watched as the entire structure lit up, all except the very top. The vial by Melaney's head shone so brightly it hurt Fiona's eyes, and Melaney's skin took on an eerie orange hue.

The realization hit her like a blow. It was almost over. They had lost.

Ivar wiped his bloody knuckles on his coat and turned toward Alena's side, victorious. Fiona collapsed to the snowy ground, anger and despair tearing at her. Her tears fell, melting the snow beneath her.

Darry, Brannon, Dakara. Where were they? Were they dead?

This was it. They had failed. Ivar took another step toward Fiona, leering at her as he wiped his hands off.

"You really thought you were gonna do something out here, miss?"

Fiona's resolve cracked. Something inside her snapped. She didn't care that the marauder watched her with a smile, or that he would kill her. Julian groaned next to her, but she made no move to reach his side again. The sky above her wavered, her vision weakening, and now she lay broken, waiting for the inevitable.

A low rumbling hum reverberated through the ground. It started as a faint whisper, like the distant rustling of leaves in the wind, but quick grew into a bone-deep vibration, as though the air itself was being pulled apart. Then came a sharp crack, like lightning striking a tree, followed by a rush of energy and a hollow roar. A portal appeared in the distance.

Bella.

Behind her was the Wickard Forest. She strained, every muscle focused on holding this portal so much larger than the last one.

A great cry rose, shaking the ground. Figures began to appear, blurry at first, but soon taking shape as they came through the portal. They were many, some human, others not. As Fiona's vision cleared, her heart leapt.

All manner of animal and beast stood at the edge of the battlefield, flanked by more shades with their familiars—creatures that stood, hovered, or crouched—all waiting for their command.

At the center of the army stood Dax, Lia, and Natalie. Movement flickered in Fiona's periphery, and then, the Leshy stepped into view. Towering above all, it stepped into view with a slow, deliberate grace, its twisted limbs creaking like old wood in a storm. Each step it took reverberated through the ground, as though the earth itself acknowledged its presence.

Flanking the Leshy were creatures of the forest, wild and

untamed. A massive boar, his tusks sharp and gleaming, snorted and pawed the ground, his eyes filled with a savage hunger for battle. A wildcat, sleek and muscular, prowled at the Leshy's side, her fur rippling in the cold wind as she flicked her leathery tongue over her fangs, anticipating the hunt. Overhead, birds of prey circled, their shrill cries echoing across the battlefield.

Behind the Leshy, more of the Wickard Forest's creatures emerged. Wolves with glowing eyes slinked through the ranks, their teeth bared in silent snarls, while elk with antlers draped in ivy stamped their hooves, ready to charge. Owls, with feathers that shimmered like moonlight, perched on twisted branches, their gazes unblinking and watchful.

Wickard Forest had come to the unforgiving mountains to defend the land.

To defend Fiona.

And the Leshy had been undisturbed by the magic of the portal.

Above them all, the predator screech of an eagle pierced the air, and Fiona looked straight up to see her golden eagle—HER eagle—swoop in an elegant arc and land on the Leshy's shoulder.

The marauders paused a moment, unsure how to face this new foe. Ivar stepped forward, his brow knitted together. "What are you waiting for?" he roared.

They took no more urging, and the marauder army charger forward.

As the army advanced, the Leshy raised one of its massive, branch-like arms, and the animals surged forward. Fiona's eagle took back to the skies.

The Leshy moved with impossible speed, closing the distance between them. Its massive, twisted form loomed over Fiona, its white, unblinking eyes locking onto her with an intensity that sent a shiver down her spine. It studied her without a word, then the forest spirit reached into the moss-covered folds of its body, retrieving three obsidian stones, each dark as night and smooth as glass.

With a delicate precision that belied its monstrous size, the Leshy placed the stones gently on Fiona's chest, one by one, positioning them in a perfect triangle over her heart. As the final stone settled, it chittered softly to itself, its voice a strange mix of the creaking of branches and the rustling of leaves in a distant forest. The sound, though alien, was oddly soothing, as though the forest itself was whispering to her.

The stones pulsed softly in rhythm with her heartbeat, their obsidian surfaces glowing faintly. Fiona gasped as warmth seeped into her skin, filling her with strength. The exhaustion that had crippled her moments ago faded. She felt solid, as if an invisible anchor had been dropped from her deep down to the center of the world.

The Leshy lifted her, setting her on her feet as though she weighed nothing, then pressed the obsidian stones gently into her hands. It watched another moment longer before it bowed his head in a slow, deliberate gesture. Then, it turned, its spear raised high, and charged into the fray.

Fiona's breath came in sharp bursts as she watched the creature disappear into the chaos, her heart still racing from the surge of energy coursing through her. She closed her fingers around the stones.

The Dobhar-chu ran past her, growling a greeting as it went, followed by a muttering Darry. "You okay?" he asked as he passed.

Fiona nodded numbly.

Brannon and Dakara and several other shades were close behind him, all waving tiredly as they passed. She was relieved to see her friends okay.

But her relief was short-lived.

She looked to the doorway. The green light was now fully illuminated. Ivar stood there, his attention fixed on Melaney, whose body twitched as if on fire. The vial near her head was almost empty, and steam rose in thick plumes, flowing into her eyes, nose, and mouth.

Alena's life force.

It was nearly too late.

Fiona ran toward Melaney, desperate to save her friend. But as she neared the door, Ivar swung his arm, sending her flying through the air. She hit the snow with a bone-rattling thud, pain lancing through her side.

"There's no hope for you here, little lady," Ivar sneered, his dark laughter reverberating in the cold air. His eyes glittered with triumph. "The transfer is all but complete."

Fiona gasped for breath, her limbs trembling from the impact, but she wouldn't give up. She couldn't.

Then, a crackling sound filled the air. A whip of fire snapped against the stone frame of the doorway, the flames sparking against Ivar's shoulder. He cursed, batting at the fire in surprise.

Julian. He stood tall despite the rivulet of blood trickling down the side of his head. A flame burned brightly in his hand, his eyes locked on Ivar as he drew the fire back like a whip once more, his deep voice a growl that echoed off the mountain. "Back off."

Ivar's expression darkened, rage contorting his features. "You know that's not going to happen," he snarled, rolling his injured shoulder as his gaze flickered between Fiona and Julian.

Fiona's pulse quickened as she saw her chance. The Leshy had given her just enough strength. She summoned the wind once more, though her body ached with the effort. The wind gathered around Ivar's legs, pinning him in place as Julian's fire snaked around his arms, the flames curling with deadly precision, searing his flesh to the bone.

Ivar howled in fury, thrashing against the invisible bonds. His massive form lifted off the ground by the combined power of wind and flame. He kicked and hurled curses as he struggled to break free, but even a being as physically powerful as he could not.

With one final push, Fiona and Julian slammed him down into the earth. Ivar's body hit the ground with a sickening thud. His form lay still, motionless, steam rising from his charred skin.

Fiona staggered to her feet, her entire body shaking from

exhaustion. "Melaney," she whispered, panic rising in her chest. She rushed toward her friend, but her heart plummeted at the sight before her.

Melaney's body jerked violently, her limbs flailing as if controlled by invisible strings. Her eyes snapped open, and Fiona gasped—her pupils were gone, replaced by a sickly orange glow. The vial by her head hissed as the last remnants of the steam poured into her mouth, nose, and eyes.

Fiona's heart raced as she grabbed the vial, her hands trembling. She had to stop it—now.

No! Alena's voice rang through her mind, sharp and deafening, as if the enemy was standing right beside her. The force of it made Fiona flinch, but she gritted her teeth and held firm.

"I'm sorry, Alena. This isn't your body." Fiona's voice cracked with determination. With all her strength, she raised the vial above her head and brought it down against the stone frame. It cracked, but the steam continued to flow, feeding Melaney's violent transformation.

Again and again, Fiona slammed the vial against the stone, desperation fueling her blows. She screamed with every blow, the sound ripping from her chest, shredding her throat, fueling her desperation.

The glass splintered, spider-webbing with cracks as the vial's surface weakened. Fiona's breath came in ragged gasps, her arms screaming in protest, but she couldn't stop.

Two hands wrapped around her, enveloping and warming them. Taking over. Fiona looked up through teary eyes, gasps heaving from her chest.

Niklaos.

He raised the vial with her. Brought it down together. Another crack in the vial.

Alena screamed again, her voice shrieking through Fiona's mind.

Fiona screamed more.

Niklaos brought the vial down again, taking over while Fiona slumped at her friend's side and wrapped her arms around Melaney, holding her close.

Finally, with a final, desperate strike, the vial shattered, shards of glass raining down onto the snow. The steam dissipated into the wind, spiraling into the sky. Alena's furious screams echoed through the air, growing fainter with each passing moment, until, at last, they were gone.

Melaney's body stilled. Fiona tightened her grip on her, fear icing her heart. Niklaos, spent, wrapped his arms around Fiona, to which she found no objection. They all laid together in the sun, the rays caressing them under the cold wind.

Then, slowly, Melaney's eyes fluttered open—clear and familiar, no longer clouded by the sickly orange hue.

"Fiona?" Melaney's voice was weak, barely a whisper. "Is that you?"

Fiona pulled her mentor close as tears welled in her eyes. "Yes," she whispered, her voice thick with emotion. "It's over."

As they prepared to head back, Fiona sat on the ground, exhausted. Melaney and Niklaos were put on horses with others, too weak to ride alone. The Leshy approached quietly, picking her up as carefully as a newborn baby. She laid her head on its broad chest as it walked towards the opening portal.

And that's when it all hit.

Fiona's tears fell freely. The weight of everything—her family's death, the endless battles, the fear, the uncertainty—crashed down on her all at once. It was as if a dam had broken inside her, releasing a torrent of grief. Her body shook with the force of her sobs, each one pulling from a deep well of sorrow that had been buried for too long.

The memories of her father's laugh, her sister's gentle touch, and the warmth of her village all surged forward, blurring together in a flood of pain. She had tried so hard to be strong, to keep moving, but now, in the presence of the Leshy, with the exhaustion deep in her soul, it was too much to contain. The loss felt like an ache deep in her bones, and the sobs tore through her with a raw intensity that left her gasping for breath.

For the first time since it all began, Fiona allowed herself to feel the depth of her pain. It spilled out in waves, unstoppable, as though her very soul was being cleansed of the sorrow that had weighed it down.

She cried it all into the Leshy's wooden chest as it walked through the portal.

CHAPTER 37

Fiona leaned against the gate to Shades Hollow, watching Cleary's stooped, receding figure as he made his way back to the village center. The moon had just begun its ascent into the sky. "Think he'll ever admit the truth?"

Julian twirled a knife in his hand, watching alongside her. "Not a chance."

Cleary walked with a puffed chest, despite his aging frame, his voice echoing from a distance as he spoke to the gathering townsfolk. "It was all part of my plan," he was saying. "I knew we could save Melaney, just had to wait for the right moment."

Fiona clenched her fists. "How can he take credit for something he didn't do?"

"People like him always find a way," Julian muttered. "People know the truth."

Brannon approached from behind them. "Forget Cleary for now. We've got bigger things to focus on. Let's get back inside—Melaney's waiting."

With one last look at in Cleary's direction, Fiona sighed and turned back toward the council building. The main hall had been opened up to air out, and inside shades scrubbed the walls with a kind of fervor that made Fiona smile. They were freshening it up as was customary when a new councilperson was inducted.

This time, it was Melaney. She was there helping, and she turned with a smile.

"He's out there taking credit again," Fiona said, stepping inside.

Melaney paused, wiping her brow with the back of her hand. "Let him talk. The village needs a new leader, and the more he runs his mouth, the more obvious it is that he's not fit for it." She set the rag down and stretched. "This place is going to be different now. Safer, better. And that's what matters."

"If anyone can make that happen, it's you."

Melaney chuckled. "Thanks, Fiona. I'm just hoping I can live up to the task." Behind her, Moirin, who looked much healthier already, launched her usual scowl at them but also helped.

"I have a question," Fiona said, returning her focus to Melaney, "about Julian."

"My answer depends." Melaney stood.

"When we were preparing to leave, I saw a memory box in his place. He said it belonged to someone else."

Melaney's expression changed, fell. "Ah, yes. I'm assuming you're asking me because Julian didn't tell you."

Fiona just watched her friend, hoping for some kind of answer. Melaney looked around her for a moment and cleared her throat.

"I wish I could give you all the answers, but the most I can tell you is that your presence here is a reminder to him."

That wasn't cryptic at all.

Before Fiona could respond, a voice called from outside.

"Fiona! Come quickly!"

It was Niklaos. Fiona exchanged a curious glance with Melaney, who nodded. "Oh, good. It's time to stop here for the night, anyway. Go see what's going on."

Fiona stepped out onto the porch and down the stone staircase, her heartbeat loud in her ears. The cold air hit her face, nipped at her exposed skin. Niklaos stood tall ahead of her, his frame outlined by the snowy backdrop. He nodded toward the courtyard, his eyes wide, drawing her attention forward. Shades had gathered, their postures straight and solemn. Their familiars rested beside them, forming an aisle of sorts. Fiona's heart quickened as she realized they weren't assembled by chance. They were waiting.

And there, at the end of the path, towering above the gathering of Shades, stood the Leshy, its twisted limbs illuminated by flickering torches. The creature's blank white eyes pierced through the snow, locking on to Fiona as if it'd had been waiting for her alone as its braided beard shifted ever so slightly in the evening breeze. Around its feet, wood animals moved—squirrels, birds, and a massive wildcat, all resting beside it. Fiona's breath caught in her throat.

Fiona stepped down the stairs, moving toward the spirit guardian. The crowd watched, but their murmurs faded into the background as she approached. She reached out, hesitating for just a moment before resting her hand on the creature's chest. The texture of its bark-like skin was rough under her palm, ancient, as if she were touching the oldest tree in the world. The Leshy didn't flinch, didn't retreat. Instead, it let out a low, deep sound from somewhere deep within its chest—almost like a purr, but more primal, like the groaning of ancient trees swaying in the wind. As though the forest itself spoke through the creature.

"I don't know how to thank you," Fiona whispered, her voice so soft it barely stirred the air around her.

In response, the Leshy knelt. Slowly, deliberately, it lowered itself to one knee before her. The motion was slow, awkward, its massive limbs creaking like aged wood, but the intent was clear. It brought its long, chipped spear forward, thrusting the butt of the weapon into the snow-covered ground with a dull thud, bowing its head low.

Fiona's breath hitched, tears stinging her eyes as she stared down at the creature. This ancient guardian, this spirit of the wild, was showing reverence. To her.

Without thinking, she stepped forward and embraced it, wrapping her arms around its thick, wooden neck. For a moment, the Leshy tensed, its hard body rigid under her touch. She could feel the tension in its limbs, the hesitation. But then, like the slow thaw of ice under the spring sun, it relaxed. Its wooden frame shifted with soft creaks as it allowed the embrace, its presence warmer than she had expected.

"Thank you," she whispered into its wooden shoulder, her voice cracking. She held the creature for what felt like an eternity, her cheek resting against its rough surface, an unexpected comfort swirling around them. The Leshy didn't move.

And then, as if on cue, a sound rose from the crowd. It started as a low murmur, barely a whisper among the gathered shades. But the sound grew, swelling and rising, voices joining together in a powerful chant. The chant grew louder with every second, the rhythmic cry reverberating through the mountains, bouncing off the towering trees and cliffs. The sound filled the air, a song of reverence and unity, and Fiona felt herself swept up in it, her heart swelling with the weight of it all.

The Leshy remained kneeling before her, head bowed, as the chant continued to rise, filling the night sky like a prayer. Fiona closed her eyes, letting the sound wash over her, and for the first time in a long while, she felt peace settle deep within her bones.

She released the Leshy and turned to face her new friends, comrades, and home. Joined them in the chant.

To the sky!
To the earth!
To the air!
To the Shades!